The
# Great Enclosure
## Book One

# The
# Great Enclosure
## Book One

## The Foundation

# Jackie Chimutashu

authorHOUSE®

AuthorHouse™ UK Ltd.
1663 Liberty Drive
Bloomington, IN 47403  USA
www.authorhouse.co.uk
Phone: 0800.197.4150

Published by AuthorHouse  09/23/2013

ISBN: 978-1-4817-6841-2 (sc)
ISBN: 978-1-4817-6840-5 (hc)
ISBN: 978-1-4817-6842-9 (e)

Edited by Sarah English

Cover Design by Tirivashe Mundondo

Therefore, a Prince so long as he keeps his subjects united and loyal, ought not to mind the reproach of cruelty . . . Upon this a question arises: whether it is better to be loved than feared or feared than loved? It may be answered that one should wish to be both, but, because it is difficult to unite them in one person, it is safer to be feared than loved . . . NICCOLO MACHIAVELLI

I wish to thank my husband Chris and my family for the support and brilliant ideas they offered. I`m also grateful to Tawanda Chikosi for his assistance. Special thanks go to Chris Ablan. He taught me to believe in myself.

*For my late dad, Samuel Sabelanga, he believed in me.*

# About the Book

Hundreds of ancient civilizations erected imposing buildings, great forts and built magnificent towns but no ancient city has held so much mystery and sparked so much controversy as the Great Zimbabwe stone enclosures of Zimbabwe, Southern Africa. The Great Enclosure takes you on a journey back to the 15th century at the height of this medieval city and unfolds a story of grand architectural mastery, radical political ambitions and a daring religious coup that have forever awarded the wonderful extensive network of granite monuments unparalleled mystery.

# About the Author

Jackie Chimutashu is a Zimbabwean and a journalist from the Harare Polytechnic. She has a passion for history, ancient civilizations and medieval monuments. The Great Enclosure is her first novel and it was inspired by the Great Zimbabwe Ruins of Zimbabwe. The book is a tribute to the architects and owners of these magnificent granite stone enclosures. Currently Jackie is teaching English at a local college and is also working on the second part of the novel.

# Prologue

## THE FIRST EVENT

### Emperor Hungwe of the Great Zimbabwe Empire

Excited screams of little children filled the air as the traveller entered the city gates riding on a donkey. A black cloth was expertly wound around his face to keep away the biting cold winds and his white robe contrasted starkly with the bleak grey weather. It was winter and he was from the north where the sun was mostly bright and warm. The chilly winds of May blowing across the county were not welcome to him.

Before him walked his interpreter—a short swarthy man wearing only black cloth tied at his fleshy waist who could speak both Swahili and the local language. Every now and then with a green leafed twig he would shoo away naked little children brave enough to come and touch the donkey. They would run away screaming and laughing and behind the black cloth, the traveller would smile. He did not really mind, he had seen more than enough throughout his life as a trader to be bothered by the children.

As his donkey steadily plodded on forward, a train of dark muscular men, carrying bags on their backs followed. Despite the long journey they had undertaken, they showed no signs of weariness and carried the various goods of great value he intended to trade with, with an undeniable air of fresh zeal.

He rode casually as one does that is so used to the place but his mind was alert and through a slit in the cloth covering his face, his eyes swiftly took in every detail. He saw women carrying water pitchers balanced perfectly on their heads, unashamed of their bare breasts. They stopped, giggled and pointed at him in hushed whispers as though he could understand every word.

For the most part, he was completely at ease with what he saw but his curiosity and appreciation of this Karanga race of Southern Africa was heightened by one fact, the mighty granite enclosures. The majesty of the walls around him in this valley astounded him.

The walls were made of granite stones which had been cut to a calculated size and carefully arranged to enable them to balance one upon the other, as bricks would, but without the use of mortar to secure the brick-work. They were tall and hid from view what lay within. But the Arab was a curious man. He would not sleep until he saw for himself the mystery these enclosures hid from the naked eye. Carefully he allowed his donkey to inch towards one enclosure and his curious mind was rewarded by a simple answer. Circular huts with grass thatching were tucked inside.

"I see you are forever an inquisitive man," said the trader's interpreter.

The Arab gave him a false, lazy smile so as not to arouse the other man's suspicions.

"The huts are beautiful master, they are plastered with dagga, a type of mud used for making their earthenware as well. They smooth it with flat-based stones to give that perfect finish. Notice that they even have doors. They call a door 'sasa' here and they use bark to make these doors." He stopped speaking and shouted an order to the carriers to hurry along in Shona, the local language, then turning to his master once again he said, "Sometimes they mix the dagga with gravel and make sure that the walls are thick. This makes it warm inside. Grass is used for thatching because it makes the huts cool in summer and warm in winter. Notice that they have even painted colourful and beautiful images of birds and animals on the walls. They are a very artistic and creative race."

The Arab nodded slowly, taking in every word, then asked in a pleasant tone, "I have noticed that other huts are outside the enclosures, what could be the reason? Could they not afford to get enclosures built for those people as well?"

The interpreter smiled and said, "Here, my master, it is not a matter of gold coins, it is a matter of class. The city may be in this undesirable valley but these people have a complex class system. Those that live in the enclosures are the royal families, the great spirit mediums and the notable people of this country. The huts outside the enclosures belong to the commoners, the workers and the no-bodies. The enclosures, master, are a sign of importance and wealth."

Once again the trader nodded his head as his eyes studied the women pounding grain and winnowing it in beautifully designed reed baskets. He heard the children laughing and saw the men staring at him. This was just another African country but it was also a nation that had made an undeniable impression upon his mind. He wanted to meet the man to whom this valley and these walls belonged and tell him himself with what amazement he had first laid eyes upon them.

News of the beauty of the goods that he bore with him, especially the cloth, raced through the nation and by midday the Emperor's chief advisor led him to the Emperor's home and court, which was set out in another granite enclosure.

He kept his head bowed low as he entered and when ordered to look up he came face to face with a tall, fear-imposing, strongly built man who stood a good four inches above him, dwarfing nearly everyone in the place. He wore black cloth of good quality which was tied at his waist and reached down to his ankles. This was Emperor Hungwe, the Lord of the impressive granite walls he had just admired.

He was dark-skinned but his skin did not owe its dark hue to long days spent toiling in the sun, it had a healthy ebony glow and showed no signs of stress from over-exposure to the harsh African weather. His nostrils were large, complementing his somewhat magnified features and, as he looked at the Arab, they flared in tune with his heaving chest covered with a mat of hair, which was bare, save for the numerous colourful beads that dangled from his thick neck. He had a broad forehead that seemed to have a set of permanent wrinkles etched onto it and it caused the Arab to wonder if it was so because of the pressure he endured in ruling such an immense Kingdom.

Gently the Emperor folded two massive hands across his chest and he tilted his slightly balding head as he casually studied the Arab, as a scientist would a foreign element. Saying nothing at all, with one hand he began to stroke the thick dark beard which covered a good part of his rotund face. All those around him remained quiet including the old chief advisor who had accompanied the Arab trader. It was evident that everyone in this place feared the Emperor and with the growing silence, the unquestionable air of ruthless authority surrounding this huge man became more apparent, slicing like sharp steel into the heart of this uncomfortable quietness. The Arab ended up by concluding that Emperor was not an easy man at all.

The cloth wound around the trader's face gave him an air of mystery, which tickled the Emperor's curiosity. He looked at him for a few more moments and, like a child eager to reveal the contents of a parcel, he said, "Remove the cloth and let the Emperor see who it is that has visited his nation with such wonderful goods."

His voice was calm, deep and commanding; that of a very important man not used to entertaining trivialities. As a traveller who could judge character well, the trader noticed that this was a man of fine breeding who revelled in his power and authority. It was he who was Lord of these massive enclosures, ruler of the Great Zimbabwe, and the coolness and dignity of his voice immediately made an impression on the mind of this intelligent trader.

Quickly the interpreter whispered into the Arab's ear and the Arab trader deftly removed the black cloth and there stood, before the Hungwe, a man of an interesting demeanour. He was light skinned, had a straight nose, dark mournful eyes and buoyant long black hair. As the Arab looked into the Emperor's small, deep, red eyes, which were hooded by thick permanently arched eyebrows, he noticed a twinkle of amusement fill them, giving them a hint of softness that had not been there previously.

The Emperor slowly smiled and the trader felt relieved. To show his gratitude the Arab whispered something to the interpreter, who clapped his hands twice and a man at the entrance raced to his side. The interpreter then whispered something to him while the Emperor and his close aides looked on curiously. The man raced back to the entrance to bring back a big bundle of goods. From the bundle, the interpreter pulled out a length of perfect black cloth and laid it before the Emperor, for no charge at all, so he explained. A gift, he also said, to show how much the trader appreciated the beauty and might of the city he was in. Hungwe was touched; cloth was of great value in the nation and he viewed the gift with true gratitude. The whole afternoon they traded and the Arab cursed himself a thousand times over. Thinking that the people he was to encounter in the thick forests of this Southern African nation would be unappreciative, he had left most of his goods at the coast but—lo and behold—he had found an organised society with a culture so strange to him, so foreign and yet so fascinating.

To show his new admirer just how much he appreciated the gifts and goods he had traded with him, Emperor Hungwe invited the trader for a feast the following night and, on top of that, he also invited his first wife Chinake. This act of hospitality had never been exhibited before by Emperor Hungwe.

The trader, who found the Karanga tribe of the Great Zimbabwe fascinating in their way of life, was also astounded by the beauty of the Emperor's first wife. As was her habit, she arrived later than everyone else. The light from the torches and the large fire that burned in the Emperor's court lit her features and gave her an added unnatural glow that made her look still more beautiful.

She had such grace and though he had since yesterday grown to also fear the giant dark Lord, he found that he could not take his eyes off his wife the Empress. She wore a simple cloth wound around her, just tightly enough to accentuate her body. Although she had a way of taunting and teasing in her movements, it was undeniable to the trader that she was wholly devoted to the Emperor. Hungwe noticed that the Arab could not take his eyes off his first wife and it pleased him. At least he had something in his Kingdom of flesh and blood which made the trader feel uneasy and weak in the knees.

As the night wore on the Arab and the Emperor exchanged ideas and facts and told each other stories. Deep into the night, most probably intoxicated by Empress Chinake's beauty, the trader began to tell a story that fascinated the Emperor. Although at first it seemed an ordinary story, it had something quite exceptional about it, as it took the Emperor to another level of thinking. With his eyes fixed on Empress Chinake, who was clearly enjoying the effect she was having on him, he started speaking.

"My great esteemed Lord," he began, "I have seen your massive walls and I have come to know that you are not savages as has been told us by those who have not had the rare opportunity of visiting your great nation. Yes, so much has been said about this Kingdom, the Kingdom of the Shona and now my own eyes have seen the power, wealth and vastness which you alone hold in your very hands."

Hungwe was impressed and his wife Chinake smiled.

"Nowhere else have I laid eyes on such grandeur, such art and such beauty as this and one only wonders how you have carved such huge blocks of granite, laying them one on top of another with no mortar. Only one Kingdom that once existed in the north can compare with your mighty walls and that is the land of Egypt, the land of the Pharaohs."

Now, more interested, Hungwe asked, "Who are these people you speak of, I would like to know? Have they built walls more massive than ours that they can compare to us?"

"No, my great Lord, they have not built anything like yours, they have built this," he said as he laid out a parchment with drawings of the great pyramids of Egypt from his robes. Hungwe was intrigued by the parchment. The structures were of a shape stranger than any he had seen before and they looked quite huge. "They had their own culture, their own art but I know you have one thing in common with them, and that is wealth, power and great creativity."

Once again Hungwe was impressed. He smiled a broad, genuine smile, much to the amazement of his men for he hardly ever smiled. "True, my Lord, only great wealth, great might, great intelligence and total control can ever get such structures built and you have all that."

"Indeed you are right," he said, "My Empire stretches all the way to the Limpopo from the Zambezi. We rule all the lands as far as your eyes can see and mighty kings like Nyatsimba Mutota of the Mbire are our vassals. My kings bring tribute to my nation and hence we remain wealthy and powerful. All the animals, all the rivers are ours to do with as we please and so too are the lives of all who are under our reign. We do with them as we desire."

Those present were shocked. Was their Emperor drunk or was he losing his mind, for never had the Hungwe been so open with anyone. Surely the gift of cloth from the Arab must have pleased him. Chinake was also happy, for her usually reserved husband had lost his guard for once and she smiled, moving closer to him. The Arab looked at her, captivated by her smile and drank of her beauty. Was she really from these parts?—he wondered, for she looked like the beautiful Ethiopian women whom he had once seen.

Now he came to the very interesting part, which got Hungwe thinking differently, and started the chain of events that were to reshape the entire Kingdom of the Great Zimbabwe. He leaned closer to him and in a hushed tone he said, "These Emperors were, with the power they held and the wealth they controlled, literally worshipped by their subjects and were to them gods, divine beings. It was this worship that made them immortal. Because they held the position of gods, in their hands was power and wealth absolute. Because they were gods to their people they also held in their hands the unquestionable power to create and destroy all creatures under their authority. Their subjects held them in deep respect and their godliness was passed on to the next reigning Pharaoh."

"Did they ever die?" asked the Emperor. In response the Arab answered yes. But that was not death in its proper meaning. They simply passed on into another world. And that was not all; their people believed that their kings would live on into the next world so they would bury them with masses of gold and many worldly possessions.

The last part was of no interest to Hungwe, however. Why would he be bothered with life after death? He was concerned with the present life and how much respect and glory he got while he still lived. Dead people never benefited from their glory. Who would notice him in the after world? After all, the Karanga religion taught them that all men became equals in the afterlife and there never was anything exciting told about the hereafter. Glory was now, not after, and he would achieve it.

What had fascinated him instead was that a living man of flesh and blood could be placed on the same level as Mwari Musikavanhu, God himself, and receive as much worship and honour as their great spiritual ancestors. It tickled his fancy that he actually could change his being and become one of the immortals. With that realization, a hidden impulse, deep within him, began to stir.

The last words of the Arab excited him even further. He had said, "With all the splendour that I see in this Kingdom, with all the glory you hold, you should be a god, only divine mortals can have what you have."

Had he said it to please the Emperor or had he been mesmerized by Empress Chinake's beauty? Whatever it was, Hungwe began thinking of attaining such supremacy. The day before he left the Arab saw the Emperor for the last time and said in a low tone, "If you really believe you can be divine and immortal then you can be. Look at all this my Lord," he said, looking around, "All this splendour is unimaginable. It can only belong to one who is superhuman, he who is a god, and he who is immortal. Let them channel their praises towards you. Change the deity of this nation, change the history. History is not made by the sane, but by those with crazed ideas, bold enough to make the sane believe in them. But remember, my Lord, this is a battle to win the mind, to control the soul, so let it be won by the mind as well." He gave him a friendly handshake, a gesture unfamiliar to the Emperor, and he left.

Hungwe was left wondering what those last words meant, but as the days went by, he fully grasped the meaning of the Arab's last statement. His battle needed cunning unimaginable, a tongue to persuade the people and to change the nation's ancient religious hierarchy. No, he would not impose it on them, but they unconsciously would all agree to make him a deity. He needed their praise and oh, how he longed for it more and more by the day. He dared not fool himself, never would he be able to take the Mwari's place but then again he could become divine if, as the Arab had said, praise was channeled to him. With his quiet reserved nature, who could ever imagine that Hungwe craved for such primacy?

But he did, because he was just like any other very powerful Emperor. In fact, although quieter, he was certainly the most power hungry of all the Great Zimbabwe rulers. In silence he ruled with an iron fist, placing his generals and chiefs in front, remaining in the rear. He had always desired to be untouchable and to leave an undeniable mark on the history of this Southern African country. He also loved life, and becoming a godly being would mean life eternal. Could that be achieved? His desire to never leave all this splendour made him think so. And it would all start with the mysterious illness of his beautiful wife Empress Chinake.

Something dark, a shadow that would grow in intensity, and with it an unquenchable thirst, was growing inside him, leading him to his goal and soon it would overtake the entire Kingdom.

This would be the first event that reshaped the history of Zimbabwe.

# THE SECOND EVENT

## King Nyatsimba Mutota of the Mbire.

It was now the middle of June and the cold season still had a long way to go. Though dawn had come, thin streaks of mist still travelled along the plains of the Mbire Kingdom and here and there icicles clung to the grass. This had turned out to be a harsh winter following a poor harvest and the bitter cold was keeping people inside their round huts. But while winter brought deep slumber to many, King Nyatsimba Mutota was finding it more and more difficult to find sleep. He had a desire that was eating at his heart.

His forefathers had lived under the rulers of the Great Zimbabwe providing yearly tribute to maintain peaceful relations. This was in the form of cattle, grain and iron tools. He had done the same for years but now he felt that the power the Great Zimbabwe had over him was stifling and he wanted to be entirely free. Like any King, he desired autonomy. How could he call himself free when he was under another Lord, the great Hungwe?

From the time Hungwe had taken over the throne after his father's death, he had tightened his grip on both the political and economic structures of the vast Empire. Hungwe could call upon the armies of his vassals at any given time and use them to take over other kingdoms. This however only added to increase his power but weakened the armies of his vassals.

No foreign trader could enter the interior without the Emperor's express approval. He posted scouts at the outskirts of the Kingdom to report any secret trading activities and many kings and chiefs who had attempted to conduct trade without Hungwe's authority were heavily punished. Without any control over trade, it was difficult for any vassal state to expand or survive.

Nyatsimba Mutota was an ambitious King and he believed his people had borne enough. He wanted to be remembered by one thing, he wanted to be the first vassal to break away from the overextended Karanga Empire ruled by the ferocious Emperor Hungwe. Now was the time to go far away from the Emperor and his people.

Somewhere a cock crowed and he was once more reminded of how early it was. Being a King was no easy job especially if you wanted to make history. So today he was going to start his first move towards the breakaway of the Mbire, a breakaway that was going to create a people so powerful that their might and number would reach out across the Zambezi and the Limpopo.

He went outside and breathed in the cold air. The sun was now throwing its glorious rays across the plateau making the clouds disappear but, alas, once deprived of cloud cover, the cold air became even more bitter. How he wished summer would come and the chilly season would go. Then many things would become bearable, even his plan to move away from the clutches of the Great Zimbabwe Empire.

Outside was his court, where his chiefs met with him, their King. There he would sit on top of a large rock with a hollow base and discuss matters with his political aides. A small white stone was lying just beneath the rock. Mutota bent down and carefully picked it up. Then cracking the stone open he leaned with one hand on the rock and started to draw something on it. This was the route he had decided to take upon leaving the Great Zimbabwe Empire.

He drew the route, across a river, and stopped a while to think. He turned his head, wondering if anyone was looking. There was no one close to him except for his sentries who stood guard a few metres away. Then with deeper concentration he wiped his nose and started to draw the route again. It went north and crossed over the lands of other Shona tribes. He had once been told of the route by his father and now he intended to use it as his gateway from these parts.

A wind blew and he hugged the cloth that he wore around him tighter to his chest. He closed his eyes and breathed in. Deep in his thoughts he saw his tribe move and become free of the Hungwe clan. He saw his people live a life of prosperity and live like kings, conquering, ruling and becoming feared. He saw himself build a wall round his Kingdom, maybe not as big and tall as the Great Zimbabwe walls but one that would also act as a reminder and symbol of his existent power and authority.

"You are up early, father. It is too cold for the King to be up and about," said a voice from behind. The King looked back sharply. He had not expected anyone to visit him so early in the morning.

He was, however, relieved to see his eldest and most loved son, Nyanhowe Matope standing behind him, close enough to see what he was doing. The King simply smiled and said, "It is good for the King to breathe in fresh air once in a while, son. You are up early yourself. Is this chilly wind good for the King's eldest son?"

"It is the best remedy father," said Matope moving closer to where his father stood, "especially when you cannot sleep at night."

"Ah my son, I couldn't sleep either. So I had to get up and take a stroll to my rock, my seat of authority."

"Then I need not ask just how well your night was, father," said Matope. "It appears it was as bad as mine."

Mutota smiled and felt some consolation for having had a bad night. His son had shared the same misfortune too. He loved his eldest son, who looked just like him. He was as tall as his father and had the same dark complexion that ran in the royal family. His round face was just showing the beginnings of a beard, which Nyatsimba knew would grow long and unruly like his if left unkempt. And as he looked into his son's eyes he noticed the same serious stare that his were said to hold. He wondered if his son possessed the same wild and restless spirit as his or whether it would mature with time and circumstances. He was the King's pride and closest confidant.

"What is it that you are drawing, father?" asked Matope moving close to stand beside his father. "Have you decided to leave your mark on the rock as our forefathers did?"

Mutota shook his head, feeling rather foolish. "No, my son, it is nothing like that. It is just something that I was thinking of."

"I see, men are drawing their thoughts on rocks," said Matope, closely studying the map his father had drawn on the rock. "But if I am not mistaken, this looks like a river and this looks like—I'm sorry: I cannot make your other drawings out," he said facing his father and looking perplexed.

Mutota smiled and said, "You cannot make it out because it is my dream. This, my son," he said pointing to the drawings on the rock, "is my escape route out of the rule of the Great Zimbabwe." Matope looked back at his father in silent shock; Mutota gave him a shrewd smile. "For so long, Matope, I have dreamt of being a free man. I believe that as long as we are subservient to another Empire we are not free men," he said, leaning against the huge rock. "Look at us, we are so many in this Kingdom and we call ourselves prosperous, yet each year our cattle, grain and even sons and daughters are claimed by the Great Zimbabwe Emperors and we say we are a nation." He looked at his son who was still staring at him in disbelief. "No," he continued, "we are slaves, maybe a bit free, but still slaves of the Hungwe of the Great Zimbabwe. We are a Kingdom within a Kingdom and what good is a King's title when he calls another King master."

"You have not changed, father," said Matope in his deep voice. His father looked confused. "Grandfather told me that you were always rebellious, never one to remain under someone's wings for too long."

Mutota laughed, showing his even white teeth, and said, "I do not deny that. I remember my day of great pride was when I was given my own gota and I was so proud of my small neat hut. It was an honour to sleep in my own room for the first time. But still I was under my father's rule. I was happy when I married and went to live on my own with my wife, your mother, and happier still when we had you." He turned once more to look at his son, who was staring at his father in great admiration. "I felt that I was now a ruler of my own home; I had my own small clan and it made me feel like a King. And then after my father's death I was appointed King. That was my greatest joy. I always believed I was cut out to lead, to rule." A look of sadness suddenly overcame him. "I thought being a King would give me all the freedom I wanted, that it would give me the wings to move wherever I wanted, but I was wrong. It made me a servant of the Great Zimbabwe; it made me a slave with no shackles but shackled nonetheless. Because you see, son," he said, his eyes looking into his son's, "in any nation the King is the only free man but he can never be free if he calls another King, Lord and right now I have nothing else on my mind except for my freedom. I want to be free."

His final words were a command, a seal that closed their present era and opened a new page into a journey from the Great Zimbabwe. Matope felt, as his father said them, that they had carried a power in them that created something from nothing, the beginning of a breakaway from the Great Zimbabwe Empire.

Matope looked at his father, he saw himself a few years from now, older, more stubborn and more determined. "Are great men who make history always this reckless, father, are they always this crazy?" he slowly asked in his deep, husky voice.

"History is made and changed by those with minds willing to go against the odds my son; no fickle mind ever makes history. You call it craziness, I call it boldness. Would there be history if there were no men like us to change the course of a river that is flowing according to the way the Great Zimbabwe rulers wish. I can change the flowing current; I want to be a King, not a vassal."

With that Mutota looked away, eyes wild and cold with his anger and hatred of the Great Zimbabwe rulers. The cold wind had gathered momentum and it blew violently against the two men. Neither felt the cold hit against their cheeks, nor against their flesh. Matope stared at his father, Mutota looked away, already lost in his dream. Another cock crowed and high above them an eagle soared and screamed. Both men looked up.

"See that eagle, my son—that is what I want to be, high and lofty, Lord of my own skies." He suddenly straightened up and went to take hold of his son's arm. Eagerly, like a child, with a twinkle in his eye he said, "Come, my eldest child, come and I will show you something, something that is bound to help you change your mind and convince you to dream my dream to a reality, come,"

He pulled him away from the rock and led him out of his compound. Three sentries followed and they went high up the hill that was just behind the King's quarters. As they walked, Nyatsimba Mutota looked about. The forests were still green but Nyatsimba could see the effect the recent drought coupled with the cold weather had had on the vegetation. Here and there, leaves were drying up and, if the drought recurred, he wondered what would become of their lush green forests and their livestock and wild animals which provided a great portion of the meat they ate. Already the crops had failed and it was just slowly becoming noticeable that the nation's food reserves were not adequate. To make matters worse, Emperor Hungwe was demanding his yearly tribute of grain and cattle. All this gave him more resolve to run from the place he had once called home.

After some time the King ordered the sentries to remain a distance behind while he trudged on up with his son, still holding his hand as though afraid he would run away. Once up the hill he looked down and in one sweeping glance he took in his entire Kingdom to as far as the eye could see. Huts similar in shape to those of the Great Zimbabwe made up villages. From a few homes, smoke from fires could be seen escaping through the roof tops and small windows on the walls. People were now moving about, attending to their daily chores. From another direction they could see the walls of the Great Zimbabwe. But the King turned his head away from all that and made Matope look north. There lay vast tracts of green forest and Matope could make out a variety of animals grazing and prancing. He contemplated the distant rivers and hills.

"Look at all that my son, that is our future, that is our history and that is the end of our servitude to the Great Zimbabwe," said Mutota, beckoning to the land with his hand.

"I see, father, I see it all," said Matope, giddy with awe.

"And, my son, that shall be ours, that and all that lies within it. We will bring down nations, we will make many serve us and we will write our own history not under the wings of another, but soaring high above on our own." Matope looked at his father, and for the first time he saw what he meant, high above the hill he felt free, and he wanted more of the feeling. He would go along with his father's plan. He wanted the freedom. Mutota looked into his eyes, he knew at that moment that he had found a worthy ally and he knew that with his son by his side, nothing would ever go wrong. Here on this hill they had begun to write their own history. The birth pangs of the Mutapa Empire had just begun. This was the second event that was going to reshape the entire history of the current Zimbabwe.

# THE THIRD EVENT

## Empress Chinake and the mhondoro Chireshe

The empress, Empress Chinake, first wife of Emperor Hungwe, ruler of the Great Zimbabwe Empire, had woken up early. She needed enough time to adorn herself in the best and finest attire she had for her meeting with the Emperor. She was his first wife and believed she was always supposed to live up to the great honour that had been given to her.

Last night she had been ill and, as always, the Emperor had ordered one of his foremost herbalists to come and see to her ill health. But strangely enough, this time he had requested the help of Chireshe, a mhondoro (mhondoros are powerful spirit mediums) whom he had never called upon before. The herbs she had been given had worked wonders and, after a painful stomach attack, she was already better. She was glad for her sudden good health because this was the day the Emperor had ordered her to come to his quarters. For a whole week she had not seen him and she craved a private moment with him.

Empress Chinake knew that her husband delighted in her looks and in her body. She had made the giant son of the Great Zimbabwe Emperor crumble, she had made him feel jealous and she, Chinake, had been able to tease him, the Prince, whom they said never joked with anyone. She felt joy at the thought of how light-hearted he always became at her sight. And it was that power that she wielded over him that caused her to feel a thrill at the prospect of spending a few private moments alone with him.

As she walked out, three sentries came to her; they had been waiting to accompany her to the Emperor.

"Let's go," said the Empress with her head held high as she breathed in the chilly morning air.

One sentry went in front and two fell behind her. She walked with grace, never missing a step and they were alert in case any trouble arose. As she walked by, people stopped whatever they were doing and either simply stared at her or clapped their hands in respect. Empress Chinake enjoyed this and it made her feel good that all life came to a standstill as she passed by. It was the law of the country that such respect was to be shown to passing royalty by all civilians. Chinake had, however extended the term civilians to mean even the Emperor's other wives. This, she knew, would keep them in check in light of the knowledge that she was the first and true wife of the Emperor, while they were mere ceremonial wives.

They arrived after some time at Emperor Hungwe's enclosure. The three sentries remained outside and two more came forward from within the walls. They were expecting her and knew who she was so they asked no questions. Taking over from her three sentries they accompanied the Empress inside the walls to show her to the Emperor's chambers. But before they took a few steps further she suddenly stopped and looked proudly ahead, her neck arched. The two sentries also stopped, confused at the Empress's reaction.

"Go," she said to the two guards who stood behind her. "Leave me alone in here. I need some time on my own before I face my Emperor and my husband." She turned and giving them an icy, unfriendly stare she said, "I am Empress Chinake, first wife of Emperor Hungwe; I know my own way to my husband's chambers. Now go."

They might have been suspicious of her intentions but they did not dare show it. Instead they nodded ever so gently and went and stood just outside the walls by the entrance. They would quickly assume their positions as soon as she entered the Emperor's chambers. She closed her eyes, breathed in and focused. She always wanted to gather herself together before she faced Hungwe. He was the Emperor and not just some ordinary man. Breathing out, she opened her eyes. Now she was ready to see her husband, the Emperor.

She walked into his chamber. It was a large, round hut, neatly built and thatched, with an opening at the other end of the room which let out air and allowed the bright light of day to come streaming in. Hungwe was standing by that window looking outside with one hand leaning against the wall. He had heard her come in but had not even flinched, though it had only been the previous night that she had been taken ill and he had sent for Chireshe to see to her illness. It was good she was now well for it meant Chireshe had seen to her illness and he hoped the mhondoro had impressed the Empress with his wit.

Gingerly she stepped forward but stopped at least ten paces from the throne. His back was to her and he stood thus with his arms folded. The Hungwe was a tall man. He had broad shoulders and a thick neck. He was strong and he looked every inch the ferocious warrior they said he was. How many times had she seen him, innumerable? How many times had she been held and loved by that man, a countless number. But seeing him always made her weak and uncertain. It was always as if it was the first time and that was what had made their marriage live on for so long with the same strange passion.

She knelt, cupped her slender hands and clapped, her face looking at the floor. Still he did not look back but kept staring out of the small opening that was letting in a stream of sunlight and a cold breeze. "My Emperor, my Lord, I greet you my husband, the great Hungwe, Emperor of nations," said the Empress.

The Emperor was listening. He was always amazed at the way his wife's voice always sounded so cool and so rich. It had been that same coolness that had caught him unawares and had made him want her. From the time they had met, it had not changed at all.

"I heard you Chinake; I heard you even before you spoke as you came in. Who can mistake your step, you move with the grace of a cat," he said and turned around. She did not look up but retained her posture, her head bowed, kneeling on the floor.

His red eyes looked at her and they held a knowing twinkle. She would not look up, nor would she get up until he gave the order. He enjoyed this part, when he played the domineering husband and she the submissive wife. Then slowly he walked to where she knelt and said with a sneer on his face, "Get up Chinake, your Emperor orders you to look at him."

She looked up, her almond-shaped eyes misty and innocent. The sneer on the huge Emperor's face faded. Her eyes always challenged him, they brought out his human nature and provoked him to feel in love. For years he had tried to avoid feeling what he felt for her but he had failed. Chinake, his first wife, always brought out his soft side and somehow managed to break that wall of solid steel that made him impenetrable to others. He looked aside to avoid the childlike look her eyes had. They always made him feel vulnerable. He held out his walking stick, she held the end and stood up meekly, and looked at her husband.

Gradually he pulled himself together and said, "You look beautiful as always, Chinake. In all these years your features have not failed to impress your husband and your King."

"I am delighted, "responded Chinake, "that my husband and my Lord finds pleasure in my sight. You look as strong as ever too. A true Emperor in all respects." And she meant every word.

"You flatter me, my wife," he said, turning to walk to his throne, "but I know you mean every word, so I am pleased."

Chinake smiled and kept on standing where she was. He sat on his high stool, which had a hollow base and a lion's hide on top, and beckoned to her, "Come, my Empress, come and sit by the feet of your Lord. Come and pleasure him with your presence and your ladies' gossip."

He smiled, she lightly closed her eyes and opened them again. Slowly and gracefully with clasped hands she walked to her husband's throne. She paused in front of him for just enough time to give him a glimpse of her lovely self then gently went to sit by the floor at his feet. And just as she made herself comfortable he quickly thrust out his hand, grasped her small arm and leered. She looked up at him shocked and out of breath. The Emperor tightened his grip, she winced in pain and tears formed in her eyes. He looked into them, saw confusion and a look that registered pain. He would have let go but instead he tightened his grip. She looked at his huge hand wound around hers and she gasped in pain.

"Now tell me woman, what worm came to my wife last night without my word and why did my wife, whose body I own, entertain a sleazy spirit medium like that in my absence?" roared the Emperor.

Chinake looked at him, he wrung her hand once more, she bit her lip to stifle a cry. In a cracking voice she said, "Because, my Lord, the worm had what the Emperor required and he had come to the Empress's chambers at the request of the Emperor. I was sick, my husband, and at your request he came."

"Then did my wife get what her pain desired from the weasel, or was it just half a night spent with a sick man called Chireshe who is as his name says?"

"My husband," said Chinake, short of breath, "This body that you see now feels better than ever before because of the weasel's medicine and truly I say it belongs to you and none other. But if you continue with your hand in this way, then this body that you boast of so much shall belong to the earth and shall be eaten by worms. Why do you harm what you desire most?" asked Chinake.

The Emperor remained quiet without lessening his grip. Then slowly the Empress looked up and said in a steady, silky voice, "You can wring my hand, my husband; as long as it gives you joy then so be it. I am your vessel."

Indeed she was right and he had been caught. Many times he cursed himself for loving her so much and for never ceasing to want her. Thus he would do such acts as these simply to humiliate her, to break her, and to prove that she was nothing more than a subject to him. But alas, she always got the better of him. She always broke him and he always lost the battle. And to prove his loss as though she had been faking her pain, Chinake slowly broke into a sly smile. The Emperor looked at her, determined to win, and tightened his grip once more making her wince again in pain. Then giving up he suddenly erupted into laughter and let go of her hand. She looked at him and despite her pain she was smiling as she casually rubbed her sore arm.

"My Empress Chinake, always so unpredictable. Why don't you tell your husband what the insane mhondoro said and did that has healed you so quickly? But first let me show you what I was looking at." He roared with laughter again, she smiled and he helped her up. They both walked to the opening on the wall of the room, with Chinake stoically ignoring her pain.

"Come, come my Empress and see your husband's vision. Only you can see my dream and understand it. It is, as yet, the one big secret one that I can only share with you."

He beckoned to her, a smile on his massive face. She walked up to the opening, happy to be a part of his 'big secret' and looked out. Right there, some distance away and before her very eyes stood a hill. It overlooked the entire Kingdom and from it, she was sure, one could sum up everything in one sweeping glance. She had never even given the hill much notice. All she knew was that it was sacred and no living soul except for the mhondoro Makona who possessed the spirit of Chigwangu Rusvingo could ever go up the hill.

"Look at that, my wife," said the Emperor pointing to something jutting from the hill. "Can you make out what it is?"

She squinted her eyes and tried to make it out then she asked, "Is it a rock? It is too far to make out."

Smiling the Emperor said, "Yes, my wife, it is a rock, a rock at the edge of the hill. A rock where the Emperor can sit and speak to his court as it sits below and a rock where the Emperor can sit and look upon his Kingdom."

Chinake looked at him in awe.

"Do you know what it means for me, my wife?"

She shook her head slowly, looking deep in his eyes, searching for an answer, then unexpectedly it dawned upon her. She gasped and nodded her head in slow realisation.

"It means, my husband that you wish to be perched high above the world looking down on all creation, with the forests below you and all mankind under your feet." Turning to look at the hill, her eyes blazing, she said, "It means you can rule from there, and on that sacred hill your throne will be. You will never touch the ground and you will soar high above the earth, ruling it like the Hungwe, your totem."

"You, my wife, are intelligent beyond my knowledge. You say the truth indeed. The making of a great Kingdom begins with the making of a court and throne that hold no questions of superiority. Yes, that is the place I secretly desire to be my court and my home. And, oh, how I wish it were so easy to do."

He walked away from the window and stood leaning with his hands on his throne, facing the entrance. His wife followed and stood behind him.

"But you are the Emperor and you can decree that it be as you wish my Lord," she said, sensing her husband's agitation. "What do you mean when you say it is not so easy? Has anything ever been denied you by this Kingdom? Use your army then to get what you want. Who can resist the might of your soldiers? They will all bow down at the mere sight of them."

"Women, you think that all wars are fought by the spear and won through blood." He chuckled and she looked confused. "Still, you speak the truth, Chinake, when you say it is easy to build this new court and rest my throne there on the hilltop. Nothing can be denied to me, as you know," he said, turning to look at her, "but it is what shall come with the making of my court high above the Kingdom. It is what shall come with that and what it signifies that worries me."

"And what is it, my husband? Tell me, for I hate to see a man of such might so agitated by what is so simple to gain from his strength. You are more than a man. All else is far below you from Kingdom to Kingdom. All else bows down to you and reveres you with awe and respect beyond imagination. See these mighty walls, what else exists like these in the world that can show the strength and greatness of a man? They worship you, my husband; they quake in your presence. Get your court built and have no second thoughts about it. If lives are lost, let it be for your name and let their blood nourish the earth you tread on. Let it add to your valour and fame."

"Then my wife shall see to it that the Emperor gets what his heart desires?"

"Oh I shall, indeed I shall. It disturbs me to see you in such distress."

Slowly he smiled one of his big smiles that never showed his teeth and said, "You will do it for me, Chinake?"

She nodded her head vigorously and said, "I will and not only will I see to it that it becomes your court, I will see to it as well that it becomes your home. That is where a man of your greatness deserves to stay. This earth we walk on is not fit for a man of your greatness. You are beyond anything and anyone I have ever known. You deserve a place among the ancestors, high up in the sky for you to rule mere men."

He stood there and looked at her as though he had not understood a single word she had said, yet he was amazed at the quick way she had uttered his very desire and thoughts. Then in a low voice he asked, "Do you think so highly of me, my wife?" She nodded. "I see," he said, lowering his face and folding his hands on his chest, "I wonder if what it is you think of me could ever be what other men deem of me. I have ruled justly as far as I can. I love the task that was handed down to me but I have often wondered if, for all I have done for the Kingdom, there is a greater reward or a greater form of living than this." She looked at him and wanted to say something but he raised a hand gently and hushed her, "I do not say I am ungrateful to my people but I just wonder if I am all that a man who is an Emperor of such esteem should be."

He sighed deeply and she gazed at him with a look of pity. He had never poured out his heart so much and so openly to her. She was touched. Here stood a great man like none other she could ever know and indeed he deserved a greater reward for his kind of leadership and position. Then looking straight into her eyes from where he stood, he asked, "What then, my wife, should this Kingdom give me if it thinks that I have ruled it justly, if it believes I have given it more glory, security and pomp than any of the other Emperors before me?"

"Anything the Emperor asks for should be his," said Chinake quickly, desperately trying to appease his agonised heart.

"But I have everything, Chinake my wife," said the Emperor Hungwe. "What more can I desire? I have all the silver, all the gold and all the animals and forests are mine, stretching from this part of the country to lands beyond our very eyes. I control all the trade and I declare who lives and who dies. I hold even the breath and peace of men mighty and small in the very palm of my hand. No, my dear wife, I cannot be given anything by my people that I do not already have in abundance."

"Then, then they should do something if my Lord desires a gift from the people. Oh I do hate to see you in such agony. Everything is yours from that which flies in the heavens to that which crawls in the ground from the Zambezi to the Limpopo. It is all yours. What then can appease the painful heart of my Lord? Tell your wife, my husband, what?" said Empress Chinake, close to pleading.

He looked at her once more, his head slightly tilted, a near invisible smile on his face. He now had her worked up and that was good. In a heavy voice he said, "Maybe I have been listening to many tales from the north. But enough of my lame talk, I do not wish to bother you any further."

In haste Empress Chinake said, "No, my husband, no, it is not lame talk. It is what you wish. And what you desire is what I shall fight to see you get. Please let me help. Tell me what it is and I shall see to it that you speedily get what you want."

"It is nothing my wife. I am a bored man. I get to think of wild things that can never be achievable. Remember the funny story that Arab trader once told us of the northern race?" She nodded quickly. "But that is rubbish. I just wondered, just wondered that was all," he said trailing off and looking into a far off place she could not see. He then said, "You will do anything for me, won't you Chinake, even support an Emperor with crazy dreams?"

She nodded her head vigorously, her eyes near to tears. He smiled a small smile filled with admiration. He looked at her and saw the resolve in her. He knew she meant every word but she did not really get the meaning of his words and his concerns. But though she was still in the dark, she was now entangled in his web.

Breathing out, he moved away from her and waving his hand in resignation, said out loud, "They just quake in my presence because I am Emperor Hungwe and they just bow down to me because I am their Lord and I would kill them if they didn't." She blinked, not knowing where the conversation was heading to, "But I want them to honour me with their all, to fear me with their souls." He walked back and standing in front of her, said in a low voice, "And I want them to revere me, I wish to be divine." He stopped and she blinked thrice. The punch from the Emperor's words had left her speechless. He laughed a coarse, empty laugh and going to stand before her he went on, "I want to be given that respect they award Mwari Musikavanhu. Then and only then can my supremacy, our supremacy and our lives be undoubtedly immortal. Chinake, I mean it, I want to become divine."

His eyes bored into hers. She felt the passion in his words and thought she could touch every single one of them. Now she understood his true worry. Yes, he was Emperor and yes, he was feared, but that had not sated his hunger for supremacy. For a man to want to be an Emperor, that was something, but for him to be elevated to a divine being, that was to her beyond comprehension. No, it was not madness but an act of courage fit for a husband like hers, the Emperor Hungwe. She was shocked and delighted at his nerve and desire.

He kept on looking at her, his eyes a deeper red, she knowing what they were trying to communicate to her. He wanted her help. She was delighted, thrilled to be needed so much. Honoured, she nodded slowly, showing her allegiance from years of understanding and whispered, "Let all that my Lord desires on this earth be his. Who am I and who are we to deny you what you deserve? Who are they to deny you spiritual greatness if it is what you wish? I am at your service and let it be known, your entire Kingdom shall serve you."

"You will do it for me, Chinake, you will get me what my heart aches for. Not only for me but for all those in my bloodline and for you?"

Slowly she nodded her head in agreement, her eyes tearful from the infatuation that she had for this man. Pressing his face into her ear he said, breathing the words in a passionate hoarse voice, "Then in return for your never-dying patriotism and love, I, your husband, will build you a home beyond your wildest dreams. With walls so thick and strong that they will never fall. As your beauty stands firm so shall they. And I will separate you from the rest of my wives so that your place in my life shall forever be marked and unquestioned. Your enclosure shall be so beautiful that none shall compare to it. I will build you a home which will stand right under my home on the hill and each day I will gaze upon it and forever be reminded of your beauty and majesty. We will make sure that we get the greatest builder in the Kingdom to do the work. It will be only for you, only for the Hungwe's first wife, Vahosi Chinake."

He ended there and his face lingered beside hers for a while. She felt his breath and she felt his need, his need for her to help him become divine. She remembered the Arab's story, something that had seemed unreal at the time but now made a lot of sense because that was the gift her husband wanted. The gift to be worshipped by his people and be elevated to immortality. In the sheer excitement of being requested to intimately serve him, she nodded again.

He then moved his face away from her and asked in earnest, "And who will support the Emperor in this crazy idea, my wife? Who will be mad enough or intelligent and courageous enough to make a nation go against the rigid religious structure they always believed in? After all, who am I to change the spiritual order of this nation, one that has stood thus for years beyond my knowledge?"

Her face fell as she searched her mind. Indeed, she knew that no one would dare do what her husband was intending, because it meant going against the ancestral spirits and Mwari, the creator of all men. Only he was considered divine. Was her husband's dream a delusion? She sighed and then from nowhere an idea hit her like a bolt of lightning. She knew who would be crazy enough to do such a thing. Someone who had visited her at the height of her illness and who had shown a great desire to talk, to be believed and could in fact be believed because she had seen him sway people in the past. And that someone was none other than Chireshe.

"I know, my husband," she cried in joy. "The mad mhondoro Chireshe will work for you. You have seen him at your court, how he can talk and how he can do anything to get an audience. Who would deny working for the Emperor? He will do anything that will give him popularity and a woman by his side."

"You seem to have an answer for everything," he said smiling. "But enough of that. Now tell me, my wife, how did your clandestine meeting with my popular and intelligent mhondoro go? I trust you did not spit bile from your stomach when he gazed lustfully at you?" said the Emperor, returning to his throne and beckoning Chinake to come and sit by his side. It was as though he was ignoring his wife's suggestion.

She was both confused and discouraged. Had he ignored her or was he simply not willing to commit himself? She had wanted to press on, but something made her refrain from asking. Feeling discouraged, Chinake lifted her eyes and looked at her husband, who was still smiling at her. Breathing in, she smiled back sweetly, ready to go and tell him all that had happened. As she sat down beside him on the floor he looked at her, saw the twinkle in her eyes and roared into his characteristic loud laughter. They talked and they dined. Chinake left her husband that day with a whirring head, proud to have been invited into the Emperor's plan. She was still determined to help.

Now alone, the Emperor looked out once more at the hill that would soon be his court and he felt pleased with himself. His plans for Chinake had gone well and he was certain she would secretly convince the devious mhondoro Chireshe to join in. She had told him exactly what he had wanted to hear about the mhondoro and he noticed that she had indeed admired his wit. Chireshe would crush any internal rebellion with his influence and sharp tongue. Already a new enclosure for his other wives was being built and his new ideas for the improved structures were paying off. He intended to do everything he had recounted to his wife with such passion.

Hungwe had come to realise that although he had wealth and power, the two would not suffice to make him divine and immortal. He needed religious control and that would start when he took up residence on the sacred hill. For now, he would let the matter rest and wait to see how far his current plot with Chinake would unfold. The hill was as yet his biggest secret, an idea to be divulged only at the right time. Thus he had told Chinake not to tell anyone about it and the seriousness on his face as he had said those simple words had made an impression in Chinake's mind.

He walked outside; it was dusk and the sun was about to set over the eastern hilltops. There lay the Kingdom of the Mbire ruled by Nyatsimba Mutota and a troubling thought occurred to him. The Mbire were growing steadily in number and in strength. They were hard workers and in the event that workers were needed to build more granite stone enclosures, the Mbire would do very well. All this they accredited to Mwari Musikavanhu, who played such an important role in their lives. They were also religious fanatics and if ever there would come a time for the small Kingdom to rebel, it would come in the name of Mwari. They were the only vassals of the Great Zimbabwe strong and big enough to pose such a threat. Was he thinking too far ahead? No he was not, he was one man who never wanted to leave any stone unturned. All gaps had to be covered but how would he see to it that any external threat was avoided? As yet he did not know how but soon he would. He rested his case and prayed for an opportunity to come his way.

The third event to reshape the history of two nations had just occurred.

# THE FOURTH EVENT

## Kwatara the dreamer

The day had advanced to mid-morning but still had an icy edge to it. Many people were now up and about. Young herders were busy whistling to their cattle and goats and several women were on their way to the river to fetch water in their large earthen gourds. Kwatara, one of the mhondoros of the Great Zimbabwe Empire, saw all this but his mind was too preoccupied with thoughts of the dream he had had during the night to be bothered with whatever was going on around him.

He was sitting in his favourite spot which he always came to each time he needed to think, on top of a large granite rock which lay among many others that were strewn all over the plateau. These were the granite rocks which were broken and chipped by the Karanga of the Great Zimbabwe Empire to make the brick-like stones with which they built their enclosures.

Sitting here among the large boulders he always found peace and space to think. The rocks were silent and made no noise. They awarded him the solitude he desired most when his mind was troubled by many thoughts. Besides, no one ever came here save for the workers from the building site. Today they were busy trying to light a fire on flat granite rocks so that they could cool them later with water and break them—a task which was most difficult in winter. He wondered what it was like to be one of the builders, burdened by the work they had to do but free from any national obligation. It was true that many people out there admired him, for it was an honour to be a mhondoro and one so young and good looking too.

Kwatara was in his early thirties and was tall and lean. He had a full mouth with dark lips set against a light-skinned face that highlighted their black colour. Many had said that when he looked at you with his large brown eyes it always felt as though he was looking deep into your soul. He had an air of seriousness that discomfited many people around him. His beard was short, dark and unkempt. He had short stubby hair, which was hardly ever cut and yet was never long because it just did not grow. He was devoted to his calling and took great pride in his work.

Looking up at the sky he exhaled a stream of warm air which mingled with the cold to form a misty breath and for the umpteenth time in his life he wondered why on earth he had been granted the gift he had. He truly wished it had been given to someone else in the Kingdom because, whenever the visions came, they placed upon him a burden so great he found it hard to carry. Ever since he could remember, Kwatara used to dream of things that would come to pass, especially things that affected his family and the Kingdom. He had been only five when he dreamt of the swarm of bees surrounding his father's cattle kraal. Two days later a swarm of bees did come and they stung many cattle in his village, killing them stone dead. Years later he was the one who warned the people about an invasion of locusts early in the rainy season and encouraged them to harvest much earlier than usual. People now knew and appreciated that he had a gift. So they followed his advice and, when the locusts came, they swarmed on the forest fields and found no crops.

His dreams had assisted his family, foretold great feats and catastrophes in the Kingdom and had warned him of the events in his life. And each time he was forced either to fight alone for the nation or to warn the people about whatever danger it was that was coming. But despite the fact that his dreams had been proved true over the years and had aided the Kingdom, it was never easy to stand up and tell people of impeding danger, hoping for them to believe his words. It would have been easier had the dream been straightforward, but this time it was more like a riddle brought upon his life to torment his conscience.

He remembered having gone to sleep the previous night a happy and free-minded man and it surprised him how he had woken up worried and broken. What he had seen in his dream so weighed Kwatara down that no words, however dear, could make him feel any better. He had had many nightmares, from some of which he had awoken shaken and trembling, but this dream had damaged his soul. There had been nothing nightmarish about it yet it had managed like no other dream before to sap the strength out of him.

Again, he felt a rush of anger and great futility, which led him to hate the gift he had and wished he were building walls and enclosures like his brother Hombasha and his father before him. But he had been given a different gift. He had the gift of the mhondoro. He was one of the few people in the Kingdom who presided over the Kingdom's sacred ceremonies. He was one of the few who could speak to the ancestors and plead to Mwari, the creator of all things, for guidance, forgiveness and assistance. He also was the only Spirit Medium who had the gift of dreams.

Now as he sat lonely and tormented he hugged his cloth tightly around his shoulders and recalled the dream despite the heaviness it cast on him. He remembered suddenly finding himself surrounded by a thick blanket of darkness. The blackness was so thick that as he groped around where he stood, he felt as though he could just feel it. And it was a strange feeling, for him to feel darkness. Then from the darkness emerged a young, beautiful girl with large and small colourful beads hanging down her neck covering her breasts. Around her waist was a lovely new cloth, neatly tied and clinging to her hips.

It was strange, Kwatara had thought in his dream, how he could so clearly see the girl in such darkness and how her beauty appealed to him. She was so young and so innocent but her face was passive as though she had emerged from a void and the void had done harm to her spirit. And from nowhere, balancing upon the girl's head, there appeared a clay pot, round and well made. The clay pot had a beautiful design which looked familiar. At that moment he couldn't place it. He knew he would be able to soon if he laid eyes on it again. Then, as if she wanted to hand over to someone whatever was in the pot, she tripped and, as she fell to the ground, so too did the pot. She screamed in pain, the pain of letting her carefully handled and beautiful clay pot fall.

Kwatara saw himself say something but he couldn't hear what it was. He saw his lips move but couldn't make out the words. He felt a compelling desire to assist. His hand reached out to help the girl but it was lashed away by some unseen force in the dark. His face writhed in agonizing worry and his mind raced. What could he do to help the girl? She looked at him and groaned. This time he opened his mouth and he heard himself speak. "Let me help you, please. Let me pick up the clay pot."

She looked at him and then to the clay pot lying on the floor and horror filled her eyes. He too looked at the clay pot and saw that one piece had broken off and was lying on the floor. His eyes opened wide and he let out a cry. Why, he thought, was he so agitated? It was just a broken piece of a clay pot and nothing more. Why was he so horrified and in such agony? Now he forgot about the girl and reached out to pick up the broken piece but with an unexpected force the girl sprang up and crushed his hand with her foot. Kwatara screamed and looked up pleadingly. The young girl looked at him and laughed.

Her previous innocence was gone, she had lost all her beauty and passiveness. Now her face was hard, her eyes stony, her tongue turned black and she spoke with venom. "Who are you to put your hand on things that do not belong to you? Who are you to think you can help? Let me alone for I am the all supreme. This clay pot is mine and that which is broken from the clay pot I shall hunt down and break to nothing because it is mine to do with as I please."

Kwatara looked at her shocked. His hand hurt intensely and this time tears rolled down his face in pain. She looked at him and laughed. She let out a horrible screaming laugh and tears ran down her face. Then she removed her foot. He remained crouching on the floor holding his painful hand. Slowly she walked towards the broken piece and stopped. A sigh of relief escaped her lips and they broke into a triumphant smile.

Kwatara turned his head and looked at her trying to pick up the broken piece but something strange happened. Even Kwatara was left dumbfounded. As she bent down casually to pick it up, the piece from the clay pot leapt up, twirled around in the air and was sucked into nothingness.

"No, no, no!" screamed the girl. She too could not believe what had just happened. It was just a piece of a clay pot and she had had it in her grasp but something had taken it away from her. She looked dumbfounded and the pain of her loss clearly showed on her face. And as though she had discovered the cause of her painful loss, she turned to look venomously at Kwatara. With a vicious look on her face she spat out the words, "You, you did this, you stole my piece, you blew it away from my grasp. You! You!!!"—the last words were a real scream.

With deadly determination she advanced towards Kwatara, hands outreached, a mad look on her face, aiming for his throat. He could not move. Her eyes glistened and her nose flared. Her lips twitched and noises filled the air. Noises of people angry, angry with Kwatara, for the voices loudly cursed his name. He could not understand why they were angry with him. What had he done? He had done nothing wrong.

Suddenly she was standing before him, her hands curled around his throat. He looked up shocked and she smiled at him. It wasn't an ugly smile but a nauseatingly sweet smile of triumph. For all his strength, Kwatara still could not fight her off. It was not because of his painful hand, but because he was immobilized. He felt emerge from the darkness the anger of everyone whom surrounded him, everyone who he could not see and he was terrified. Their anger seemed to hold him in place, to keep him nailed to the spot. Lifting his head he looked at the angry woman in front of him and tears filled his eyes. Was he going to lose his life to her?

Slowly her hands curled around his throat, amazingly soft and well groomed hands. It was as though he had seen them somewhere and at one time had felt them somewhere. What surprised him was that, as soft as they were, they had an unearthly strength and the stare from her eyes held a madness that was unquenchable. Kwatara felt the life go from him the minute her hands folded around his neck. But before she could choke him to death a strong wind came.

Kwatara looked up and so did the young girl. The wind whirled around him and turned into a whirlwind that separated them with such force that it ripped the girl's hands away from Kwatara's throat and hurled her to the other side of the room. Surprisingly, Kwatara remained where he was, untouched by the wind. He looked at the girl and saw her painfully try to get up. And she succeeded in spite of the force of the wind working against her.

Kwatara looked at her and saw the desperation on the girl's face. He saw the energy she used as she reached out for the clay pot which now lay between the two. Once more the wind worked against her with such a force that it nearly ripped her hands from her body. But still she tried and the mhondoro felt sorry for her.

The whirlwind swelled in size and moved towards the clay pot lying on the ground. The girl screamed. Kwatara could not hear the scream but he saw the way her mouth opened wide with horror and how her eyes widened into madness.

The wind remained relentless and now blew with a force that rendered in vain all her efforts to retrieve the broken piece. She writhed on the floor and kicked. Kwatara was amazed at her determination and force. But what he was seeing could not be compared to the sight he witnessed a split second later. An unseen force lifted the clay pot, twirling it in the air like the broken piece before and then it was thrown to the ground. It broke into many pieces and each broken piece was sucked once more into oblivion. What remained was one larger piece, the zigzag pattern quite clear on it, resting on the floor all alone. The girl let out an animal-like scream that filled the air above the force of the wind. Her hand shook as she reached out for nothing and she convulsed into sobs. With tear-filled eyes she looked at the broken piece and for the first time she appeared helpless and lonely.

Kwatara looked at the remaining piece and saw how disfigured it looked. It had many cracks and had lost all its shine. He felt a pang of pain. The wind abated, the whirlwind disappeared. Only the silent darkness, the girl and the piece from the clay pot remained. Suddenly Kwatara was taken out of the picture and, noticing that she was alone, the girl frantically looked around. The darkness started closing in and the girl became afraid, afraid of something Kwatara could not see but something that was happening around her and only she could see. For now, as Kwatara dreamt on, she mumbled words of mercy, her lips moving, trying to say things that could not come out. She moved about on the floor as though searching for a place to hide, but the darkness still came and, as the final blanket of blackness covered, her she screamed.

All that remained in the end was the last broken piece, all alone and abandoned. The girl was nowhere to be seen. Kwatara was very saddened by all this. He turned away and moved into a bright light. It was then that he had woken up. And now he was here and nowhere near to finding out the meaning of his dream. This frustrated him. What if something big and terrible was about to happen in the Kingdom and he was not able to help?

He sighed and shook his head. Seeking some consolation he cupped his hands, bowed his head and silently he clapped. He needed someone to tell, someone to talk to and right now prayer seemed to be the only solution.

"O great ancestral spirits, you who are above, I come to you with a burdened heart and though I do not shed tears I know you who are in the skies can feel my pain and see the fear that is rocking my mind." He stopped clapping and, locking his fingers together, he clasped his hands. With his face contorted in pain, he looked up at the sky and said in a hoarse whisper, "Oh how can I make you understand, but I know you do. I need to know the meaning of my dream for it has burdened me so. Plead on my behalf, great ancestors, and beg Musikavanhu Mwari, he that created me and my gift, to direct my steps so that I can guide this nation, for I would never live and forgive myself if I fail the gift and mission you gave to me." Silently he clapped once more and a tear escaped his eyes. For a long time he remained silent and felt utterly forlorn.

From somewhere in the sky a bird screeched. He looked up shaken out of his thoughts by the cry. A child let out a laugh from nearby and the wind blew clouds over the sun, banishing the warmth and bringing a shadow that slowly covered the rock-filled place. Kwatara suddenly felt scared. He realised without knowing how he knew, that a shadow was also creeping over the Great Zimbabwe nation and one that could be too great for him to stop on time. Quickly he got up and started for home. His usual place of solitude was not doing him any good at all today.

# Chapter one

## Many weeks later

Being late in July in the southern hemisphere of Africa the winter season had reached its peak. Many would have been found huddling indoors by a warm fire, but that was not so in the Great Zimbabwe nation. Already hundreds of workers were toiling in the cold, for the sake of the Great Zimbabwe ruler, the Hungwe. He was erecting a new enclosure for his other wives.

Down here in the valley, the cold was merciless, it bit into the bare feet of the workers and clung to their naked backs. Their teeth chattered noisily and many of them sniffed and coughed painfully. Slowly they worked on the granite rock, chipping it with chisels made by the famous ironsmiths of the Great Zimbabwe Empire. It was not really a hard job to do had it been summer and if they had been working casually but, alas, they were under immense pressure to finish the enclosure. This was Hungwe's experiment to see how well his dream enclosures would look like. For with Hungwe, everything had a purpose.

The morning mist still hung around the sanctuary thick and blinding, but fear made the workers hardly miss a step. They worked, they moved around and they toiled in utter silence save for the singing to complete the mighty walls of the great Hungwe, Emperor of the Great Zimbabwe. Gradually the sun made its golden entrance. It was greatly welcomed and was a consolation from the cold. A few people started humming, and this deep murmur slowly broke into song which brought warmth to the dry mouths and lips of the workers.

One might have presumed that Hungwe and his forefathers built these walls for protection, but in truth the Great Zimbabwe rulers did not really care for this; the enclosures and their alarming majesty were a sign of power and supremacy, for nowhere else in the whole of Africa would walls and enclosures so great be built and found. And today the King's son was coming to inspect this enclosure to see if it was beautiful and strong enough to impress his father.

To announce his entrance the horn sounded, loud and crystal clear. The drums were beat sharply for all to hear. This was the way they heralded the approach of the Prince. No slave, no worker and no civilian were to stand in the way of the crown Prince.

People scurried to the sides of the walls and hid themselves from view of the approaching royal entourage. No one spoke and the minds which had only moments ago been dulled by the cold, suddenly became alert. From one entrance the royal guard appeared, the horn sounded once more, this time louder. In their midst was the Prince whom they guarded like a god. Chikomo was his name and his father the Hungwe had assigned him the task of overseeing the works of the master builder.

Slowly the young Prince moved around with his convoy and the master builder following at his heels. He was Hungwe's second son from his first wife Chinake. His guards flanked him, ready to kill even a fly if it came his way. He was clearly enjoying the attention he was receiving as he assessed the progress of the enclosure.

"The walls are strong enough now," said the master builder. "I am sure that my Prince finds the size and shapes of the rocks to his utmost liking," he finished, bending low.

Chikomo sniffed loudly and hugged his thick animal furs around him. He did not even look at the master builder but turned his eyes to look at the trail of workers moving with rocks in pouches on their backs. The master builder and his junior looked at him, anxiously wondering if it was just the way he naturally looked or if he was angry at them. The Prince was not too good-looking and he had about him a definite air of arrogance that could be sensed from afar. It was as though the word "Prince" was written in bold letters from his forehead to his toes. Then twisting his mouth proudly, he slowly turned his large, unfriendly, cold eyes to look at the master builder. The man would have loved to look back at his master but the sight of his emotionless, unfriendly, ugly Prince made him cringe under his skin.

"What is the matter, master builder?" he asked in his rasping, cold voice that added a chill to the cold wind surrounding the men. "You cannot face your Prince, or is his face so ugly that you would rather look at the dirt and see it as more beautiful than the face of your Lord's son?"

Quickly the master builder looked up, his eyelids batting a hundred times faster. A chilly wind blew again and he shivered in spite of the thick animal hide that he wore around himself. He furtively blinked at his junior and when he saw the fear in his eyes, he turned to look at the Prince and spluttered an answer not even audible enough for him to hear himself.

"My King, my Prince, no indeed do not take any grudge against me. I merely looked to the ground as a sign of respect, that I should not annoy my young majesty with my humble stare. Indeed why would I want to continue to stare into the eyes of a Prince, my Lord?"

Chikomo smiled a slow and queer smile that appeared like the beginnings of a bulldog's snarl. Then he burst into a laugh that made even the workers stop and stare in wonder. His guards raised their eyebrows, the master builder and his junior looked at each other worriedly.

"The blood of the Great Zimbabwe, the blood of the Hungwe, is fear inspiring and even our laughter causes fear," he suddenly stopped smiling and with gleaming eyes he looked at the master builder who was attempting to break into a smile meant to match his masters mood. "You are indeed a genius master builder, my grandfather was not wrong to appoint you to this position."

With a serious look his eyes moved from the top of the wall they were facing right to the bottom. The eyes of all those around him followed and stopped where his stopped. Then he went to the wall and the people gathered around him. He touched it and ran his hand down the rocks that miraculously made a solid wall with no mortar.

"We are geniuses, are we not, to balance these bricks, one on top of the other with nothing sealing them?" he said proudly, turning to those gathered around him as he gestured with his big arms.

A murmur of agreement rose from his entourage. "These walls are so thick and so tall that no enemy can penetrate. Imagine surrounding your Kingdom and all the thousands of people in it, safe from the enemy, is that not a master stroke of genius?"—followed by another and now louder murmur of approval.

"Ah yes, my master builder," he said, turning away from the people to face him, "We may have a long way to go but indeed we are proving to be the masters of builders, the Lords of Kings. But we are too mighty to think of protecting ourselves with walls. Our army is too powerful for any other in this country. Let these walls be built for the show of supremacy and may they become stronger and more beautiful." Those around him spoke in low tones of agreement. The master builder simply looked on, wondering what would come next. He dreaded the very presence of this young Prince. He was so unpredictable.

Chikomo came towards him and placed his hand on his shoulder looking directly into his face. His eyes were red, from heavy drinking most probably, but they were also void of feeling and full of evil. The master builder smiled. It was a pathetic smile. It was apparent that he feared his Prince and all more so since he knew that this young man was bound to do anything he pleased to anyone: he had not been wrong in his fear of what the Prince could do. With his eyes fixated on the old man, his long uncut nails dug into the master builder's flesh. The old man winced in pain and tried hard not to cry. Gradually Chikomo let go and, like a drunk studying the effect of his work, he dreamily stared at the old man and sneered then said, "So I will tell my father that he can sleep in peace. Things are moving on rather smoothly, as I can see." He smiled his queer smile again and painfully the master builder nodded his grizzled head.

"Winter is still with us, we have enough time to make many more rocks and many hands to do the job. The people who serve the Hungwe know no winter hindrance, sun or cold; the granite shall be broken and the enclosure shall be finished at the Emperor's appointed time."

Though it was so painful the master builder dared not even rub his shoulder or look at it. He could only breathe laboriously and respond, "It is an honour, my Prince," and the Prince ever so slightly nodded his head.

"I shall be going now, old man," said Chikomo wrapping the furs around him. "It is too cold here for a young Prince to stay. But do not forget, you work for your Lord, conqueror of many, you build for a mighty Emperor and so let it all be fitting for the great Hungwe."

The master builder nodded his white head politely. "Yes, my Prince, indeed it will be fit for my great Emperor, the Hungwe."

The Prince smiled, breathed in and clapped his hands just once. His servants and his guards gathered around him as though to shield him from the bitter cold as he moved away. The workers scurried out of the way, or they stood still and dared not move before the passing Prince. Satisfied with the sensation he was causing, the Prince smiled his queer smile.

As soon as they were sure the Prince was truly out of eye and ear-shot the master builder's assistant named Gweshe gingerly placed his hand on his master's shoulder and asked, "Are you hurt, master?"

"More than you can imagine," replied the master builder wincing in pain. "That young man has an ugly heart, uglier than his brother Perayi's."

"It is funny that he enjoys inflicting such awful pain, in all this cold, as though we are not doing enough. It is winter and it is hard to break the granite, let alone heat it. Work is slow and yet they want us to perform miracles."

"It is not strange, my young man," said the master builder, turning to look at his young assistant, "because that is the only way they can maintain such a huge Kingdom. Who can build all this with soft hands," he said, looking about. His young assistant's eyes followed his gaze. "Let us work for these kings of the earth and hope that their wrath will not be against us. Winter is still with us, we will work hard to break the rocks. If we fool around and focus on other things, our heads could roll. So let us hurry along and get back to work."

"They say that he loves testing his dangerous herbs on people and he gets them from the various traders who come into this Kingdom from far off lands," said Gweshe ignoring Hombasha's order.

"Then maybe one day they shall turn against him. It is dangerous to fool around with such herbs. You never know what may become of you in the end."

"Then go and see someone who can assist you because he may have inflicted more than just the pain on your shoulder, the Princes are all an evil and ignorant lot. Their whole thinking ability has been eaten up by wickedness and, I tell you master Hombasha, that they shall cause the ruin of the very walls they hurt and kill others for," said Gweshe in a voice full of concern.

"You are now talking too much, Gweshe, how many times do I have to tell you not to talk about royalty and important people as though they are nobody? You shall end up under the whip one day," Hombasha reprimanded him harshly.

"I am sorry, master, but it is not good to see one whom you admire so much being hurt for nothing. Do go and see someone about the shoulder tomorrow, please."

"I will, but the Prince may come back and see us talking. Now please let us get back to doing our job. We have a lot to catch up on." Hombasha knew that if he entertained Gweshe further, all this lame talk would end up in gossip and his very words would end up on everyone's lips and in the Prince's ears.

The young assistant would have loved to ask more and to discuss more but the master builder moved away quickly, rubbing his shoulder. He knew from experience that it was wiser to keep his loathing of the young Prince to himself, lest one day the young man he called his assistant would sell him out. Yes, Gweshe was loyal but he had a bad habit of gossiping and it was actually unhealthy to say anything before him. Hombasha had learnt long back that he was good at his job but also better at hearsay. Though he had never said anything about Hombasha, the master builder thought it was better to avoid giving the man any temptation to do so. As he walked away he stopped for a moment and felt pain shoot through his shoulder. Gently he rubbed it and was amazed at the swelling that was quickly gathering there. He looked back and saw his assistant looking at him with a concerned face. In return he gave the young man one stern look and that saw him hurrying off to his duties.

Much was said about the young Prince Chikomo. Many said he loved messing around with dangerous herbs which traders from the north and the east brought to the Kingdom. The master builder hoped the young Prince had not placed some poisonous herb under his long nails. He tried to think positively but the pain kept coming back. In the end he gathered up courage and painfully walked to his duties on the enclosure. Very soon it would be finished and the King's other wives and their children would come and stay here.

Looking at his shoulder once more, he thought he saw the swelling redden and to make himself feel safe he promised himself he would call on his young brother the mhondoro called Kwatara. He was not just a dreamer, but like most of the spirit mediums in the Kingdom he knew a lot of very helpful herbs. Then he looked at the wall they were building once more. It was coming on beautifully. It was funny that the very man who was building the best granite stone enclosures ever was the one the young Prince had carelessly hurt. How thoughtless to try and destroy a man who was doing such great work for the Kingdom.

And indeed the master builder was doing a very good job, but the best was yet to come. Very soon, a more majestic enclosure that would rise up to six meters in height would be built through his genius and live on to this very day to profess the majesty of the Great Zimbabwe rulers. His hands would carve dwellings so ingeniously built as to cause great controversy in centuries to come as to their builders and origins. Together with the effort of the ironsmiths, the royal family and the workers themselves, by the time the city of stone was finished it would house over eighteen thousand people, standing as the greatest stone structure in Africa, only then to be abandoned.

# Chapter two

Mutota and his son Matope sat in a round hut, which the King used for his private discussions. Outside it was very quiet and here and there crickets chirped. A large fire was burning, keeping them warm. It had been many weeks since the two had gone up the hill to view their future land.

"The fire is one of Mwari's greatest gifts, my son," said Mutota as he reached out his hands to the flames, rubbing them together. "I have always wondered what we would cook with or what would keep us warm on such miserable nights." Matope, who was sitting on a stool beside his father, gazed admiringly at the older man. He was proud of him and he knew the way his father believed and honoured Mwari. Religion played a very important part in the Mbire Kingdom.

"He created the earth and all in it. Men were meant to eat, father, and to eat cooked food and not to live like the wild animals of the forests, hence the gift of fire," said Matope in his deep calm voice.

"Indeed he gives to us all," now we wait for him to honour us with a plan and an escape, my child. We wait for Mwari to make us conquerors," said Mutota raising a fist in the air and Matope responded with a reassuring smile. "Tekeshe Chingowo shall be coming soon," continued his father. "I sent word for him and I know all this may appear too hasty for you, my son, but we need to make preparations if a way of escape from the control of the Great Zimbabwe rulers is to succeed."

"Nothing planned for the love of a Kingdom and from the goodness of the heart can be too hasty, father," said Matope. "We just need to proceed with caution if we are to achieve our plan. We simply have to wait and see if Tekeshe Chingowo is for the move and I know that, with him by our side, nothing can go wrong."

"He is on our side. Last year when we sent our tribute to the Hungwe of the Great Zimbabwe, Tekeshe lost out on a lot on his grain. He was unhappy and he hinted that if a chance came, he would run away, but to where, on his own with his family? The Kingdom soldiers would track him down and kill him."

"Then at least we have one reliable ally," said Matope to his father, who had moved even closer to the fire. "What we now need are a cooperative people. Trouble may arise if one half agrees and the other disagrees."

"That," said Mutota, "is what we shall discuss with Tekeshe. "He is the army general and a strategist. He will know what to do and just how to make the people understand and agree to our mission. He will know how best to mobilize the people and the army. The thing is we have to make him into a true soldier, a warrior of the Mbire state."

"I do not understand father, "said Matope looking confused. "Tekeshe is the best soldier you have and one who will die for the Kingdom. I find it a natural born instinct in him to lay down his life for the Kingdom."

"I do see the same in him," said Mutota standing up and looking very serious, "but he needs to be rejuvenated. He needs to be moulded over again and attain a fresh zeal."

"But I have never seen him anything less than a great army commander father," said Matope in defence of the man Tekeshe whom he admired. "He has a bold and no-nonsense way of grooming and addressing the army."

"Your heart and eyes are still full of youth and innocence, my child. How can you tell how brave he is and how firm he is? Our army has been inactive for years. We are under the Great Zimbabwe rulers. Who are we to go about pillaging as they do and fighting others who are also their subjects? Years of servitude have done harm to our true warriors."

Mutota looked at the flames, picked up a small stick and threw it into the fire. It crackled and hissed then burnt out entirely. Matope looked at his father. He seemed to have aged by more than a year in a few days. His excitement and the pressure to move from the Great Zimbabwe plateau were taking their toll on him.

"And," said Mutota at last after a brief and thoughtful silence, "he needs to be, placed in the real situation, groomed only by words to appreciate our true cause and then made to believe in our dream. The first battle is that of the mind."

"I see what you mean, father. In any case he is our best hope. He is a soldier, feared and respected, a strategist like you said and a man of the people, a protector. He is bound to get the people's support sooner than any of us."

"And as leaders, we should know that it should end only with his service to us. Understand this, my son," said the King, crouching before Matope and giving him a stern look, "once the army has too much control over people and excess influence, rebellious thoughts start to spin around in their heads. We should make sure that Tekeshe understands he is answerable to us. As soon as he appreciates and knows his position he shall fight for us and never against us."

"And how shall we achieve that, father? It is good you have everything planned and thought over," said Matope, beaming in admiration.

"Simple, my son: give the man his rightful position, but spell out his limitations as firmly and as ingeniously as you can. Then make sure he understands his job, part of which is to work so that the people should respect you as King. I should not lift a finger, my son: those that serve me like Tekeshe should work for the respect and furtherance of my crown."

Matope simply looked on in amazement. He had learnt so much in the space of just a few days and he wondered why his father had never taught him anything like this before. At that point, they heard footsteps outside. A deep growling voice came from the entrance outside in the dark and said, "My King, I beg your permission to enter."

The King recognised the voice and said, "Enter Tekeshe, we have already waited too long for you to come."

Tekeshe entered. His eyes blinked against the light from the bright fire indoors and they quickly scanned the whole room. They came to rest on the King and the Prince. He crouched on one knee, cupped his hands and clapped in greeting.

"My King, my Prince. Your humble servant has come upon your request. Forgive me for being late. It is the cold weather that delayed me so," said Tekeshe, his face hung low. The King maintained a serious stare and, beckoning with his hand, he said, "Arise Tekeshe, worthy soldier of the Mbire. It is indeed cold outside. Take a stool, sit beside your Prince close to the fire and make yourself warm. The King wishes to discuss serious business with you."

Tekeshe arose and took a stool from the other side of the room. Then seated beside the Prince, his spear beside him, he once more cupped his hands and clapped. "Greetings my King." The King clapped back. "Greetings my Prince," and the Prince also clapped back.

Once the formalities were over the King cleared his throat and started to talk.

"I shall not delay either of you for the night grows colder and we all need to rest. Tekeshe, my worthy soldier, on so many occasions you have shown a great zeal for this Kingdom of the Mbire and you have not let us down on any point." Tekeshe nodded his head slowly in agreement. "I have no need to doubt your allegiance to the Mbire Kingdom. But it is not because of that that I have called you. It is because at one time you suggested an idea to me which has come to fruition in this very heart of mine; you expressed a desire to be autonomous," said the King and his eyes carefully watched Tekeshe as though searching for something, not on the man's outside features, but deep inside him.

"May my King tell me all he desires," said Tekeshe, in the humblest growl he could muster. "His humble servant is listening."

Mutota was listening carefully to Tekeshe as he spoke and watched his facial expressions. The King saw excitement written all over the face of the giant army general and he observed the way he tried to control his rising eagerness. The huge man's nose flared and his eyes widened slightly. The King had not seen this expression on Tekeshe's face for a very long time. Dejection had reduced Tekeshe to a mere soldier, now something of his fear-inspiring warrior's heroism was returning.

# Chapter three

Hombasha, the master builder, whom the Prince had tortured with his hands on that fateful morning, had been doing this job from boyhood. His father had been master builder for the Great Zimbabwe rulers before the present day emperors. Life had been a lot easier at that time because, though the then rulers had been smitten with a passion for building, they did not exhibit cruelty to the workers.

For as long as he could remember he had enjoyed shaping the granite rocks that lay abundant on the hills surrounding the Great Zimbabwe area. He had worked beside his father and beside many other workers and he had been honoured when, after his father's death, he had been crowned master builder. That had been his lifelong dream.

It was his father who had improved on the smoothness of the walls. Earlier on, the walls had been made of rough, uneven blocks coarsely fitted into each other and even boulders from the surrounding landscape were incorporated into the walls. But Hombasha's father had refined the technique by chipping and shaping the granite blocks into finer, brick-like structures. Granite naturally breaks into even slabs, hence it was not difficult to break it into portable sizes. These were then placed one on top of the other because no mortar was used, each layer slightly more recessed than the last. The end result was a remarkably finished surface.

The Great Zimbabwe walls needed great artists with great foresight and talent to build them. They had to be able to command and to coordinate the workers and the supervisors so that no sloppiness took place. Hombasha was one such man. He had such a high drive and such a huge amount of energy. With the Emperor's father he had received his honour and had loved his work, but with the present Emperor something had gone wrong. Work was no longer a pleasure but a trial to be borne because one had to stay alive.

He was at his home now. As master builder he stayed within one of the enclosures. He was sitting in his hut, a big fire was burning and his brother Kwatara the dreamer was sitting on a stool beside him. The winter darkness covered the Great Zimbabwe like a thick cloak and reduced visibility within the stone walls almost to nothing. Here and there, fires lit by the soldiers and the sentries and by people in the huts within and outside the walls shone, lighting the place up a bit.

Hombasha sat on an animal hide, his back bare and the marks of the Prince's nails clearly visible on his shoulder. His younger brother, the mhondoro Kwatara, was with him tonight, attending to his wounds. Despite the bright fire in the round hut, Hombasha shivered.

"You shiver from the cold, my brother, or is it the pain in your shoulder?" he asked gently, as he massaged the shoulder with soft leaves dipped in hot water.

"I am old, little brother," said Hombasha, in an unsteady voice. "There is no way that I can withstand the pain. The young Prince is a mad man. How could he easily dip his crude nails into my flesh like that and for what reason? Have I not served his father as per his expectations? I should have called you two days ago but I thought it would easily heal; now it has grown worse."

"It is because you did not rest. Heaven knows what was in his nails. I hope he was not testing any strange herb on your flesh."

"Oh, how I wish I was younger, little brother. I would have done something. I would have . . ."

"Hush, big brother, do not shout. It will do your weak body no good at all. And remember, walls have ears." He dipped the leaves into the water once more from a small clay pot and gently massaged his brother's shoulder. The older brother winced in pain. A tear rolled down his cheek and Kwatara felt his pain.

"It is good you came to attend to me, Kwatara. The leaves and the water are doing me some good. I wonder what I would do without you."

Kwatara smiled gently and said in his soft voice, "You have two wives, they would have seen to your injuries. And you have sons, Hombasha. You are not a lonely man."

"Yes, that may be so, but they are not mhondoros. They do not have the gift that you have or the gift of healing. Ah, the pain was so unbearable in the morning but I had to work because those were the Emperor's orders. Now you have made me feel better," said Hombasha.

"Don't mention it, my brother, at least you are no longer concentrating on your pain. It will heal faster that way if you ignore it."

Hombasha turned to look at Kwatara and spoke in a lower tone, "My brother, do you think it is only the physical pain that I feel, no. It is the shame that that young man inflicted upon me. It is the emotional pain that I am feeling. How can one be so cruel, so unkind and yet so young? They appoint him overseer of the building yet he does not even know how to lay one stone upon the other."

Kwatara kept quiet for a while then answered, "Because they have the power to do so, Hombasha. They are the kings and they are simply making a statement. Unfortunately, the Prince did it on a poor old man like you."

"After all that I have done for them . . . After all that our father did for their fathers. And you, you are their most important mhondoro, their greatest spirit medium. If they are not happy with us or with my work, why can't they just demote me?" asked Hombasha bitterly.

"Because you are the best and they know it," said Kwatara consolingly. "You ought to know by now, brother, that these people of the Hungwe have become too powerful. They control the trade, they control many kings and they control gold and the forests. Power corrupts minds but puts you on a spiral down that path of destruction."

Hombasha kept silent for a while as he looked at his hands. Then raising his head slowly, he said, "These hands have been faithful, they have never lied. They have worked proudly all these years. And to think I always thought highly of the Emperor because his father was a good man. I regret the years I have wasted." He looked down at his hands and started to cry.

Kwatara knelt before him. He looked very concerned and unhappy. "Do not cry, my brother. You are hurting already. It is bad for a man to cry. Besides, it is not the Emperor but his son who has done this to you."

Hombasha looked up at his young brother and wiped away a tear. "You are lucky you are just a mhondoro. They fear your power. They need you to continue to make sacrifices and to pray for them." He looked away. "They know they cannot do without their intercessors to

Mwari, but as for me, there are many out there who can do what I can do. Very soon they will replace me. My gift is accursed."

"That is where you are wrong. Right now they need the walls more than anything. You say you are cursed by your gift, yours is one you can control and one with an end you can foretell. As for ours . . . ," his voice trailed off.

Hombasha looked at him intently. He sensed something in his young brother's tone that alarmed him. Though Kwatara had said it softly, Hombasha sensed there was something more to what he had said than merely some kind sentiments designed to console him.

"Tell me, Kwatara, what is on your mind. What is it that your superior mind has seen that we have not? I do not like the way you have spoken," said Hombasha in a very concerned voice.

"It is nothing, my brother," said Kwatara, sitting down with a heavy sigh. "There are some things that we can prevent, but then there are other things that we see and yet can do nothing about. What happens when you see things that shake your entire frame and you wish you could do something about them and yet you cannot? You wish you could understand them yet they are so confusing. Now you are sick in the flesh but I am sick in the mind. My soul is tormented, I can at least heal you but I cannot heal myself. Hombasha, I wish life was different."

He looked truly tormented and desperate, like a little brother appealing to a big brother who sadly could only lie down and do nothing to heal him. Suddenly he had turned from the stronger, consoling brother to the one who needed care.

Hombasha shook his greying head and, looking uncomfortable, he said, "You have said too many things all at once. I do not like your words or the sound of them. I remember you did the same when our mother died, and when our father died." Then looking horrified, he asked in a loud voice, "Don't tell me, please, don't tell me. Are you going to die, young brother, have you foreseen your death or—rather—mine?"

Kwatara looked at his big brother and smiled his casual smile again. Slowly he shook his head. "You think too far ahead, Hombasha. You always have. No, I have not seen anything like that, but," he stood up, facing Hombasha who looked up at him, "I have never lived in a dream. I have never before been so shaken with life. I actually fear like never before, brother, and I ask myself questions like a madman. I desire to know and to know so much. But let me bide my time."

He stopped there and he bent down, took the leaves and dipped them once more into the clay pot and started massaging his brother's shoulder. Hombasha was too stunned and now seemed oblivious to the pain. So, his little brother had had a dream and that dream had shaken him. So many dreams had in the past, but he had hardly ever spoken of them as he had done tonight. Hombasha suddenly felt weak and desperate. Right now what Kwatara needed was a pillar to lean on and he just was not strong enough.

He turned his head slowly and with a worried stare looked at his young brother. Kwatara may have read his thoughts, may have seen the worry and the confusion in his brother's eyes. But he just smiled and once more dipped some leaves into the hot water to rub onto the painful shoulder. Hombasha looked away and this time he felt the pain and winced.

Meanwhile Kwatara worked in thoughtful silence. His mind was filled with the dream he had had many nights before. Like most of his dreams he knew it had something to do with the Great Zimbabwe nation, but he did not, as yet, comprehend its full meaning. Somehow, he felt in his gut, that things were about to change and to change drastically. His face became heavy and his mind filled with blurred images of the dream. Hombasha looked at him and saw the faraway look in his young brother's eyes. Kwatara sensed that he was looking at him and glancing up he smiled a reassuring smile. He did not want his brother to worry. He had said too much already. He started to hum an old tune and Hombasha, smiling, joined in. It had been their favourite from childhood and it was what they always used to soothe their pain in silent, brotherly understanding. But as Hombasha looked at him he saw not the happiness that was to be derived from the tune, but fear and doubt on his young brother's face.

He wished he was strong enough to pressure his young brother into telling him his problem, but he had also noticed Kwatara's polite obstinacy and so he had shelved his desire to question him further. Still, it made him feel inadequate. All their lives he had been the father figure and, despite Kwatara being a mhondoro, Hombasha had had the role of being the head of the family. He would not push Kwatara tonight. He knew that one day Kwatara would tell him and he hoped that when that happened he would have the answers Kwatara needed.

# Chapter four

While the brothers talked, a thin trail of ghostly mist had formed and now wound around the walls of the Great Zimbabwe sanctuaries, creating an eerie picture of the enclosures. Very few people were about and those who spoke, even inside their homes, did so in hushed voices. The thickness of the night seemed to weigh heavily on the shoulders of the people. Only those folks, who desired to discuss and plot dark deeds, met and sealed their deals without fear of being noticed under the cover of such blackness.

The dark winter nights were despised by many, but not Chinake the Empress. She found solace in them. To her, darkness was like a thick cover that hid a person's wildest passions and concealed his most hideous desires. Moreover, she believed the darker it was, the better it was, for every inch of people's moves and secrets would remain concealed unless divulged. The light from both the sun and the moon held no secrets, but the darkness held mystery and kept from so many eyes the truths of people's lives.

Now, as she lay on her back, she absentmindedly stroked her hand in circular motions and felt its smoothness. The copper bangles on her wrist tinkled and shone in the glow of the light of the burning fire. She believed and knew there was none other like her in the Kingdom. She had been born the only daughter of the late King's army commander. Her father, now deceased, had given Chinake, not her beauty, but aggressiveness and had taught her how to use her brain.

And so many battles he had won for the late King that apart from her natural beauty, they were her father's mighty feats that had made the late King's son, her now reigning husband, notice her. Chinake's mother had instantly seen the young Prince's eyes on her daughter. She had passed on to her the same cold and conniving spirit she had. In her veins had flowed the desire for power and fame which her husband had given to her, but for her daughter she wanted more. And so she had groomed her to attract the Prince. "Never be too forward and never be too shy," was always her advice, "But make sure that once you grasp his heart, you twist it so lovingly and firmly in your delicate fingers that you ensure he will never leave you. The chance for royalty comes once in a lifetime and your beauty is not to be wasted. Use it, for men are so gullible."

Therefore, Chinake had listened to both her parents and she had heeded their advice well. She had such innocence and beauty but could easily flaunt her mischievous side. She was fun and knowledgeable and a brilliant love strategist. She always attacked from the rear, knowing the Prince was mightier in wisdom and power yet never planned defeat but victory. Her two natures excited the Prince and her beauty made him crave her hand in marriage.

Then she had been blessed with three strapping boys. Of course, they did not possess a single inch of their mother's beauty, but they all had her devious mind and cold spirit. She admired this in them and, despite their looks, she adored them. They worshipped and loved her too with a fierce passion.

Perayi, the first, was not interested in stone masonry, but was in charge of a special unit of the army who were nothing but a bunch of mercenaries. He was the exact replica of his father with the exception of the curly hair which he had inherited from his mother. His voice did not have the same coolness as that of the Emperor but had an icy feel to it that showed a total absence of mercy and tolerance. Unlike his father, Chikomo her second son—the one who had inflicted injury on the master builder's shoulder—was of average height, which actually made him look short among his brothers. He had large eyes bordered by bushy eyebrows that nearly met at the centre. His large flat nose, which was set in between two chubby cheeks, closely resembled that of his father, and he had a habit of flaring its nostrils, especially when he was addressing a person of a lower rank. Tapera, the last, was in charge of nothing but he was feared enough to occupy a position of authority. Something of his mother's genes had dominated in his body structure. He was tall, but slender and not as heavily muscled as his two brothers. He had the same curly hair as his mother, but his eyes, mouth and lips closely resembled his father's. He loved to see blood flow freely and even his other brothers felt uncomfortable with him.

Both parents had played a great role in mentoring them. The Empress had taken great care to make her sons understand and overly appreciate that they had royalty in their blood, and her sons breathed and lived in that belief.

As she gently continued to stroke her hand, she thought of Hungwe's need for her assistance and excitement soared up every inch of her body to her very soul. How could a man of such wealth, such power and fame be like everyone else? He had to be different. Each era held its own history, this era, the Empress was sure, held the creation of divine Emperors. After all, she believed such power and strength her husband held could only belong to godly beings and not to men. The Arab's story had sounded like a fairy tale before but now it was the most logical thing ever for great men like the Hungwe. She was determined to help her husband attain his glory.

All she had to do was to unleash her feminine prowess—just a little, too much would spoil everything. Then the match would begin with her making the first move as soon as Chireshe arrived. She had heard Chireshe speak as he had attended to her. At first he had irritated her and had on more than one occasion failed to hide the desire he felt for her. But what she had noticed, despite his irritating manner, was that he had a way with words and a powerful one at that. At times, she had found herself listening to him and even believing his endless speeches. Then she would shake her head and return to reality.

Later that morning, when they were together once more, she gathered up her courage and repeated her idea of using Chireshe to the Emperor. He had not been too eager to agree and had smiled slowly and weakly, saying to her, "You are an impossible woman, my wife; to think a woman of your beauty would talk of a weasel like Chireshe."

Those had been the magic words, the words that had given her the authority to hire Chireshe to carry out the Emperor's bidding. It was as though the Emperor wanted to have everything to do with Chireshe but wanted nothing to do with him at the same time. It was as if he was setting himself apart from all her plans, giving her the freedom to plan and to help but still binding her to secrecy and to his power. She had known him for years and so slowly she said, "It is I, your wife, who desires you to be the divine being and so let it be known you have played no part in this." And thus she had placed the entire burden on her shoulders.

He had simply grunted and had said nothing, then smiling he had once more held out his hand towards her. She knew she had to tread carefully and she would, lest it was her head on a silver platter. Empress or not, the Emperor she knew was still unpredictable, and his glory and privacy meant more than the life of anything he held dear. Chireshe was to help blindly, for a reward, and she was to encourage him to do so.

A day after she left the Emperor's quarters she had started her research by inviting mhondoros to her court and dropping a question or two. They all believed that only Mwari and the great ancestral spirits of the land that guided the people were divine, and no man could be considered as such. She carefully listened when the mhondoros spoke and had quickly gauged from their speeches that all of them were too weak to invoke the Emperor's outrageous desire. Her heart had thus settled on Chireshe as the only mhondoro crazy enough to assist the Emperor in his cause, and to sway other mhondoros to their side. She also knew the reason why the Karanga feared and revered Mwari was because he was Musikavanhu, the creator of all men, and he was omnipotent and immortal. He was unmatched in power and strength. Further to that, she had been taught that Mwari and the great spirits of the ancestors were firm, punishing all men who went against them severely. This she had brushed aside but had kept in her heart one very important fact, the fact that if Mwari was fear inspiring, too great to overthrow and totally immortal, that was exactly what her husband would become.

It could have been a crazy idea but the more she had thought of it, the more it had made sense. Was not the Hungwe, her husband, a creator of these mighty walls? Was he not the owner of lands too vast to be mentioned? Did he not control trade and wealth in the Kingdom and were not the animals in all these forests his? Then in what way was he incomparable to Mwari? He had to be worshipped because he craved it and certainly he would then cease being bored. She would make sure of that and had devised a plan, a plan that would see great changes being made to the Great Zimbabwe and it would start by the simple entrance of two virgin maidens into her quarters.

From the darkness outside someone said, "My Empress, we are here with the maidens."

Joy flowed through her and she closed her eyes in relief. The first chapter in her quest had begun, just as planned and it had arrived right on time. If everything went as planned, what could go against her plan to make her husband divine? She sighed as she rose up from a wonderfully woven mat. This was a present her husband had given her. A trader had given it to him in return for a leopards hide and only the Empress had it. It made her feel special.

"Let them in," she said in her clear, soft voice. The maidens were pushed in and clumsily they stood before the Empress. The Empress looked at them. They looked back at her, blinking their eyes against the bright light in the room, having come from the darkness outside. She smiled at them; they became more frightened. She approached them and they huddled close to each other. Approaching the first maiden, she ran a soft hand over the girl's shoulder and licked her lips thoughtfully. The girl just gaped at the Empress. She had never felt such soft hands before.

"Mm-mm," said the Empress. "Not bad."

Then she came to the second girl. This one was terribly shy and close to tears. The Empress walked around her and fingering the numerous colourful beads around her neck, she sighed. Then calling out to whoever it was at the door, she said, "They will do." The voice outside simply grunted and the footsteps left.

The girls remained standing; the Empress kept looking at them and without warning, as though bored, she suddenly turned around and went to sit on her mat.

"Sit on that reed mat over there," she said, without looking at them, and beckoning with her hand. "You make me uncomfortable just standing over there and gawking at me."

The girls did not move and the Empress looked up. Her beautiful features became cold and stony. Her eyes held a command in them that was further reinforced by the icy voice with which she spoke. "Little fools; you dare remain standing when the Empress has been kind enough to offer commoners like you a seat in her house!" her last words were nearly a scream. "Now sit and don't you dare shiver like cold chicks. You had better put on your best faces because you should not fail me in what I am going to do. If you do then I shall make your lives a living hell." She nearly snarled.

The two maidens, a moment before mesmerised by the Empress's beauty and immobilised by being in her presence, suddenly sprang to life and went to sit on the reed mat, cross-legged. They really were just children. "And there you are sitting like babies." They both looked at the Empress wide-eyed. "Fold your legs and sit gracefully. Slaves, are you taught nothing better than to be so common?" she spat.

Quickly the girls sat as commanded. The shier one of the two was nearly crying. "And don't you dare shed a tear, girl, or I will make you mourn," hissed the Empress. The girl gazed at her in horror and was so sure she saw the fangs of a snake, for she held her mouth and gasped. The tears dried up before they left the eyes—fear can work wonders on the imagination. Suddenly the Empress's voice softened and her features became warm once more. The girls were once more taken aback by the rapid and seemingly deliberate metamorphosis that took place.

"Now pay attention, my lovely maidens. It took my trusted guards a week to find and choose you. You are the beginning of a wonderful plan to make history in these walls. You should feel privileged to be in the presence of royalty. Is it not an honour to have the chance to abandon your miserable cold huts for just one night, to leave the winnowing baskets for a day and to free your sorry heads of the water pitchers?" She looked up and with a thoughtful look on her face she said, "It is like living in a make-believe world in that your normal day-to-day lives will cease henceforth." Looking at them with a serious stare she said, "I will need you to oblige and this is no request but a command. For if you don't I will make sure that you pay dearly with your lives and," she paused, an evil twinkle coming to her eyes, "the lives of all who share your blood." The wind blew, the flames leapt about and a monkey screeched in the distance. The girls breathed in, the Empress simply smiled her sweet warm smile as she waited for Chireshe the mhondoro to come.

She knew Chireshe had a weakness for beautiful women; he was a glutton for feminine beauty. What she wanted done did not suit anyone with scruples or morals; it required a wild man who was on the brink of madness and who cared nothing of human norms and ethics. Apart from all that, Chireshe was a witty man. He could out think anyone and prove himself correct by unabashedly trampling on the truth before the eyes of everyone. He had the brains the Empress was after, the coldness and the cruelty as well as a strong influence over people and he would prove to be very useful indeed.

She would present herself to him as a vulnerable female and he, of course, would play the part of the rescuing knight in shining armour. She knew his desire for female splendour superseded his fear of visiting the Empress without an express command from the Emperor himself, and made him numb to all fear-inspiring penalties. Here was a man, thought the Empress with a sly smile, who would risk the sharp blade of the Emperor's knife simply to be in the presence of forbidden beauty. Tonight it would take only a few hours with Chireshe to make him wag his tongue and make damnable promises.

# Chapter five

Chireshe sat in his big round hut in utter silence, staring at nothing. How long had he wished for such a glorious moment to come? Anticipation swept through him making him shiver and he started to chuckle.

Just a few nights back he had been called to attend to the Empress, the Emperor's wife. He had rushed there, not because she was the Empress nor out of fear, but firstly because it was an honour to have the Emperor call upon you in the event of an illness, secondly it was a huge show of trust and thirdly it was because of how much the Empress excited him. He was the most knowledgeable in herbal medicine yet each time she had been sick, only the other healers had attended to her. The Emperor did not seem to want him anywhere near his wife and he could guess why.

He had a reputation of flirting dangerously with beautiful women, even the married ones, and his weakness for attractive women was widely known. Surprisingly, despite his unattractiveness, many women had fallen for him. Chireshe knew and accepted that he was ugly and had found a way of compensating for his looks. He knew his herbs better than any other mhondoro in the Kingdom, possessed a clever mind and a sharp tongue as well. He could outwit anyone in any conversation without forceful, rude language, but with the use of his mind, the right words and expertly timed gestures. Very few men had ever been able to out-argue him and thus he had gained a reputation among the Emperor's mhondoros in the Kingdom.

Chireshe's sixth sense enabled him to understand the human mind and behaviour. It taught him that what controlled the man was the mind and he who could control those minds and understand them was the master. It was a pity, though, that he had used this gift to lure many women to bed. It was a good thing he was impotent, otherwise the nation would have been filled with little boys and girls who possessed his comic looks. In consequence of this failing, he had never married. Of course it had caused him pain, but as the years wore on people had stopped wagging their tongues about it and life had taken the path it was on now. Still, he enjoyed fun with the opposite sex and had many gruesome tales that flitted after him on how he treated his women in and out of the bedroom.

The fire burned brighter as he stared at it with his big eyes and he recalled the one thing his tongue and wit had not been able to win. This was the hand in marriage of a particular beautiful young lady and it had been the only time he had ever had the courage to ask for a woman's hand in marriage. His nerve had cost him his pride and it had left a scar running so deep and painful he had never dared to dream of marriage again. A torn man, he had walked away from the girl's house with one vow, that one day he would win her body, married or not, for he knew then that he could never win her love.

Years had come and gone, folding and unfolding into each other. No opportunity had arisen and the dream had seemed to fade with age and time. Could it be that he who seemed to know everything had been wrong? No, he couldn't be, so he decided to place conviction in his dream. Though a mhondoro, Chireshe was not a religious man at all, yet because this woman obsessed him, he made a vow to base his hope in time and hold onto faith and providence. One day he would get the opportunity to court her and if he could play his cards well he could even win her over. Beautiful and proud Empress Chinake would one day be his.

How true was providence? All these years he had seen the Empress grow up and had never been given the chance to speak to her. All these years he had watched her married to the Emperor just hoping for a chance and now it had come, the night he had gone to see to her illness. And she still could, after all these years, take his breath away. He had not laid a finger on her, that would have spelt certain death but he had spoken to her, yes, he had been her only chance of survival after the sudden poisonous attack from the fish she had eaten and he, Chireshe, who had been denied her hand in marriage by her mother, had healed her. He had healed her when no other man could and yes, yes indeed, her very life had lain in his very hands. His to snuff out and his to preserve, but to preserve he had chosen because his time had come and he was going slowly, like the worm he was, to weave his way through to her and one day possess that startling beauty.

And what of that fateful night when his pride had been wounded, when the Empress's late mother had denied him the chance to marry Chinake? He hated to think of it but now it was going to be all right. He told himself he could finally reminisce in peace. She had spat in his face with her words. He, in turn, had angrily waved a finger of warning at her. Yes, he had told her that she had no right to be so rude because he knew of Chinake's true paternity, the Ethiopian trader with the looks of an angel who had come to trade with the late Emperor, he was Chinake's father.

He, Chireshe, being Chireshe, knew the truth. How had he known? He had declined to tell yet he did say he had proof. Chinake's mother had searched her mind for the one person who could have told Chireshe the truth, then it had hit her like a vicious bolt of fiery lightning. Chireshe's uncle, the one who had looked after the mhondoro from childhood, had given her the medicine that had helped her conceive Chinake. She had five boys and no daughter. She had wanted a daughter so greatly. Chireshe's uncle had been the herbalist who had tutored Chireshe. He had given her the herbs to eat, the herbs that would help change the child's sex.

Then during that week the Ethiopian trader had arrived. He had been honoured by the late Emperor with a feast for he had brought many precious goods for trade. Chinake's mother had noticed his beauty, the large watery eyes, the curly black hair, the beautiful face and tall figure. He looked like a woman and was actually too beautiful to be called a man in these parts. How she wished she could have a beautiful girl like him. And how she would make the men fight over her. She had been no better than her daughter Chinake. Being the then Empress's cleaner she had the opportunity to see the Ethiopian and somehow she managed to end up in his arms and in his bed. The Ethiopian had not found her strikingly beautiful but she had been quite some entertainer. He had left with no regrets whatsoever about this woman and the city and he had also left his seed behind. Months later she had given birth and the beauty of her baby had astounded the entire Kingdom. "She is going to marry the richest man in the Kingdom," her husband had said to his wife as he held her in his arms. "And she is going to make us very proud and very rich." Not a word of her daughter's true parentage did she utter over the years as Chinake grew into an astoundingly beautiful lady. And her husband never appeared to suspect any foul play. All was well.

And marrying the Emperor was exactly what happened. The Emperor's son had seen her and had fallen for her, despite his cold nature. She had won his heart because her mother had taught her well and she had it all. What else could the Emperor wish for? But before Hungwe had sought Chinake's hand in marriage, Chireshe had gone first to see her father. Though Chinake's father did not like Chireshe's looks, he was willing to give his consent. Chireshe was by then a respected and popular mhondoro who was slowly rising to fame and wealth. When he had told his wife, however, a dark anger had clouded her face. She did not shout at her husband, but had politely told him that there were far richer men than Chireshe who had eyes on their daughter. Being a quiet man, he had obliged and had given Chireshe the excuse that it was still too early to seek Chinake's hand in marriage.

Chireshe understood the message but was still determined to win Chinake. She was too beautiful to let go. He yearned to lay his big eyes on her and feast on her beautiful form each day but, alas, she was seldom to be seen. She was supposed to remain indoors most of the time lest her skin became tarnished. The only work her mother taught her was what was personally required by a husband and nothing more. Her mother had high hopes for her. In time Chireshe, who had vowed never to marry, had lost his fear and could not contain his desire anymore. Thus he had approached Chinake's mother for her daughter's hand in marriage and that had been a disastrous mistake.

She had not just laughed at him, she had done so cruelly. Yes, she did not have her daughter's beauty but she had given Chinake that same scheming mind, the same voice, the same laugh and the same coldness. As soon as she got over the shock that Chireshe knew who Chinake's real father was, she retaliated in the coldest hearted manner a vixen of her type could.

"So what if I lay with the Ethiopian trader and so what if you know? My husband is too happy to listen to you. All he knows is that he has a daughter who will one day marry the Emperor's son. So you think I broke my back that night to give birth to a daughter who would marry you, Chireshe? Ha, what a stupid thought. No, I broke my back after eating all those herbs your dear old uncle gave me so that I could give birth to a daughter who would one day marry a man of wealth, real solid wealth. Those beautiful looks of the Ethiopian have finally paid off and my angel, my Chinake, will rule you one day." And she had laughed, a laugh that still haunted Chireshe to this day. He could still see her head tilted, her white teeth showing and her long neck arched. And he could still see himself humbly make apologies and humbly painfully, walk away. A few months later Chinake married the Emperor's son Hungwe and indeed she landed into solid wealth, like her mother had said.

Now the same woman whose mother had snubbed him years ago had called upon him once again. Chireshe glowed inside and his curiosity grew making him overly excited. Why had the Empress called upon him herself? By rights it was supposed to be the Emperor alone who ordered any mhondoro to attend to his wife, but she had requested an audience with him and had done so on such a dark mysterious night. Was it a trap? If so, for what reason? Had the Empress found out what Chireshe knew about her true paternity and decided to do something about it? He wondered. But he had waited all these years just have a private moment with her; would he let this moment, no matter how dangerous it appeared, just slip by? No. How strange it was, he thought, that a woman could make a man so reckless. He had always been a good judge of situations but now obsession blinded him beyond thinking. He tried to focus, but the only thing he could think of was the Empress, his beautiful Chinake who had been stolen away from him by the Emperor. How he had hated the Emperor all these years for stealing his beauty.

Now he would stand before her and hear what she had to say and cleverly devise any means possible to get to her. Yes, he would play along and help, even if it was for the sake of the Emperor, but he would also make sure that he was in total control and could arrange for all things to work together for his good in the final end. He was already in control. But first he needed some advice, support and reassurance from the only friends whom he trusted to keep his secrets.

He looked around in his hut as though he did not remember where he kept his most treasured possession, that which had seen him come so far. It was a sinister gift which people whispered of only indoors lest he heard, for they feared him so. Indeed his uncle had loved him a great deal, for he was the only child of his sister and had been a most intelligent, enthusiastic student. It was his uncle who had looked after him from childhood when his mother had died of tuberculosis, for no one had really liked Chireshe because of his looks, but beneath that lay an intelligence and an understanding of human psychology that was unparalleled, and his uncle had noticed it. He had therefore left his brilliant apprentice and nephew a rare and mystical gift he had received from a dark, curly-haired trader from the East in exchange for ivory. The gift diagnosed ailments and gave prescriptions, telling him just where to find them. It was Chireshe's biggest secret and the very thing that had made him prosperous.

He walked to a heap of animal hides and gingerly put his hands underneath, feeling for a leather pouch. He found it and gently withdrew it from beneath. Holding the pouch ever so gently in his hand, he went and placed it on a reed mat that was close to the fire. He then went and took a small earthen bowl and scooped water into it with a gourd. With a cooking spoon he had picked up from a clay pot full of cooking utensils, he lifted some grey ash from the fireplace and mixed the ash and water. That done, he sat cross-legged on the reed mat and picked up the pouch with his left hand. With great care, he placed it onto his lap. Gently he scooped the ash mixture out onto the small bag and closed his eyes. His face became still; all body movements ceased. From the look of things, Chireshe was now deep in meditation. After a few moments he opened his mouth and, in a deep voice, he chanted something in a foreign language:

> *"O hijau merambat bijaksana salah satu dari timur, saya memanggil Anda keluar dari kantong Anda untuk melihat apa yang menyebabkan rasa sakit kita dan mengucapkan kata-kata yang begitu bijaksana."* The pouch that had been flat came to life as Chireshe intoned and something inside started moving. *"Memberi kita kesembuhan sejati kita dan membuat kita bijaksana, membuat kita tahu."*

"O wise One, green vines from the east, I am calling you out of your pouch to see what is causing our pain and to utter words so wise. Give us our true healing and make us sage, let us know."

Finishing, he slowly opened his eyes and blew at it. As though the mixture had not been wet, the ash lifted off in a small cloud of grey dust and a loud, eerie sigh filled the room.

Chireshe opened the pouch and out slithered two little green scaly serpentine creatures gliding onto his hand as though they were on an oiled surface. As they escaped from the pouch, their scales glistened in the light of the burning fire and, like the petals of a budding flower, the scales opened up one after the other from head to tail emitting an ethereal rustling sound as that of the dry leaves of a tree being shaken by a wind. Moments later, slithering and resting upon Chireshe's hand, was spectacle that had never ceased to amaze and baffle him from the day his late uncle had given him this mystical present. It was a cross between two little green snakes and two little green creepers. For though they had leaves, they also had eyes and scales but Chireshe's uncle had called them creepers and so Chireshe had also called and seen them as thus.

One coiled itself around the wrist, sending a tingling cool sensation that travelled right into his bones. Chireshe shivered and with inquisitive restless eyes, it looked about like an excited child. The other gently coiled itself around his hand and settled there in between the thumb and the forefinger. With its head lazily resting on Chireshe's hand, it looked at him with dreamy eyes.

The restless one started to wriggle about excitedly, its head bobbing to and fro inviting Chireshe to do something. Knowing what it wanted he chuckled and with his other hand, he stretched out a finger to scratch it. Both sighed in contentment, as though both could feel the action—and then a very strange thing happened. As soon as he started to scratch it, his finger went right through and poof!—a shiny green mist escaped the little creature's belly, shimmering in the yellow glow of the fire.

One moment it had been whole with a skin that Chireshe could feel and the next moment its belly had disintegrated in a tiny puff of shiny green fog. Stranger still, in no time at all the emerald mist coalesced and once again the creature was whole, curling around his wrist as though nothing had happened. He chuckled at the way it tickled him.

"Aahh Chireshe," they said in an eerie double whisper, "How happy you are our friend's nephew. So happy indeed." They possessed a strange way of dragging words out and speaking in unison.

"Yes, yes, I am," he said with a gleeful smile. "The Empress, my secret desire, oh yes the one I crave for, has asked to see me again of her own will, not the Emperor's."

"Aahh the Empress has asked you to go and see her again. Oh it was good you healed her; how fate has looked dearly upon you and given you joy."

"Oh indeed and how I thank you my friends for the cure you gave, you who are so wise. I have prayed to the ancestors for so long for her, she who was snatched away from me by the Emperor so long ago. And now she has requested to see me. I, Chireshe, who was wrongfully denied her hand in marriage by her mother. Oh may the snakes spit on that evil woman's grave." He screwed up his face in total disgust.

"Oh yes, that woman did deny you Chinake, so beautiful, so lovely," came the double voice again as the creepers writhed and unwound themselves on his arm. "How she brings you joy. So she has called and, oh yes, you are so happy because your love has desired to see you, and at night. Such secrecy and such mystery, just what you desire. Aahh," they ended with a sigh.

Chireshe laughed and wiped away another tear from his eye. "So I shall go, but tell me, my friends, how is it that I look. For it is the beauty of my life and dreams, the beauty of worlds that I am off to see."

He thrust out his hand and the creepers said in unison, "You look fine, Chireshe, finer than the Princes of the north who brought you this beautiful cloth you have wound around you. But be confident, for you know not what roams in the minds of royalty."

"And indeed I shall. Now I will go and you shall remain here to watch over me till I return."

A whisper from the creepers signalled the end of the conversation and the creepers uncoiled from his hand and slithered like two little snakes back into the pouch. Gently Chireshe tied it again and placed it back in its hiding place till next time he needed their help.

He got up to leave for the Empress's quarters. The game had begun and, like a dutiful servant, he would play along but win the game in the end. Strange things were at work in the Great Zimbabwe Kingdom.

# Chapter six

Chireshe, the most devious of the Great Zimbabwe Kingdom's mhondoros, was now standing before the Empress in her quarters. He wore around him a black cloth and had many shiny copper bangles on his wrists. He had in his hands a short donkey tail which he constantly stroked.

He had large crazy eyes that darted restlessly here and there as though looking for something to steal. Though he was quite tall he was skinny as though he was always on a diet. He had a chocolate brown, shiny skin, which the Empress had always thought he oiled with snake fat because it never showed any dirt. The people believed that, once a mhondoro used snake fat to oil himself, he never caught any dust, just like a snake. His mouth too was strange: the lower lip protruded and he had a habit of twisting it about. His head was round and very bald. Chinake wondered if a single strand of hair had ever grown on it from birth. In contrast to his bald head his eyebrows were bushy; one might have expected him to have sported a beard but that too was absent from his clear face. All in all he was not pleasant to look at at all. The Empress's sons were actually no better-looking but they were not as weird as this mhondoro that stood before her. She was grateful for the way he had helped her with her stomach-ache and fever a few nights back but she had viewed him with the same distaste on that night as well.

"My dear mhondoro, Chireshe, the greatest of them in the Kingdom," purred the Empress in a deep velvety voice, "I am honoured by your visit. Do take a stool and sit close to your Empress." She beckoned delicately with her hand as she remained seated on her mat.

She cast him a sweet smile and tilted her head ever so delicately and so seductively that Chireshe could not help but tremble with excitement. He knew that she did not take pleasure in his looks, because he was an intelligent man whose eyes were quick to notice and judge, but he was always weakened by her beauty and grace. Her feelings for his looks were currently overshadowed by the way she made him feel when he looked at her.

Mumbling his thanks, Chireshe went and took a seat close to the Empress on a high stool with a broad hollow base. The Empress turned to face him and focused her eyes on him. He felt his knees weaken and he nearly dropped his donkey tail. He realised that if he kept on with the eye contact things would go drastically wrong. So he looked sideways.

"It is a cold night, Chireshe, I am happy you braved the cold wind to come to your Empress at her humble request," said Empress Chinake with a dreamy look in her eyes.

"I could not refuse the request of my Empress, whose husband has been so kind to me in times past and present," said Chireshe truthfully, trying not to fully focus on the Empress.

"The Empress of the Great Zimbabwe is most humbled by her faithful subject. And on such a cold night like this," she shivered slightly rubbing her delicate shoulders enticingly, "I will grant you a gift of warmth. True warmth, beautiful warmth like you have never been given, my friend."

She looked up, showing the full length of her beautiful neck and with such delicate hands she clapped just once. Instantly from outside entered two maidens; they walked in and stood before the Empress. They were adorned afresh with lovely colourful beads around their breasts, covering them entirely. Around their small waists they had tied new, expensive looking cloths which clung to their hips, accentuating their shapes. The quick and intelligent Chireshe was swift to notice style and beauty. And he judged that what stood before him was the best.

The Empress, seeing the excitement rise on Chireshe's face, smiled a smile of satisfaction. He was mesmerised and gawked at the two maidens. His lower lip trembled and his large eyes widened. His breath came in short gasps and he flared his nose like a bull. What beauty was this that stood before him that he had never seen in the Kingdom of the Great Zimbabwe? And it was so young, so unblemished, so tender. He was transported at once back to the days of his youth. She had judged the man so well, he loved the mere sight of beautiful maidens.

"My Empress," he said at last. "Are these your visitors, my Empress, or are they your new maids in waiting?" he did not take his eyes off them.

The Empress looked amused and said in a humorous tone, "No, my dear Chireshe, these are to be your winter gift, a gift to keep you warm, a gift for your humble services. You who have so far not failed your Empress, deserve the royal gift of living and breathing beauty," she said, looking at him closely and stressing the word "not".

Chireshe unsteadily stood up, his face covered with excitement. He looked like a horrible clown and the girls cringed. But they had heard the Empress, not only they would be killed but their entire clan would lose its life if they failed her. Noticing their reaction she cast a cold, quick glance at them. That was enough reprimand. They flexed, as best as they could, eyes full of tears and remained standing as gracefully as their scared selves could.

Chireshe approached them and walked around both of them, happy and looking like a mad man. He nodded his head and mumbled a stream of inaudible praises. The Empress kept a close eye on him.

"Oh my Empress, such lovely tastes you have," he said hoarsely. "Who could have ever known that such beauty lives within these walls of the Great Zimbabwe? My eyes have been opened. The night is suddenly so warm."

The Empress smiled an icy smile. She knew she had his attention now, she knew he was in her clutches. For what seemed ages she had planned and had waited for the right time. Everything was coming together and she was sure she would succeed. Then Chireshe broke into one of his hysterical bursts of laughter. He did that each time he was elated by something. And the Empress's fears rose. She nearly scolded him but checked herself on time.

"Shut—quiet, Chireshe. Do you want the whole Kingdom to hear that you have visited the Empress at night?"

He immediately clamped his mouth and wiped away a tear. Going close to the girls he reached out to one of them. Her eyes widened and so did his. His lips trembled and so did hers, from fear. The Empress sensed something going amiss and a warning sounded in her mind. She was not only devious but quick to notice danger—not danger to the girls but to her entire planning.

"Chireshe, the girls are yours," she said urgently. "The Empress requests your presence right now. The night is getting late and it is too dangerous for you to remain in these quarters. Leave them, I command you and attend to your Empress." She spoke sternly; he was whisked out of his euphoria. The girls were safe, for the time being.

Shaking his head as though to clear it, he went to sit down on his stool and gathered himself together. Once more he sat facing his Empress and she clapped her hands. The girls got the message this time and they scurried out, glad for the time being to be out of the mad mhondoro's way.

Chireshe quickly turned to steal a glance at them as they left and, with a gleam in his eyes, he rubbed his chin, thinking of the joy that lay ahead. He believed this was going to be one of the warmest nights ever. So maybe the Empress had not brought him here to set a trap for a secret he alone knew. The night was still young and the game was just beginning. He would wait and see.

"Now sit, Chireshe," commanded the Empress, making herself comfortable on the mat. "The night grows old and so much is to be discussed."

Her voice was no longer smooth; it was no longer sweet but held in it an icy impatience and urgency. Chireshe, now fully recovered from his ecstasy, turned around on his stool and looked at the Empress and as though she had not been cold a moment ago, her warmth returned; she smiled sweetly again, instantly getting the insane mhondoro's attention. She was now ready to throw her arrows and knew they would hit the bull's eye.

"I am sorry, my Empress, but your humble servant was carried away by the beauty of her Majesty's gift to him. It has been so long since these poor old eyes of mine have seen such beauty," said Chireshe, in the most convincingly humble tone he could gather.

The Empress smiled and slyly put one finger on her mouth. She knew how innocent it made her look and just how it affected Chireshe. He quickly looked away shyly and said, "I'm sure the Empress does not wish to detain me any longer lest my presence shall become a problem. I am waiting to hear my majesty's request."

Slowly she got up and stood before him. Chireshe sensed her presence in front of him and dared not turn his head. She made him feel so vulnerable.

"Look at me, my dear mhondoro Chireshe, the Mighty mhondoro of the Great Zimbabwe. Look at me and tell me openly, where have you seen such beauty?" said the Empress, in a deep imploring voice.

Slowly Chireshe turned his head. He did not understand where all this was coming from nor where it was leading. He was and looked confused, but he was Chireshe and he enjoyed mystery so he answered earnestly, "Nowhere, my Empress. Nowhere in this land so vast and so full of people. Nowhere, not even among the traders that come and go from the city have I ever laid eyes on such beauty."

And Chireshe was right. The Empress was a rare beauty in her own right. She had chocolate brown skin, unlike the darker skins of most other women of the Kingdom. It was smooth and healthy as though she bathed in waters from a land above. It spoke volumes of its owner and the care taken to keep it thus. Her hair grew wavy and dark on her beautiful head and her teeth were perfectly white and even.

Her lovely big eyes and long eyelashes gave her the innocent look of a mere child. At times the eyes held a naughty twinkle in them when she laughed, she could also turn them into soft, kind, deer eyes. Then they could hold an icy cold look that completely overshadowed all her soft beauty and highlighted that well hidden dark nature inside her. One thing she knew to do very well was to bat her eyelids and she understood the effect they had on poor, unassuming men. She could look at them squarely in the face and make them melt, and then she could stare deep into their souls and make them fear her.

Then there was her neck, long and smooth, usually adorned with the most colourful and lovely beads from all over the lands they traded with. She usually craned it as though to straighten it but in truth it was just to show off its smoothness and splendour. Her hands were soft, very soft. Chireshe had had the rare opportunity of feeling them when he greeted her on one occasion. She would make sure that the handshake lingered on long enough for any man to wonder days afterwards how they could be so soft and fine. And she had a lovely figure. She had married the King when she was only fifteen. In quick succession she had given birth to her prized three ferocious looking boys. Oddly, the strain of giving birth had not made her body sag, but if anything had made her look younger and more beautiful than before.

She was an unusual first wife. While many first wives ended up fat and shapeless, mere masses of human feminine creatures, Chinake had achieved over the years an unequalled beauty. She had not been driven to carelessness by her seniority as first wife, but she had managed to claim and seal her position as the true wife of the great Hungwe by maintaining an undisputable beauty. Chireshe believed that the Emperor would not find even if he joined the faces of all his many wives, such exquisiteness as he now beheld in Empress Chinake.

Chireshe had on occasion heard that she used a secret potion from one of the Eastern traders who had once come to the Kingdom to trade with the Emperor, to make her skin look more youthful and to cause her figure to look shapely and slender. But he knew the truth to all these rumours, which made him angry because he was so fond of the Empress, too fond in fact. He knew the simple answer to this was that the Empress was just a beautiful woman, blessed with such a gift from her original seed and further to that, she had the time and the resources to manage to take care of herself. Now he was here alone with her on such a dark night and she was asking him if he knew of any other beautiful woman like her. What on earth was she driving at?

"When I hear it coming from you, Chireshe, I know it is the truth, because you are a man of your word and an honourable man for that matter," said the Empress, in an earnest, hoarse voice.

This was one part of her nature which Chireshe found most intriguing. She could possess such sincerity and show such attachment and love for something that it was shocking to hear people say she was evil. Then she could be so callous and cold that it was also amazing to hear anyone say she was kind. All the same, Chireshe had a love-smitten boy's admiration for the Empress; he would do anything to please her highness.

The winter wind howled outside and made the leaves of the few trees in the enclosure rustle. Empress Chinake shivered and placed two pretty hands on her shoulders. She breathed in, sighed and aimlessly looked about. Then casually, with the sureness of a cat, she started walking to the other side of the room. As she sauntered past Chireshe, her body just, ever so slightly, brushed his leg before he had time to move them away. Chireshe felt excitement rise up his chest. He nearly trembled but held himself in check just in time. The Empress did not even turn back but kept on walking. She knew that the desired effect had taken place. Then, from a neat pile of rugs, she pulled out a beautiful rug of lovely knit and colour and she wrapped it around herself.

Chireshe would have loved to look but respect demanded that he turn his eyes away and look down on the ground. The Empress walked back but this time she did not sit on the mat, she stood just behind the mhondoro and said in a low husky voice, "Now tell me, Chireshe my friend, what do you think of my husband, the King?"

Immediately Chireshe looked up. Was this the trap? His eyes held questions in them and fear. What really was the Empress getting at? But he was also cunning. He knew that if it was a trap, he was already too deep in it because he was here, at night in the Empress's quarters, alone with her. She had laid her trap so well and he had been so gullible. He had been so pleased to be called upon by the lovely Empress and the idea of coming to see her on such a dark night held in itself a mystery that had tickled his curiosity. Chireshe decided he would answer and go along with the flow. If need be he would use his brilliant mind to extricate himself from this one. He had escaped many life-threatening situations before, and all he had to do was to consider the Empress as just another witty opponent.

"I hold the Emperor in great esteem, my Empress," replied Chireshe, in the steadiest and most earnest voice he could muster. "He is a man of great power and wealth and wisdom. Otherwise there would be no such Kingdom without all those attributes."

The Empress smiled. She hugged herself more tightly with the rug and slowly walked past Chireshe. His eyes followed her, his mind churning with activity. Facing the wall she said, "I wonder why you echo my thoughts, Chireshe, you act as though you can read your Empress's mind. I have heard I am beautiful and that none other in this Kingdom can equal me. They say my husband is the greatest of the Hungwe, the greatest of any Great Zimbabwe rulers."

She suddenly turned back to look at Chireshe. The flames lit up her face and gave it a strange glow, her eyes were alive and her breasts heaved up and down with her laboured, excited breath. Chireshe watched and took in all this with awe. Something had excited the Empress. He waited to hear what those beautiful lips would utter next.

"Then, Chireshe, does not my husband deserve more than just being an Emperor? Do I not, with all you have said, you who are so genuine in heart and mouth, do I not deserve more than just being an Empress?"

She spoke with such force and energy, Chireshe felt the house become warmer. He listened in wonder, not really knowing where all this was leading. In a wave of renewed energy she walked towards him and knelt before him. Chireshe was shocked. This was not right. He was not comfortable with this stance. He looked around like a cornered beast. His heart raced. How could the Empress kneel before him? This was sacrilege to the royal throne. What would become of him if the royal guard caught her in this position and what would the Emperor do?

He held onto his stool to steady himself and to prop himself up in a bid to stand. But before he got up, the Empress's soft hands gripped his, pressing him down onto the stool, her large eyes, deeply imploring, looked into his and rendered him too weak to even think or protest. The softness of her hands pressed into his rough palms.

"Chireshe, listen, I beg you, listen," she implored, in the voice of a child.

Chireshe swam in her innocence and looked in her eyes. This was not right, his intelligent mind kept yelling, but—God—she was so beautiful. Just listening to her and looking at her made what was so wrong feel so right.

"W—what is it my Empress," he managed to splutter at last. "What is it that makes my master's Empress kneel before me?"

The Empress looked up with the most pitiful eyes Chireshe had ever seen. Eyes that were imploring and in need of wise words. Eyes that held the mhondoro transfixed and unable to move. "Tell me, Chireshe, is it not mockery that my husband, as great as he is, should be nothing but a mere Emperor? Is it not mockery that, with all that he owns, he should be nothing but ruler of the Great Zimbabwe? Do I deserve nothing other than the title of Empress? Is there no greatness beyond which a man like the great Hungwe deserves? Is there none other beyond that title? Do we not, with all that you claim we are, deserve to live in greater splendour? Tell me, Chireshe, you whose mind supersedes all, tell me: am I wrong to say all this?"

"My Empress, your servant does not know what her majesty desires. He is agonised to see her in such agony of heart. Indeed your beauty and greatness is famed, the royalty and might of the Hungwe is unrivalled.

But do please get off your knees. You offend the crown and my heart is troubled by your act of humility before me, a humble servant."

Chireshe, who was quite an intelligent mhondoro, still failed to grasp the meaning of all this. Somehow the Empress was playing with him, playing around with words, gently leading him off to some place. Should he get out of it now—or maybe, just maybe, he could go along and see where it all ended? After all, he was in the presence of the Empress, and men like Chireshe enjoyed being in the presence of beautiful women. He would tag along and give her what she wanted. The Empress's kneeling was indeed making Chireshe feel awkward.

Slowly the Empress rose and Chireshe helped her up. She stood facing him, a tear falling down her cheek. Her lips trembled and her lovely nose flared. Chireshe was at a loss. He did not know whether she looked more beautiful angry, sad or happy.

"My Empress, now you cry, what is it that makes you so sad and so excited at the same time?" asked the now agitated Chireshe.

She simply stood there, staring at him as he stared back at her. She so beautiful and also so in control, he a mere rag doll being controlled by the strings of the Empress's beauty.

"My husband deserves more, Chireshe. Tell me, my worthy servant, great mhondoro of the Great Zimbabwe Empire, what will it take to make my husband into what he is worth? What will it take to make him—divine?" she ended there with an air of finality.

Chireshe opened his mouth in shock but, seeing the resolve on the Empress's serious face, he just as quickly closed it. He was intelligent, and now he understood the meaning of all the Empress's kindness and actions. But he would steal every opportunity to toy with her. For as much as she thought she was making him dance, he was making her sing for him. Quickly his mind raced. She wanted his help for sure and would he deny it? No, he would not lose a single chance to be with her, to win her one day even if it meant helping her husband the Emperor, for it also meant extending his chances of getting what he wanted all these years.

The Empress's request was not only strange but too vast to fulfil. Yet his mind was big enough for the bait and he would swallow it. Chireshe enjoyed sparring and sparring with royalty was particularly gratifying. It was this that had brought him to this point in life. He was not only a mhondoro but an intelligent orator, a demagogue who could convince crowds, and he knew the Empress had noticed this. The mhondoro also knew that the stakes were high, but so would be his esteem and position.

He would not disappoint the Empress. She had called him here because she believed in him and trusted he would deliver what she wanted. It was to be as she desired. And so he would deliver the answer that she wanted to hear. It was really that simple. A door had been opened for him and enter he would.

# Chapter seven

The howling wind brought further despair to the already bleak and cold night, muffling the voices of the three men who were huddled together, planning an escape from the Great Zimbabwe Kingdom. Temperatures had fallen drastically throughout the Kingdom of the Mbire but such was the zeal possessed by these men that they did not notice both the intensifying chill and the wailing wind outside.

The King had finished his briefing to Tekeshe Chingowo and he believed he had done it to his best. He needed the army general's support and his strength lay in his words. They would persuade the general and bind his loyalty to the King. Mutota knew that Tekeshe was a very well respected army general. His soldiers loved him. They listened to him and he was crucial to the success of the breakaway.

"Now what do you say, my dear army general, to our plan? Is it just a fantasy or is it something that can come to fruition?" asked Nyatsimba Mutota sincerely.

"Your desire is most welcome, my King," said Tekeshe. "To be free in a foreign land is better than to be servants of another Kingdom in your own land. I have served this Kingdom for many years and I have groomed many young men to become worthy soldiers. But I have also wept at the fact that so many of them have been taken to serve in the huge army of the Great Zimbabwe rulers. I call myself an army general of the Mbire Kingdom, but I have never been free enough to serve the Kingdom I love most."

Mutota looked at this man and believed every word he said. He now saw that Tekeshe loved this Kingdom with a passion unequalled. He was now eagerly and openly displaying his desire to serve the King, a desire which was close to mania. It was his service to the crown of the Mbire that he lived for and in truth he was such a loyal servant that he would serve even if his life was at stake. The King felt proud to have chosen this man to be his army general.

"And to be free is an expensive thought, my friend. It comes with a lot of courage, force and bloodshed as well," said the King softly and thoughtfully.

"Then it would mean we definitely need the support of our people," said Matope. "If they fail to rally behind us, we will certainly lose the battle. It is a pity they may most assuredly choose to stick to the Great Zimbabwe Emperor. They have been servants for too long and most feel as though they are part of one big Hungwe family."

"It will prove a tricky and tough job to rid the entire nation of a servant's mind," said Tekeshe thoughtfully. "They say they are your people but they fear the Hungwe of the Great Zimbabwe more than they respect their own crown. We must find a way of making them agree to our plan."

"I do not really blame the people, my son," said the King. "We have been servants of the Great Zimbabwe Empire for too long. That alone can make many believe that it is normal to serve rather than to be free. Some even take pride in being slaves. It is like that with men who have been harassed for too long. They simply become too submissive. And remember the law that we all obey, the Emperor is the law and he who disobeys the Emperor dies."

The King stood up and once more crouched before the fire. The leaping flames were reflected in his tired eyes but his mind was alert. He had thought of an escape route and already he had mapped out the path to be taken on foot, now what was needed was the strategy. Then he spoke loud and clear, well above the wind, for the other two men to hear

"The most loyal servants a King can ever have are his army. The soldiers enter the army knowing full well that they are to lay down their lives not only for the Kingdom, but for what the Kingdom represents and desires. It is the army that will do the work for us Tekeshe," said Mutota, tuning to face his army general.

"My Lord, do you mean to say that we shall use the army to force people into accepting to break away from the Great Zimbabwe Empire? The Hungwe would find out and we will be done for. You know how fast such news can spread and how rebellious people can be against a ruthless army," said the frightened Tekeshe.

"And that would be the worst mistake ever, father," said Matope. "Once the army has been given that much rope, even Tekeshe will not be able to stand in their way. A simple taste of power can drive a man beyond control. While the thought of freedom never existed, men will remain subservient, but the minute it is introduced it will blossom into an insatiable need, not only to be free from the Great Zimbabwe rulers but from the Mbire Kingdom as well."

Mutota was listening to them intently. He stood up and walked to stand behind his son. The other two men turned and looked at him. Gently he folded his arms behind his back and looking at the ground asked Tekeshe, "Tell me, Tekeshe, how many able and reliable, worthy soldiers do we have?"

"Over two thousand sir, including those who were enlisted this year. There are many young men whom we took into our army to train and so far they are doing very well."

"Then I will tell you this. You say that it is not good to give this army too much rope over our plan for fear of a mutiny and civil war, and you are right. But we will use psychology, my men. This will be a battle of the mind, a war to win the way they think, to remould it and then to win the soul of the soldier." The others stared at him as he tapped his head, trying to follow where the conversation was headed to this time. "We will reshape their cause, enough to get their warrior blood roaring inside them. We will revitalise their lost pride and when the time comes they will not fear to help us lead the people out of this land."

"And how will we achieve that, father, without raising suspicion in the Great Zimbabwe? Once they hear of a rejuvenated Mbire army they are bound to attack us and disband it," said Matope in a worried tone.

"And remember, their army is very big, they will send it together with the armies of other vassals and crush our private little rebellion like an elephant's foot crushes a fly," added Tekeshe.

The King smiled a smile of admiration and said, "I admire the way both your minds work. Together you will make a formidable team of great thinkers. What I did when I thought of a breakaway was to come up with a workable solution. You see the soldiers will work against the Great Zimbabwe Empire without even knowing it. They will neither fight nor force the people to believe in our idea and leave, but they will lead the people out of the command of the Great Zimbabwe."

"Then tell me, my King, I am now more than ever curious to know of this wonderful plan you have," said Tekeshe, looking eagerly at Mutota.

Mutota nodded his head and came to sit by the fire close to the men on his stool. The other two moved closer to him and pricked up their ears.

"This, gentlemen, is my plan and I am sure that both of you will love every bit of it," he said with a smile. They too smiled, eyes twinkling in anticipation. And the King began to talk.

# Chapter eight

Kwatara, the mhondoro, was now on his way home. He had left Hombasha, the master builder, feeling much better as to his shoulder but rather worried about his younger brother's words. Kwatara wished he had not been so transparent. He wished he could have hidden his worries and kept them to himself. But he knew Hombasha would have picked it out. He was a very observant man and very meticulous. He left no stone unturned.

That had been the master builder's gift from childhood. He could notice the most minuscule detail and straighten things out by his great gift of observation. This was why he had easily become the master builder at the Great Zimbabwe. Hombasha was neat. Each part of the wall he had built was straight and firm. If a brick or a stone went even slightly out of place he would notice, despite the length of the walls and their height. His sharp eye never missed a detail and hence he had easily noticed that Kwatara's mood was out of place. And, as always, just as he straightened the walls of the Great Zimbabwe, he had tried to set his brother's mood right.

This time, however, he had not succeeded and as Kwatara walked home, disjointed parts from his dream once more haunted his mind, especially the parts that were most terrifying. They came to him in all their vividness and did not fail to make him feel worried and afraid. Now and again, he shook his head and shrugged his shoulders as though to rid himself of a burden, but still many parts of the dream mercilessly clung to his poor mind. And the surrounding darkness was not helping much. He wished he could get back home soon. His wife would be worried by now. It was rather late, so he quickened his step, wishing it was summer instead of this miserable winter cold. As he turned a corner he heard something and stopped. Hurried footsteps and voices were coming his way. He moved closer to the wall he was walking along and in the darkness he could make out two figures moving and whimpering. Kwatara had grown up with a gift of making out voices, even in the dark.

The whimpering most probably came from girls, not women. He figured out the other voices that followed were those of men, most probably soldiers by their gruff sound. Now they were just in front of him and he sank into a wall, but one of the soldiers saw the silhouette of a body and demanded, "Who stands there? Answer or I will strike with my spear."

Kwatara knew better than to keep silent, despite the fact that he was a respected figure in the community. "It is I, Kwatara, the Emperor's mhondoro. I am coming from my brother's house, the master builder, Hombasha. He was taken ill and he needed my help."

"Oh I see," said the soldier, "We shall not detain you, most respected one, let us be on our way."

They moved on and before they went far, the moon came out for the first time that night casting brightness on the darkness and making everything once hidden visible. The wind had blown the clouds apart and the light from the moon shone with a welcoming brightness.

Kwatara looked back to see the people who had stopped him and noticed something that stopped him dead in his tracks. He saw a young, beautiful girl look back at him with pleading eyes. She had around her neck an abundance of lovely red beads that covered her breasts entirely. The cloth tied around her waist was, as far as Kwatara could make in the light of the darkness, quite new. Right there before Kwatara was the very girl from his dreams! He was stunned and immobilized by shock.

"Get a move on girl, our Empress will not like it if you delay in getting home to warm your master's bedding," said one soldier as he roughly shoved her on, while the other gave a crude laugh. Kwatara saw the girl turn her head away and move on. He could not believe what he had just seen. His hand quickly went to his neck as his breath became constricted. Sweat filled his arms and they became sticky. Why was the girl he had seen in his dream with these soldiers? Where was the clay pot, or was she just an image meant to fill in the role of the real woman or situation represented by the clay pot in his dream.

Then from behind him came some more footsteps. These were in such a hurry. They were accompanied by inaudible mumblings and giggles from the owner. Quickly he spun out of his current fear and thoughts. Kwatara did not want to believe whom he thought these belonged to. But by the light of the moon, he was proven right. It was Chireshe and what was he doing all alone in the dark, coming from the very same direction as the soldiers and the girls and mumbling in excitement?

Forgetting his current distress Kwatara looked about and saw a tree close to the wall. He hid behind it, squeezing himself between the tree and the wall. Then he held his breath and wished that the other mhondoro would not see him. But Chireshe was in such a hurry that he noticed absolutely nothing and, giggling and mumbling, he went past.

Kwatara remained where he was for some more moments, his mind a whirlwind of thoughts. He was puzzled. Those were the Empress's soldiers, but who were the girls? And could Chireshe be the master the soldiers were talking about? Could he be coming from the Empress's quarters so late at night? Kwatara knew that no man was allowed by the Emperor to even go near Empress Chinake, let alone at night.

Slowly he came out of his hiding place as soon as he was sure Chireshe was gone and stared on after the other mhondoro for a long time. Suddenly his head turned sharply towards the direction from which Chireshe had come. He thought he had heard some more footsteps and he was sure he had seen the silhouette of a man. He squinted his eyes but it was difficult to make out anything. Still he was certain he had seen a person move in the distance.

No matter, he finally told himself. There was nothing so strange about people moving about in the dark within these enclosures. The only thing that had unnerved him about it was the fact that he had just seen a figure from his dream and what connection, he wondered, did Chireshe have with the girls? He had never liked Chireshe. While no other mhondoro or chief had ever been bold enough to challenge the quick witted and sharp tongued mhondoro, he had been the only one who had stood up to his crazy words and arguments. He despised the way the mhondoro spoke and how he could easily make people believe his endless words. Some had thought it was hatred and jealousy, but he knew that one day Chireshe would sway the nation to absolute madness if he was not checked and he had made it a point to keep the mad man in place. But right now he needed to go home and, deciding to save his strange discovery to mull over another day, he turned and he moved on. He would bide his time, he knew answers would come.

# Chapter nine

While Kwatara headed home, Chireshe was also hurrying back to his home. The slight wind that had risen sent a chill right into his spine. He wasn't as young and as fit as he used to be and this hampered his desire to catch up with the two soldiers and the girls. But he did not really worry about that. There would be plenty of time to get to know his two young lady friends better. What a beautiful way for fate to lay the starter meal for him before he finally feasted on the Empress. Life in the Great Zimbabwe could never be more attractive for the wild mhondoro than it was now.

The soldiers had already gone, having left the girls in the hut he had instructed them to. He decided to visit his private hut first and enquire from his two friends, the creepers; they had to know this. It was hard to imagine that a man of Chireshe's intelligence could find creepers better friends than humans.

Getting inside he performed the same ritual as before and out wiggled the two green creepers with the same sigh. Somewhere in the other hut close by the girls heard it and they whimpered in fear but they could not run away for both hands and feet had been skilfully tied by the two cruel soldiers who had accompanied them to Chireshe's place.

"Tell us, Chireshe, tell us what happened. Has the Empress found you pleasing?" they asked in unison, sending out an excited rustling noise.

Chireshe smiled. These days he had nothing but good news.

"Oh yes she has. She invited me because she wants my help. My specific help. Yes, only I, Chireshe, can help her and I will."

The creepers emitted a sigh and Chireshe chuckled as they tickled his hand with their movements.

"And what has she asked of you, Chireshe, tell us please, we itch to hear."

He laughed and once again tears rolled down his large eyes. It seemed as though they always fell freely on his happy occasions.

"Ah the fools, they want to become divine, yes they want me to make them, immortals and they believe that I can because I am the only one with the nerve enough to convince the masses that he, Hungwe can be divine."

He laughed again, a manly cackle that ended up choking him and made him splutter.

"Oh such fools," joined in the creepers. "Gods are born, they are not made. Immortality comes with death, do they not know? When the will to live on this earth ceases and one is transported to another realm beyond, where life never ceases. Only in death is immortality."

Chireshe stopped and wiped his tears away. Had he heard correctly what the creepers had said? He stared at them, unbelieving at the words they had put in his ears. Immortality is the price of death. Was the Emperor designing his very own death with his own desire? Was this an omen for the Emperor and his bloodline? Then another chilling thought crossed his mind. There was nothing wrong with the Emperor's death but could his desire to become immortal also cause the death of Chinake.

"You cannot tell me that," he said, suddenly sober. "Should all my joy be for naught, shall my Chinake die, because the Emperor wants immortality? Then I shall not aid him. Not if I am to lose even the mere sight of that beautiful woman."

"Your desire makes you worry. Aahh Chireshe, passions as yours can be so imprisoning. But why does she need to suffer, she is not of the bloodline. She is one with the Emperor out of wedlock, not by blood. But for her to die is a choice, your choice."

He was slightly relieved and he wiped a bead of sweat from his shiny forehead. Like a drunken man, he sat down on a stool and finally said, "Oh what should I do, I need a plan and a beautiful one. I have made a promise to the Empress and I dare not disappoint her. You should have seen her, such a fragile creature, all her hope in me for that thief the Emperor. Oh how I want her. Tell me how can I help?"

They wound themselves around his wrist and coiling around each other they said,

"You ask us Chireshe, you with the mind of today and ages beyond. You, who knows other minds as well. How can you have known how to make men believe by your tongue? In your voice is the potion the Emperor needs to make him what he wants, so pour it out. Just be patient and watch and learn and yes, you will win your war and Chinake will be yours."

That was the answer, his voice, words and his quick mind. He rejoiced.

"Yes I will make her mine and as for the Emperor and his sons I will make them immortal, I will do it for them, for like you have said, only in death is one immortal." Then suddenly he stopped as he heard a whimper outside. "Ah my ladies, my gift of human warmth, with such eagerness they await me," he snickered.

"Yes Chireshe, so lucky are you to get your true desire. Go now and enjoy the sweat of your patience," said the creepers with one eerie voice. And with a big smile on his face he carefully returned the creepers in their pouch and placed them under the heap of animal skins. But before he left he sat down to evaluate the facts. The girls could wait.

He now knew that there was no trap being laid but that the Empress genuinely needed his help. To make the Emperor a divine being? How ridiculous it seemed but was it not true that in nations far from theirs, other kings were gods? It was. He had heard the traders from the north say so. Now their Emperor was dreaming of becoming a god as well. Would it work in these parts of the world, in a place where the only divine beings were meant to be Mwari Musikavanhu and the ancestral spirits? He wondered, but maybe it was worth a try because the more he would entertain the royal family the more the Emperor would get to trust him and the closer he would get to his goal.

Chireshe had studied the man, and he had concluded that the Emperor was not as soft as the sheep's wool he wore over his crocodile scales. There was something unnerving about him and something dark and hidden. Chireshe had his dark side as well and maybe that had picked on the truth behind the Emperor. So he had to tread carefully, very carefully.

Certain things did make him wonder really and sent tiny warning bells ringing. Never before had he been called to see to the Empress's ailments, but maybe it was because he always tore off his guard in the presence of beautiful women. Definitely, he decided the Emperor had chosen him to come at this very appointed time to see his wife because he had a special purpose for him. It was as if he wanted to make it look like a coincidence, and did Chinake know? He couldn't tell. Perhaps it had been the Emperor himself who had given his wife a small dose of whatever it had been that had made the fish poisonous. He checked himself in time. It was like him, Chireshe, to think wildly. He needn't go so far, not just yet, but tread carefully he would. If he became too knowledgeable it could spoil everything. He needed the current lack of knowledge to maintain his innocent stance. The Emperor, he told himself again, was too sleek. It could all go very badly for him before he got his hands on that precious beauty, Chinake. He shivered again at the very thought of her.

Had it been the dark, cold and windy night which had made the Empress's request less dangerous but more of a mystery or the desire for a great adventure? An adventure that could change the entire history of the Shona. Whether for good or for bad, Chireshe didn't mind. Going against the odds and proving himself made his blood roar. It excited him and he lived for it. No wonder the Empress had asked him to do something so outrageous.

So the Empress had known his nature and had wanted to use his ingenuity. The fact that the she had taken time to study him and desire his very personal assistance was a great honour. He marvelled at her wild suggestion and wondered dreamily how many other wild thoughts roamed around in that beautiful head of hers.

Of course he knew that one way or the other she thought she was using him, but he was no fool. He would use her too, in fact, he would use the entire royal family to get what he wanted. As long as he played the dumb spirit medium he would be safe. He would do all they asked him and he would get closer to his love. Yes, his love, for only she had ever made him feel anything that he knew was love.

And what then would happen in the end? Would Chireshe be given a golden crown and be made into a small god next to the royal divines? He chuckled at the ridiculous thought. He knew that he would only be wasted and given to the dogs. Those who had not played a role in it all would be given the chance to sit next to the royal family and sup with them. This was a rebellion, a revolt over an age-old deity, more dangerous than a violent, bloody, political coup. And as soon as victory was won he would not be needed. Why would an Emperor like Hungwe desire to share his glory with a man like Chireshe? If Chireshe could win the day for him then he could certainly take it away as well. This was war; if you could stab someone's back then certainly, someone could stab you too. So contingency plans had to be made. First he had to win, then he had to escape, but to win he had to keep an eye out for anyone who could ruin his plans. Once again he stopped and his lower lip trembled as he tried to think of some of the people who could try to stop him from assisting the Empress and the Emperor. Immediately a face sprang up. His nose flared in anger and he spat at the very image that had come into his head: it was that of Kwatara. Only Kwatara was ever bold enough to reprimand Chireshe in public.

Damn that young mhondoro and his dreams. He was his only known and true enemy. Maybe he already knew what was going on; he therefore had to be watched and finally destroyed. This was war, a war that if won would change the entire shape and faith of all the Shona people. He needed a plan and he would, as days went by, see how he could carry out the huge task placed upon him by the Empress. Poor people, if only they knew what was coming their way. He chuckled. He had no hard feelings whatsoever. After all, all is fair in love and war.

# Chapter ten

Empress Chinake had made sure that she had a sentry follow Chireshe home after he left. She had told him to stay in the shadows because Chireshe was a sharp man, never to be underrated and he knew his surroundings well. The young guard was to make sure that the old man was not seen by anyone dangerous enough to hamper her progress. The sentry had returned and had told her that he had gone home unseen; for some reason he had not told her about Kwatara. It was he whose footsteps Kwatara had heard just as soon as Chireshe had gone past. The Empress had been proud of his discretion and work and to make sure he kept his lips sealed, she promised to send a goat to his home the following morning. He was happy and he left.

The same guard who had been sent by the Empress now stood in front of the Emperor, relating the story that Chireshe had been to see the Empress and that he had been given two beautiful maidens. At the end he added the fact that he was sure he had seen Kwatara come out from behind a tree and look on after the passing figure of Chireshe. With these last words he had been dismissed by the Emperor with high praises, and was told he would be called upon again.

Hugging himself and rubbing his shoulders, the Emperor stood pensively looking into the blazing fire in the centre of the room. He was a man who played his cards well and close to his chest. He never left a stone unturned and though he knew Chinake adored him to pieces, he still had her constantly spied on. This time he had fooled her entirely. He had a mission, she was his pawn and he wanted to know whether or not things were proceeding as expected. So he had changed her guard of honour just two weeks ago. The older sentries had been assigned elsewhere and one of the replacements was this younger and less experienced sentry whose serious and innocent features simply yelled, 'trust me' to people. How predictable the Empress was. She was such a schemer and yet could be so easily manipulated and used by the Emperor.

He stood close to the fire that burned brightly in the centre of the room and crouching down, absentmindedly started to warm his cold hands. Had it been on another occasion, the Emperor would have been infuriated to learn that Chireshe had been to see the Empress without his permission. Instead, it made him smile to himself and chuckle softly into the bright yellow flames. It was amazing how carelessly well thought of words could be thrown about and achieve a goal beyond anyone's dreams. Like a greedy crocodile, his wife had swallowed the bait, inviting Chireshe along.

On many occasions when he held court with his council of chiefs and mhondoros, the Emperor had noticed how quick-witted Chireshe was. He was bold enough to raise any point, no matter how outrageous and strong enough, to support his craziness. He brought life to the court, usually sombre because of the protocol of respect the council had for the Emperor. Chireshe was also clever enough to be disciplined and humble when displaying respect for the entire council and the throne. He was a great orator, maybe the greatest ever the Empire had known. The sentry had told the Emperor that Chireshe had gone back home a merry man, and knowing the mhondoro's weakness for beautiful females, the Emperor at once knew that the prize he had been given by the Empress had been enough to get his mind working towards the Emperor's goal. Already he had won Chireshe's heart.

Hungwe had noticed how everyone shied away from Chireshe's sharp tongue, all except for one younger mhondoro. As the picture of Kwatara came into his mind, the Emperor sighed loudly and rubbed his beard. This one the Emperor had noticed, was not afraid of Chireshe's fast double-edged tongue that could slice you up and leave you bare for all to see. This one was cool, too cool for comfort in fact.

He was always composed and was not afraid to speak against any wrong in the court. The mhondoro who roamed in the Emperor's mind right now was a true worshipper of Mwari and he openly disliked any who blasphemed or spoke against Him. His name, the Emperor had learnt as time went by, was Kwatara and he was a man who highly respected religious protocol. Over the years, the Emperor had also learnt that he was loved by the people because he was a dreamer and his dreams had saved the nation on many occasions.

When the young sentry had mentioned seeing Kwatara come out from behind a tree, the Emperor had not been amused and he had wondered why the mhondoro was out so late. Had he been spying on Chireshe? But the guard had dismissed that suggestion and had told him that the mhondoro's older brother, the master builder, lived somewhere in the direction from where he was coming. That explained his presence, but still the Emperor was not happy with the fact that Kwatara had seen Chireshe and the girls on that particular night. Hungwe was a very cautious man and he became the second man that night to decide to keep an eye on the young mhondoro, in case he ruined everything. All he had to do now was to set the stage for Chireshe to pick up the remaining pieces and then he would concentrate on one major external force, the Mbire Kingdom. From the time he had spoken to Chinake and won her support he had been thinking hard about Nyatsimba Mutota and his people. In the end he had come up with a plan.

The morning before the council of chiefs and kings, he would hold a briefing on the pressing matters to be discussed at his *dare* or court; his sons as well as the most important chiefs in the Kingdom would be there. The Mbire Kingdom had not paid tribute and this would be his vantage point over them. He knew the council was not too happy with the lack of payment, drought or no drought, and coming from the Mbire, their largest vassal, he would make it look like sacrilege and not mere failure. He would only slightly highlight his concern about this to his sons and his council would seal the doom of the Mbire. They would see that the Mbire deserved a worse punishment and not just the one that had been decreed by the council; it would get a punishment that would destroy its very existence. Once again, he planned to stay in the dark and remain the innocent ruler while others took the fall for him.

The Emperor rose up and hugged his massive shoulders. His hands were now warm, indeed the heat from the fire had warmed up his entire body. The room was also quite warm by now and he relished in the feeling it gave him. Outside it was cold. This winter had been one of the worst and the Kingdom had been attacked over and over again by sharp and bitter howling winds. He was one of the lucky few to always have a large burning fire and warm coverings at night. Yes, one of the lucky few.

Life for the people was not as rosy as it was for the royalty and the few who lived in the protective enclosures.

He walked up to the small window in his room and looked outside. It was pitch black. A small cloud covered the moon, cutting off its light, then slowly it drifted past. The light of the moon shone and made the night a bit bearable. The Emperor imagined life in utter darkness, life in death where you were not mighty, never recognised and quickly forgotten. It was a formless, cold life, in a lifeless, blood frozen body.

And where did people go when they died?

Would he become a great spirit and one day possess one of his descendants? He did not know and did not even want to know. He was Emperor Hungwe with nothing to fear but he was afraid of one thing, death. To him it meant being no more, losing his glory and all his wealth. It was horror for him to imagine a life without all these comforts, a life without all this protection and a life without all this praise and awe from the people.

Was he insane? No, he thought not. He was just a man who had ambitions, ambitions to be greater than any other and a man who knew how to get what he wanted out of life. He had been lucky enough to hear the right words at the right time and to know how to make them become a reality. He was not like Chireshe intelligent beyond doubt but only living for the moment. Nor was he like Kwatara, a stupid man, he thought to himself who knew the power of Mwari Musikavanhu but was too submissive to even try to be as supreme. A docile mhondoro willing to be led by a being he had never seen and who would even lose his life for this abstract being.

Hungwe viewed himself differently. He would become the divine being the people saw and heard. He would never to leave all this grandeur which his forefathers had prepared for him, but live on to generations unending.

The cold wind blew another cloud over the moon and the night darkened once again. A few stars became visible where there were no clouds but they were not strong enough to shed light into the dim night. Looking up, he thought to himself, he was going to become the moon, strong enough to shine and cast light over darkness. The stars were like his wife and children as well as the rest of the Hungwe clan. They were like his kings, chiefs and mhondoros who did his bidding. They would move away one day, but he was determined to live on. Someday his home would be above, like the moon, and his wife's enclosure would be a sight to see. Superior beings deserved nothing less than the best, that would last forever

In a few days' time at the council meeting in his court, he would make sure he played his game well. This time he removed the Empress from his game and it was time to place the chiefs and the mhondoros. His game was played not to protect the Empress but the King. And it was the King not the other side knocking his own team down, in order to leave himself standing.

# Chapter eleven

The warmth from the early morning sun was rendered useless by an icy, cold wind but the three men were oblivious to the cold current. They had slept late, once again, planning their breakaway and had woken up early. So excited were they all that sleep hardly came and for each of them dawn came slower than on any other day. As before, they had met at the King's quarters but this time to accompany each other to the first point of their intended plan.

The King walked with a brisk new step, which his son gathered had been born of his plan to break away from the Empire of the Great Zimbabwe. For years he had never seen his father walk with such determination and with such a spring. Now, however, he saw a rejuvenated man who would die of sorrow if his plan did not succeed. Hence, as he looked at his father walk boldly alongside them, he prayed that nothing but the best would happen to their intended plan.

"You did well to send the messenger, Tekeshe," said the King. "I'm sure that any day from now, the Emperor will be hearing from him and hopefully accepting our humble tribute of two hundred worthy soldiers, trained to outrun and overcome any army between the Zambezi and the Limpopo. It was their request in case their vassals failed to pay tribute."

"I told him to tell the Emperor your exact words, my Lord," said Tekeshe. "He, too, believes what I told him and he made haste because last year he also lost out on a lot of grain and he was relieved when I gave him the message. I am sure that, even before he left, he told as many people as he could and the word is already all over the Kingdom."

"I still say it was good you thought of the plan, father," said Matope. "The Emperor is a wise man. If he had heard of us regrouping and excessively training our army, his suspicions would have been raised and he would have sent spies to come and investigate."

"You are not wrong," Tekeshe said. "The Hungwe is not a dull leader and he is also a soldier. Besides, all rulers spy on their subjects, especially if they believe the subject is powerful. But if we play our game well, we will outwit him." Mutota and Matope were listening attentively. "And to overcome a man is to know his mind," went on Tekeshe, "and we have one advantage over our Emperor, we know him but hopefully he doesn't really know us. From what I know and what I have heard it would be too dangerous to underestimate him or to overrate ourselves. He has been known to ruthlessly quash any rebellion and he will deal more harshly with us."

"I have always thought that he is far more ambitious than any other Great Zimbabwe ruler," said Nyatsimba Mutota. "Silent men are usually like a soundless, deep flowing river, innocent on top but murderous below. They say he is a true gentleman, reserved too, yet I cannot stop thinking that it could be just an act."

"Some say he is a deep thinker, clever and bright," said Matope slowly.

"Ah, but it takes two to play a game. So we have joined in his game. If you want to win a war, notice your enemy's strengths and turn them into weaknesses," said Mutota. "He uses his chiefs, his family, his mhondoros, as well as his soldiers; we shall use ours as well. It is a pity he decreed that this year, in the event of failure to pay tribute, we were to hand over a certain number of men to assist his army. It is a pity for him but a blessing for us, for we shall use his very words against him."

"But how will the army react to the idea of being traded for tribute? Will they not rebel, father?" asked Matope looking very concerned.

"It was the Emperor's decree that all who do not have this year's tribute should bring to his Kingdom soldiers, young and able bodied. If they rebel then they do not rebel against me, but against my Lord, the Hungwe," said Nyatsimba Mutota as a matter of fact.

"To rebel is to declare a mutiny, my young Lord," broke in Tekeshe. "And we all know that any soldier who revolts is handed the death penalty. You do not become a soldier of the State to rebel, but to obey orders and serve your country. When they were recruited into the army they knew the consequences, and to serve your nation goes beyond fighting for it with the spear, but includes doing what it takes to save your people."

"Tekeshe is correct, you do expect revolts and deserters in the army, but you deal with them ruthlessly and in that way you instil discipline. These measures are necessary if you want to have a well serving and obedient army," said King Mutota. "Do not worry, our army is made of worthy men. They are not mercenaries but disciplined soldiers who simply need a lot more tough physical training and psychological fine tuning. And if they prove they are not worthy enough, we shall make them worthy."

"We shall then have to work hard on getting them all physically fit. It would be useless to have an army of weak men. Lack of stamina always affects a soldier's confidence," said Matope.

"That is why," said the King, "we need as much grain as we can lay our hands on this year. This is the year of revolt and we need a strong army to back us up. We also need a great deal of cattle for food as well. We cannot allow our soldiers to go hungry or to think of how to fend for themselves and their families. This year they need to concentrate on nothing but fighting."

"Focus is essential. One day a soldier, tomorrow a farmer, the following day a beggar. That will not make a good soldier," said Tekeshe. "What else do you think we should do to make a great army, my Lord?"

"We need to work on their minds," said the King, stopping a while. "The mind is the central place for fear and courage. It makes a man. A man is great if he believes he is great and he is pathetic if he believes he is nothing. We need to talk to them, to drill their minds with great words of encouragement and bravery. To teach them to believe in their greatness and strength and to teach them total allegiance. Then our mission will be complete."

The others simply stared at him in awe and it was Matope who broke the silence by saying, "And to think that we have just a few months to complete all this. We therefore have a lot of work to do and we need total commitment ourselves." The other two nodded in sombre agreement. "What else do you have to add to this Tekeshe? I am learning a lot from both of you and I do find most of your ideas quite intriguing."

"I am not sure how to put this but if I may, my King, do not think that I mean to say your first wife has ever been against you, allow me to suggest this one very important fact," said Tekeshe, in a humble tone.

"Go ahead," said the King, warily. Matope cast the army general a questioning glance.

"I suggest that you fully involve your wife, the Queen Tashonga. This will, if I may suggest, bring support from her family. She comes from a very large family, whose forefathers have been mighty chiefs with great influence in the land of the Mbire. At the same time, if she is involved, I am sure she will as composed and as wise as we know her to be, bring balance into our plans. My father always told me to learn to place my wife first in my dreams as long as she is wise, because wise women bring sanity to all men's plans."

The King nodded, relaxed and looked thoughtful. "Secondly," said Tekeshe, "your sister, tete Rungano, is very influential. Make sure that she, too, is involved. I have observed the way she motivates women in times of stress. We need her to do the same in our plan. She loves you a lot and is a child of your mother. Women have a passionate love for their families and homes; we need their support."

"I hear what you say. I had not really thought of it," said Mutota, "but as soon as our campaign looks promising then I shall give her the word. Indeed, my wife comes from a large and influential family whose support or resentment can easily affect our wishes. She is by our side, don't worry. As for my sister, we are very close, she will help."

"We have always been made to believe that women are weak. They are in the physical sense, but they are also the mothers and wives of these men whom we wish to train for the day we leave to take over nations. And if we start by showing the King's first wife respect and seeking for her help, then we are bound to succeed," added Tekeshe.

Looking at the giant army general Mutota smiled. It was Matope who said, "It is amazing that you, a fierce army general, thinks like this. I am amazed. I now see there is a soft side to every man."

Tekeshe smiled softly and said, "I have a soft side and at the same time I am a strategist. There should be no stone left unturned. This is serious business. We need everyone on our side; well at least as many people whom we can get". Pointing ahead he said, "Look we are nearly there. Just beyond those trees our army awaits us."

\*　\*　\*

They walked in silence for a few moments and coming upon the plains they saw, already gathered there, hundreds of the Mbire state's soldiers. The King's messengers throughout the land, as planned, had sounded the horn last night, and this had called all the soldiers to the plains. The King was impressed that they had managed to come so early and gather so obediently. That was a good first sign. But more was needed to be done and said. The greater work still lay ahead.

Now flanked by his son Matope and Tekeshe, the army general, Mutota the Mbire King sat on a large rock, looking at his army. Yes, they were a real army; they looked serious enough but compared to the Great Zimbabwe warriors they were a sorry lot. On some faces he saw strain, on some he noticed dejection and on others there was even a hint of humility.

He had been correct last night, they had an army with soldiers but they did not have warriors. And what they needed was not a mixture of tough and easy-going soldiers, but a true breed of fighters, brutal enough to make the trek to the new land, intelligent enough to lead and guard its people against enemies and vicious enough to fight other states taking them over along the way.

Before today, the King had felt sorry for the men in his army. But today he was glad that most had been pushed by the Empire to the brink of a breakdown. He would work on this so cunningly, that each would, one day when the time was right, simply wake up and beg to walk away from the Great Zimbabwe Emperor.

Tekeshe looked at the King and the King nodded. He stood up, a tall and fear-inspiring figure with bloodshot, sharp eyes that commanded respect by simply looking at them. He held a spear in his hands and raising it in the air, he yelled, "Hail, O King! Hail O King of the Mbire! Hail your King, mighty warriors of the Mbire! Hail the mighty Nyatsimba Mutota!"

"Hail! Hail! Hail!" they all shouted, spears raised as well. The King nodded in response and raised his spear to the sky as he sat.

"Now kneel and greet your mighty King as warriors do!" he shouted again, above the wind.

They all crouched on one knee and cupping their hands, waited for the signal. It came from one man who clapped three times. As they clapped they said in unison, "Hail, hail O King of the Mbire. Hail to the one who is the son of the earth. Hail to the one who is a mighty warrior. Hail our King. Hail our King."

Once more, the King raised his spear and the clapping stopped. Then Tekeshe raised his spear in the air and shouted, "Fall into your lines, great soldiers of the Mbire! Show your King how well trained his army is! Show your great King the allegiance his army has!"

They fell into their lines, spears tightly held in their hands. They stood in their ranks with the lowest ranks standing at the back. The King beckoned to Tekeshe and whispered in his ear, "Go down to them. Walk in their lines. I will come with you. Look for those who deserve to be trained for our mission; to become part of the special Mbire army that will lead the people out of this land, while those that do not qualify shall simply remain as the supporting units."

Tekeshe was surprised at this request. He had thought that the King had simply come to address the army and to boost it with wise words. This proposal, however, took him by surprise. Even the soldiers would be surprised once they saw the King and Tekeshe come down and do the selection. He breathed in, looking at his army. He had many questions to ask but he had not the guts to displease the King who had so much faith in him. So he would deliver.

"And how shall I find such men, my Lord?" asked Tekeshe in a whisper.

"Look not for the young and able bodied only. You have known most of these men for a very long time. They may be older but brave enough to withstand the test. They may be much younger or of a lower rank in the army but obedient and courageous enough to go through with what we seek of them. Ignore the bold faces. They are usually a front. Look for the truth. You will know it. I will help you. It will not take us just a day but four at the most. We need at least two hundred such men. We shall not get tired and I dare not give the duty to anyone else but you, because we are both of the same heart and for the same cause."

Tekeshe nodded thoughtfully, trying hard to absorb all that the King had said. Then Mutota turned to his son and said, "Son, take my seat. You should get used to it. Very soon it will be yours. Learn from today to live and think like a King. Now notice what we are about to do and keep it in your mind. You will be a greater leader than I someday," and he smiled at Matope. Matope nervously smiled back and as his father rose from the rock, he timidly went to take his place. His father smiled at him, encouragingly. Matope realised what this meant. Things were moving so fast.

All the army looked at him as he sat. So did Tekeshe with a hint of amusement on his face. This was a clear sign before all the Mbire army that Matope was the successor of Nyatsimba Mutota. Tekeshe and Mutota went down to the soldiers. They started their job. The second phase of the plan to breakaway would be completed in four days.

# Chapter twelve

The month of July was over and a windy, cold August was present. It was another day and the Great Zimbabwe Emperor was holding court with his kings and chiefs, as well as with a few notable mhondoros. The council gathered on various occasions to discuss and iron out pressing local and external matters, which kept both the Great Zimbabwe Kingdom running and their vassal states in check; but little did they know that the Mbire King was busy mapping his way out of their grasp.

Emperor Hungwe sat on his elevated stool. He looked bored, but that was his usual look and people were now used to it. It was rare to see him smile or laugh or even chat with anyone. Hungwe preferred being alone, thinking and scheming. He was a man who delighted in his own thoughts and company; a man never easily understood and one whom everyone feared. His true nature was always veiled and his features made his feelings unreadable. It was difficult to even strike a true friendship with the man. The only man whom he could have a somewhat personal conversation with was his advisor, an old man called Shamai. He had been chief advisor to his father and the personal discussions they had only went as far as the politics of the nation and no further. No one ever advised Hungwe on his personal life or politics, he had made it a point. No one ever invaded his privacy.

All his life he had believed loneliness to be a friend that offered him the best possible advice, rather than seek friendship from the mouths of many men who considered themselves intelligent. And these were his kings, his chiefs and his mhondoros. But his father had taught him well and no matter how much he delighted in his solitude, he had been made to understand that he needed the company and use of other men. No ruler, his father had told him, could survive without his subjects and their allegiance. Worlds were never conquered by men single handedly, but by rulers who could gain the faith, support and fear of people.

Thus, despite being bored by the presence of so many people around him, the Emperor, on rare occasions, listened to their thoughts, which he took and twisted whenever he was on his own to suit his desires. He would silently sit in the court as matters of state were discussed and new ideas broached. He would look into their faces carefully and listen to their words intently. All the time he would be rubbing his beard calmly and slowly, taking in what was useful and throwing out what he considered junk, which was most of it. Hardly ever would he open his mouth to say anything and he had found out that this tactic worked as it gave his words a lot of weight. But today was different; he had an agenda and he would listen.

The chiefs, as well as some mhondoros, were seated a distance away from the Emperor on small stools. The court had been called to discuss tribute payment and other problems faced by the Empire, which needed immediate solving. Even Chireshe and Kwatara were there to listen to the day's proceedings and so was Hombasha. There was the upcoming ceremony of first rains too. The Empire was quite large and the ceremony was difficult to plan. It needed time and dedication and so it would come last. His chief advisor, old Shamai, stood up, greeted the Hungwe and the entire court by clapping his cupped hands, then addressed the entire gathering. It was his duty to brief the Emperor and to introduce to the court the day's proceedings.

Hungwe lifted his head and looked at him. He saw the same expression that Shamai always wore, an expression that never revealed what he was thinking. Even when offended, he never divulged his feelings. Hungwe wondered how much anger he had hidden over the years, how much boredom and how many frustrations he had veiled behind his mask. He was the one man Hungwe did not fully understand. Maybe it was because he was also like him, though the similarities rested with the Emperor's better side. Shamai could be so unemotional, even when being battered by pressure and words. He could be so silent, at times one would think he ought to burst. As he addressed the men, Hungwe noticed the never-ending dignity the man possessed; a quality that had made him one of the most feared advisors of all time.

"We welcome our great Hungwe and the crown Princes to the court. Our Emperor has graced us with his presence and it is now time to discuss the matters at hand. Let our behaviour, today, show respect to our Emperor and with our hands, may we offer our praise to our ruler, Hungwe."

The men present cupped their hands and clapped. When they were done, Hungwe lifted his walking stick which had carved at its tip the face and beak of the fish eagle, the Hungwe bird. That was a signal that all proceedings could start. Shamai then stood up and said, "Will the chief of the court Magura stand and bring to the attention of the court the first matter at hand."

He sat down on his stool and an elderly man, one of the senior chiefs of the Kingdom with a black cloth carelessly wound around his waist, rose up. Hungwe noticed that he had been there when he had briefed them about the tribute issue and he became more alert. Would his dart hit the target, he wondered.

After greeting the court, the chief said in a loud voice, "Our Great Lord and ruler Hungwe, we, your kings and chiefs of this vast and terrifying Great Zimbabwe Empire, hold you in great esteem. And if we do, so shall our vassals. However, it has come to our attention that so many of them are failing to honour our great ruler with the required amount of tribute. Their failure shall not only do damage to the image of the great Hungwe, but shall also affect our nation and our people who have for so long thrived and fed off their smaller states. So far, not even our biggest vassal state, the Mbire Kingdom, has managed to send tribute."

Hungwe listened attentively and yet not as eagerly lest he sold himself out. He was satisfied, his plan had worked. Indeed it was beautiful to be an Emperor.

A murmur of agreement rose and he went on to say, "How then, my fellow men, shall we be able to sustain our Kingdom of such great expanse? How shall the might of our Lord be upheld if what is to be given to him by his minor subjects is too little or nothing at all?" The great number of men at the gathering all agreed loudly. "Our Emperor has been too kind to these nations and never has he raised his concern over their tribute, but this time he has openly stated his disapproval of such behaviour and we shall not take it lightly."

The men present agreed. True, Hungwe had never raised concern about tribute but that was because it had always been paid on time. This year, however, the drought had ravaged their small nations and nothing, so far, had come.

His eldest son, Perayi, rose from where he sat close to his father and stood proud and confident. Something of what the chief had said had caught his attention. Seeing him stand, the chief immediately excused himself and without a word gave him the floor. The Princes never needed to follow protocol. Casually he said, nodding and clapping his hands to his father, "Excuse me, father, great Hungwe of the Karanga. May I add to what your chief has said?"

His father, the Emperor, nodded, smiling. This was the moment he had been waiting for and Perayi, seeing the smile on his father's lips, became more confident. He turned to face the gathering of chiefs and kings and said in a loud, authoritative and booming voice, "It has caught my attention as well, o great chiefs and kings of the Great Zimbabwe, that many small kingdoms are now unfaithful when it comes to paying tribute. I was there when my father showed his concern over this matter and it did not please me to see the great Hungwe so unhappy." Once more the men solemnly agreed. He went on, "It is a law that they pay their tribute in the form of cattle, goats and grain to the throne of the great Hungwe, but they have not. We should stop accepting every excuse they are giving to us. Let us, as we agreed before, take their soldiers, but this time let it be known that we will only require the young and able-bodied men." There was a loud cheer of agreement.

The dart was still on its way to the target. The Emperor shifted in his large stool and rubbed his beard with a twinkle in his eye. Perayi, noticing that he had got his father's attention as well as that of the entire court, stepped down and walked to where the chiefs and mhondoros sat. They all turned to look at him and he saw alert men, keen to hear his words. But for many it was fear lest they should be caught dozing while the son of the great Emperor was talking. Even Kwatara turned to look at him and Chireshe paid greater attention. Something was beginning to form in Chireshe's intelligent mind.

"Our Emperor is a great man, greater than any in this part of the world," boomed Perayi, as he pointed to Hungwe with his hand. "How many can oppose him and stand? None! But look at how a worm is eating its way into the core of our might and position. It was only a little hotter this season but so many claim that they cannot pay tribute because their crops failed and as great as our Emperor is, as great as we are, we sympathise with them, that is an outrage!"

All the men in the court nodded and agreed. Chireshe became more interested. His idea was slowly gaining flesh. "Let us not stand silent anymore and entertain excuses. These small kingdoms are ours. We should make them work for us, for our prosperity. Look at how long we have ruled in this very land, building enclosures and conquering nations. They tremble at the very name of the great Hungwe, our Emperor, and yet, somehow, we have become so sweet that they dare say they cannot give us what we desire as tribute. Who are they and who are we? Who is their Emperor but the great Hungwe and which King in these lands is mightier than he—none! Let the tribute be paid and let his name stand and become greater!" roared Perayi in a passionate tone that threw the men into a frenzy of excitement.

The Emperor was secretly thrilled. He had thrown his second arrow and it had struck home. He knew that very soon the words he had not placed in the mouths of these men would simply flow out. Somehow, fate had smiled at him. Now the court he had been finding boring had suddenly become very intriguing. He looked at how such a few words from the right man could change the minds of people. He noticed how the right person could excite men and turn them into thoughtless believers. But he was not the only one who noticed this. Chireshe now had a near complete idea forming in his mind. He knew now how he would make the Hungwe's dream come true.

All the mhondoros and the chiefs were cheering and talking excitedly except for one, Kwatara. There was something familiar about the voices and the frenzy in the court today. There was a different and yet familiar spirit present. Not one of solidarity but an uncomfortable one which he couldn't exactly place. It was as though this present spirit was just forming, not yet complete, but getting stronger as it evolved into something formidable. He shook his head. The whole court was alive with murmurs of agreement.

It was Tapera's turn now, the youngest of the Emperor's first three sons. He stood up and, addressing his father first, turned to greet the court. He then said, walking to where his brother stood, "We are a great nation, full of pride. I support what my brother has said. How can we sustain a great Empire as the one we have? How can the name of our

Emperor, the great Hungwe, ever live on if the once heavily flowing tribute is now just trickling in? We are the Great Zimbabwe, we rule. Our Emperor is Lord of lords and our army is the greatest. Let us then enforce a rule that no excuses shall be taken for lack of tribute. We will annihilate whole villages and make an example of the unlucky few, and the entire Kingdom shall be forced to work and produce food for us. Those that are ruled by the great Hungwe shall live to please him alone. Why should such an honourable name be placed in question?"

Another loud cheer of approval sounded. It was typical of him to say such words. Hungwe understood his son could dream of nothing but bloodshed and sharp knives. How he wished his son would thrust one of his knives into the flesh of Nyatsimba Mutota of the Mbire, but soon, soon the time would come. Patience was what he needed and not bloodshed. A map towards total supremacy was being drawn and soon all the points would be complete.

The chief who had risen first to speak rose up again, and excusing himself before the whole court said in a loud voice, "Then my fellow chiefs and mhondoros, we demand an army of fit, able bodied young men from the defaulting nations."

A noise erupted from the whole court. Excited voices spoke up and here and there more suggestions were given by the chiefs and mhondoros of the Great Zimbabwe.

Chireshe looked on, in a manner very unlike him, silently observing and retaining important facts. He saw the men filled with excitement; he relished their thick minds and quick, ignorant decisions. They would do. This platform would do. Now he had discovered his vantage point. With the right words he could sway all of them and make them believe that Hungwe was actually a divine being, worthy of praise. Using better words than these silly Princes, he would make them see reason. Yes, he would win the day for the Emperor and at the same time, realise his dream. Quickly he scanned the whole arena and saw all the men talking and cheering excitedly. All of them, even Hombasha. He appeared to be discussing a point with a man beside him. He looked at Shamai, not that he was of great significance but it was important to know what they were all thinking; like always, however, there was no reaction whatsoever. It was his usual style to remain nonchalant in the event of a loud argument in court, not even a twinkle of the eye. And then his eyes fell on Kwatara. Was he just passively looking on or was that wonder and confusion on his face? Chireshe could not tell but it was important for him to be able to because this man was his major opponent. He would find out. It would help him to know who was on his side in his new intended plan and who was not. So far, only Kwatara was not showing exactly where he stood.

And while the whole court was slowly coming to order, the most unexpected event happened, Chikomo stood up. Everyone became hushed. It was on rare occasions that the Prince ever spoke during a court meeting. He usually remained seated like his father, looking on as though he was watching a dreary drama unfolding before his very eyes. He raised his hand. Chireshe braced himself; this was proving to be more exciting than he anticipated.

He stepped down from where he sat beside his father and went to stand beside his brothers. He greeted the court and after asking for permission from his father to speak, who waved him on, he said, "My fellow men, I admire your care and pride in our Kingdom. Indeed, I stand proud to have such a supportive council of mhondoros and chiefs, and it is wonderful for us all to unflinchingly support the throne. Without a doubt it is what we agreed upon, that in the event of failing to pay tribute an army of young men was to be provided. It was a noble idea then but look around you, our grain reserves are depleting. A large army will be our strength but it will strain us." He looked around and everyone looked at him. Then he breathed in and said with a voice full of confidence, "Soldiers need to be fed, they need perks. They need taking care of but," he paused to get their attention, "workers do not need the same kind of attention. They will work for the State and work for their own food as well. Yes, they may give us their able-bodied men, they may even train them but, and listen to me well here, how much time and food shall we lose further, training a bunch of no good young soldiers because their soldiers can never be as good as ours. Let them bring us well trained young men and even their daughters as well, because if the Hungwe and the Great Zimbabwe are to remain in power and total authority, we should break the very backbone of these smaller states, their young men and women. Yes, they will bring us their young soldiers but let us benefit entirely. They will not be soldiers because, for now, there is no war to attend to, but they shall work like brutes in our fields and on our enclosures. They shall be turned into helpless slaves who will despise their kings for bringing them here and their very backs shall turn against their own fathers and rulers. By the time they return, if ever they do, they shall return broken in spirit, with broken hearts and broken torn backs, to broken kingdoms unable to even know the difference between a chisel and a spear. And our Kingdom shall rule through their sweat forever."

What was this that the Hungwe was hearing? Truly, was he not born to be a supernatural being when everything was working out so well for him? For days, he had thought of how to delete the power of the Mbire Kingdom. Never again would he despise his court. Luck was surely backing him up. He had not thought it could be this good. While all his sons had brought forth ideas that were in line with their interests, this one was the best. Chikomo went on speaking to everyone's amazement.

"We will build great enclosures, massive walls beyond everyone's dreams and we will be a mighty nation whose evidence of greatness will live on to generations beyond even our imagination. Their very hands shall build gigantic walls for the Great Zimbabwe people while their very states perish without their young and able-bodied men and women. Let their young armies be brought, yes, and let hundreds be brought, but why train their armies? Rather let us destroy them and make them know that only one army exists, that of the Hungwe. So much for a hot season and so much for not giving us their grain and cattle. Now they shall suffer true heat!"

The men cheered. The Emperor smiled. Hombasha was disgusted at everything. Why take soldiers and turn them into workers. Why increase the number of workers when already there were too many and becoming difficult to take care of and control. And how on earth would they find food for themselves if they were busy working on the enclosures. He knew that one thing was certain, Chikomo wanted to increase his influence in the Kingdom and if it took a thousand whipped, malnourished workers to do so then so be it. The ache in his shoulder increased and he turned to seek out his brother. Even from this far off distance, he needed Kwatara's reassurance.

Kwatara was somehow confused. He had seen the men excited before in the court but not this elated. There was a strange atmosphere as well as an uncanny resemblance to the shouting voices in his dream. They were not saying exactly the same thing but it was as though this part was a prelude to the real event foretold by his dream. He shook his head and looked about. He listened to the men talking and looked at the Emperor.

Maybe the Emperor was finding all this as ridiculous as he was. Casually the Emperor turned his head and looked away from the excited mob and straight into his eyes. Why was the Emperor looking at him like that? Was he searching for something on his face or for support, or were those squinted eyes, eyes of hate. His thoughts interrupted by a voice that suddenly shouted,

"Hail to what the Prince has said!" It was one of the mhondoros who had stood up to support Chikomo. "How else can we be remembered if we do not leave a symbol of our greatness behind? We are such a mighty nation and we fear no one. Let us, I say, build more such beautiful enclosures. And yes, they will bring us their young men but like the Prince has said, they shall build and in turn enhance our greatness. Hail to the Prince!"

A shout of approval came from those present and the mhondoro sat down smiling and nodding his head to those beside him. Chireshe rubbed his chin in delight. The Emperor looked at him and saw his excitement. His dice had landed on another perfect six. It had not failed him.

Chireshe was beside himself with joy. How easily men cheered to evil ideas and how easily they were confused and then convinced. This was the season of psychological bashing and he would unleash his power of mind control. Now he knew how well his idea would work. No, swords could not win such men onto your side, but words and a suitable atmosphere. Both would slice through the hearts of these gullible, noble people of the Great Zimbabwe and win the day for the Emperor and for him as well. He breathed in a sigh of exultation.

# Chapter thirteen

The council's meeting at the Emperor's court had gone quite unexpectedly for Chireshe. He had come out excited and his mind a whirlwind of thoughts. A burning question in his mind had been answered and he now had a solution. So excited was he that, uncharacteristically, he did not even stop to talk and greet the other attendees but had rushed home. He had to think and sort some ideas out. Lame talk would disrupt his line of thought.

As he hurried home, he thought once more of how the proceedings at the Emperor's court today had done him an immeasurable favour and he let out a chortle of gratitude. Just when his think tank was about to burst in trying to find ways of bringing the Empress's ideas to pass, the court had provided him with an answer.

He now knew how he would fight his battle to win the minds and hearts of the Karanga of the Great Zimbabwe. First, he would deal with the lay men in one simple way and for this he would need the help of the Empress and her sons. The final battle would be fought at the Emperor's court. There all the important men and women met and there they would be persuaded and cajoled until they only knew one thing, that the old order of their religion was gone and that Hungwe now stood as the Divine. All along he had wondered where to begin, now a battle ground so simple had been laid before him, plain and bare.

He had seen the way the Princes with their simple, brave words had turned the entire court into a frenzy, rallying behind the Emperor. The so-called wise men were extremely susceptible and as long as the Emperor's eyes were before them, they would shout, jump and kill just to please him. Chireshe had observed the way the men had greedily swallowed every word that had been said, which supported their Emperor without even stopping to think. They were very patriotic and patriotism, Chireshe had noticed, was a tonic for blind loyalty. Whatever silly thing the leader said, the blinded patriots would gobble up. Like a bunch of hungry chicks in a nest, they never asked where their mother had obtained the food or what it was. Their mouths were always open, ready to eat up anything, poisonous or not.

And such loss of sight always made Emperors, like Hungwe of the Great Zimbabwe, get whatever they wanted. Chireshe believed he could do better than the Princes and the Emperor's chiefs. He was a brilliant persuasive strategist. He had carefully learnt the tricks of persuasion, mastered them beyond the original thinkers and now he was using them to get his way. He had a way of framing words making them give the desired meaning and effect. As ugly as he was, he could use his big eyes to gain empathy and he was brilliant at gestures. The mhondoro knew when to throw his hands in the air, when to break into a freakish smile and when to pace about, making people believe in the seriousness of his words.

He got home, stood in the centre of his hut and rubbed his hands gleefully. Laughing like a scared hyena, he went to the heap of animal skins and took out his little pouch. Once more he mixed the grey ash and water, sat down and poured it onto the pouch, releasing the two little creepers that escaped from it happily with their peculiar sigh.

"Aahh Chireshe, how excited you look. It looks like it has gone well with you. Have you found a way to win your bloodless war? Tell us, tell us for we are too eager to know." With this they writhed about excitedly on his wrist and he looked at them with clear-cut joy.

"Yes, my green friends, yes it went well with me. And yes, I have found a way to win my war and with it my Empress. But do not judge me when I say I shall work for the Emperor, the thief who stole the woman I desired, in so doing I shall work against him as well."

"So clever you are, so clever Chireshe," said the creepers in unison. "Oh tell us how the master of minds will win the day and his love?"

At that, Chireshe stood up and like an actor, he said aloud, "I will speak before the entire council of chiefs, kings and mhondoros. I will tell them to see the greatness of the Kingdom. I will blind them with the power and vastness of the Empire. I will trap them with the reality that without the might of the Hungwe all will be lost and I will make them see that even their breath hinges on the mere existence of the Empire but more so—yes, more so on the existence of their ruler, our majesty. Yes, I will tell them that."

"Yes, yes Chireshe our friend, you can, you can and you will and they will believe," encouraged the creepers, as they wound and unwound themselves on his wrists excitedly.

He paused to take in a deep breath, then seeing his entire picture come to life he smiled, like an evil imp, and said aloud, "I will make them feel as though they owe the Emperor a favour. I will build an image of authority and power before their eyes like they have never seen. I will wear them out with my intelligent words and I, Chireshe, will make them believe that before them stands a being of such divine power, enough to make their age old belief in their religious hierarchy crumble to dust." Then suddenly he stopped and a mocking look of sadness came across his face. The creepers noticed this and they stopped their movement as well, sending out a rustling sound. Someone had come up in his mind and as though to make himself certain the person was not going to be a threat, he said aloud to himself, "But I know that Kwatara, humble and obedient Kwatara will stand firm and will not be swayed by my words. Yes, his true nature will blind him. He will not see that he is alone and he will oppose me. Oh, how I fear what will happen on that day when you oppose me. Oh, I tremble."

The creepers sighed in agreement. He shivered in pretence and hugged his shoulders. Suddenly he laughed out loud, a laughter that made tears roll down his eyes and ended in a cackle. Smiling to himself, with his face staring in the air at nothing and eyes bulging, he said aloud once more, "I know what you will say to me, Kwatara. You will say, 'Oh Chireshe, are you not afraid of Mwari, he that created you and the world? Do you not fear his wrath for those that speak against the order ordained by the ancestral spirits and try to be their equals? Know this," he said, wagging a finger at himself in the air, with an evil smile, "'know this, you miserable mhondoro, you are a mhondoro, sworn to serve Mwari Musikavanhu and the crown. Sworn to guide the people spiritually. What will become of you when you declare a mere being divine?' Yes, Kwatara, that is what you will say to me and before the court as well. You, Kwatara, you who fears no one when it comes to supporting an abstract deity."

The creepers wiggled on his hand and sent out a strange, whispery laugh that filled the entire room. "Oh Chireshe, you are so fearless, but Kwatara will do you harm. He is so jealous of you. What will happen then?" they asked in a loud, rustling voice.

He stopped, looked serious and folding his arms, he answered, "Nothing will happen to me, Kwatara. Nothing, because for years I have fooled the entire Kingdom and they have thought and believed that I am indeed a mhondoro of great acclaim because I am a master of persuasion. I speak and people listen and follow. I shall lead them in thinking and I shall be their heart and brains. And you shall be left alone with no one on your side."

"Yes-s-s," agreed the creepers. They were as evil as their master.

Chireshe then calmed himself and sat down on a reed mat. That was his favourite place when he needed to think. He put his hands on his cheeks and started to measure the pros and cons. Enough of the comedy, he now needed to get serious. Very soon he was supposed to make the people believe that Hungwe was a supreme being, one equal to the ancestors, a godly being who needed the type of respect awarded to beings of such eminence. That was not a joke to people who believed in one God, not of flesh and blood, and that only the ancestral spirits were divine besides Mwari Musikavanhu himself. He suspected he would face some resistance, but because the masses feared the Hungwe and his vicious sons, the court drama would suffice. There was only one major obstacle, Kwatara. He was a hindrance because he was a true and straightforward man. Chireshe may have disliked him but that was one thing he could not discredit about Kwatara. He was a man of honour and quite intelligent in a reserved way. There was belief conflict there because of Kwatara's staunch faith in Mwari, as well as his knowledge concerning the religion. It posed a danger to his deal. Chireshe had seen Kwatara openly and skilfully defend the religion. He would have to undermine Kwatara by his use of words and support from the people who, bless his soul, were generally very ignorant and fearful of opposing the Emperor. His best hope rested on the people's lack of confidence and the surprise attack he would launch.

He therefore needed to talk to the Empress further. The continued talk about the army at the court today had given birth to an idea in his mind. He would discuss it with the Empress.

He also admired the three Princes and the way they had stood up for their father. It was amazing, thought Chireshe to himself, the Emperor never even had to lift a finger. His sons did the talking for him. And when they did, they imposed to the utmost fullness their father's authority and ruthlessness. He saw the way they did not leave the topics they had broached, open for discussion, demanding nothing but support. They were like their father's echo, an echo of his ideas. They were also his shield, tough and stubborn. Added to that they were his greatest and worthiest supporters, apart from their mother Chinake. All around them was an aura of selfish pride and ruthlessness that made even Chireshe wince. The Princes were cruel and spoilt, but in this case, such unworthy upbringing would be of great use.

He also needed the Emperor's other wives present. As he had hurried home past their enclosure, an idea had sprung up in his mind. They barely ever saw their husband, the Emperor, and some had not seen him for years. They hardly ever got the chance to show how much they appreciated being his wives. He doubted that they loved him nor did the Emperor have any feelings for them because most had been given to him as gifts from lesser states to maintain peaceful relations. It was just loyalty that bound them to him and the pride of being called the Emperor's wives. Letting his mind wander, he wondered how a man could juggle twenty wives or so. Well, that was not his problem; he shook his head to regain focus. The important fact was that they were his wives and they doted over him.

They had to be invited to the court on that fateful day and it would be an honour for them. In their large numbers, their ululation would save the day for him. He also believed Chinake would love to see them there. It would give her an open opportunity to show off her closeness to the Emperor and prove she was in total control. A lot needed to be discussed, however, and mapped out before the great day. He made a point to see the Empress as soon as possible. This time, he told himself, he would call the shots. It was the Empress who would be listening to him and not the other way around. He could not wait to see her and lay out his plans to her.

And then, yes, he would talk and discuss with the other mhondoros and chiefs. Yes, he would pop a question or two here, a compliment about the Emperor there, and seek out their thoughts. He was a good reader of gestures and facial expressions. The stresses in people's voices told him if they were happy, tense, lying or genuine. From tomorrow onwards, he would be busy talking and he made a bet with himself that no one would care because Chireshe was known for talking and nothing but talking. By the time he saw the Empress he would know how many were on their side; if it was a safe number then no time was to be lost. Nevertheless, he needed to be certain just in case Kwatara got the support he did not deserve. The man still roamed his thoughts as a dangerous opponent.

"Tell me my friends, you who can see more than I. Can the mhondoro Kwatara have seen anything by now because if he knows then my entire dream is doomed? I need to know for only Kwatara can stand in my way. And if you know what he has seen, please tell me I need to be on guard?" he pleaded with the creepers.

"Oh Chireshe how the man troubles your poor soul but alas, we cannot read his mind," they said together.

Chireshe looked deflated and begged, "Please help me my friends, I need all the knowledge I can get if I am to win this battle. Kwatara is stubborn, he can ruin all our plans."

"You insist, Chireshe, because your mind is troubled yet you know that we are only healers and not seers. Nevertheless, you are a dear friend. Let us join therefore if it will give you peace," they said in a consoling tone.

Chireshe was pleased that they had finally decided to help and he hoped he would get the solution to his problem.

He held out his hand and with his eyes closed, he whispered in the foreign tongue once more, "*Menjadi,*" meaning, "Become" and he blew air into their faces.

Immediately the restless one stilled and closed its eyes. The relaxed creeper suddenly became alert and moved towards its friend. They coiled around each other and as they did so, their leaves miraculously joined to become one single circular leaf. At the same time, they started to merge from the bottom to the top until one snake-like creeper was formed.

It sent out a loud rustling sound and its leaves vibrated. Winding itself around his hand, it whispered, "Oh, he is a tricky one, so cool, so reserved and so unafraid. The one who sees ahead, beyond all. But he has seen, yes he has, because he should see as is his gift. Worry, yes, about him, for he will speak against you indeed."

"Still I need to be sure, very sure, and how can I be when I know not what is in his head?" worried Chireshe aloud.

"Ah Chireshe," came the double voice again, "Study the face as you always do. Does he unnerve you so much you even fear to look at him? See his face, his way of moving. Then you will know that he knows something is on its way, something that will affect the nation, as is his calling to defend it by what he sees. His mind is his to conceal or to reveal what he knows. We are but healers and not seers. All we know is he has seen something and so be careful."

Chireshe got the message but was crestfallen for a while. How he wished the two creepers could have helped further but he knew their strength could go only thus far. They were only for herbal knowledge and were not mind readers. He would have to find out for himself before he launched his killer punch in the Emperor's court. His final decision was that tomorrow he would start his research on who was and who was not on the Emperor's side. As long as the numbers were large then he would go on with his plan.

Nothing was to go wrong for on that day, his future with Chinake in his arms would be determined. Yes, the Hungwe would rise, but he would rise under the shadow of a mighty mhondoro and when that shadow left, the Hungwe would be left exposed and his fall would begin.

# Chapter fourteen

Emperor Hungwe could not help smiling to himself. He stood by the small window looking out at the hill. Of late this had become his favourite pastime. Each time he looked out at the hill he visualised his new home right there on top. He could see himself sitting on that large rock that overlooked the entire Kingdom. He could also see himself holding court with his subjects. Even before living there he could not help feeling the wind freely rubbing his cheeks. That would be his final stamp to immortality. He would live high up in the clouds among the ancestors. Living on the sacred hill, who would deny him divinity? He would claim his position among the ones that that were immortal.

Then his mind trailed back to the day's proceedings at his court. They could not have gone any better. The destruction of the Mbire Kingdom had been mapped out for him and he had not even said a word. His original plan had been to punish the Mbire and to give the mhondoro, Chireshe, an idea on how he was going to introduce his bid to supremacy, but his sons, oh bless those ruthless boys, they had done much better. Once again, in utter silence, he had achieved his goal.

From behind him, as he mused, a voice came accompanied by the clapping of cupped hands, "My Lord, my Emperor. I do hope I am not disturbing you."

He did not want to look back but he changed his mind. The man's voice behind him belonged to his chief advisor. With an effort he turned back and saw him kneeling on one knee, his face looking at the floor. No one ever looked directly at the Emperor unless directed to do so.

"My friend and my chief advisor, Shamai, it is a pleasure to have a visit from you. Do get up and look at your Emperor," he said, trying not to sound impatient.

Slowly, without losing respect, he got up and clapping once more he said in a humble voice, "I hope I find my Emperor well today. I also hope I am not disturbing him because he is exhausted from today's proceedings but important news has come to my attention, my Lord. In fact, two important issues of great concern have arisen and I thought that it would be expedient for you to know before night time and to sleep on them so that tomorrow you may, if possible my great Lord, provide us with solutions which require much speed."

He had said a great deal at once. This was not like him. The Emperor looked at him in slight surprise and amusement. It had to be very important for the chief advisor to come on his own and so late in the day. He was now rather old, and though Hungwe would have liked a much younger chief advisor, he had not wanted to let his father down. Before his death, the Emperor's father had appointed Shamai to carry on as Hungwe's chief advisor and so far, things had progressed well despite Shamai's age. He was wise and rational. He also loved the Emperor and feared him at the same time. His father had not made a hopeless dying appointment.

"You say so much at once, old man," said Hungwe, coming down to stand close to him. "Look at your Emperor and tell him what it is that ails you so much that you think I should sleep on it. I do not need more troubles. I have enough to sleep on already. Now speak and stop being afraid."

"My Lord," began Shamai, "the exact thing we were talking about has been fulfilled already today. Just after we left the court, I was called upon to see a messenger from the Mbire Kingdom."

Hungwe looked at him and his boredom turned into curiosity. The Mbire Kingdom and its King were a thorn in his flesh and the mention of its name aroused his curiosity. "And what did he want that has made you so uncomfortable?" he asked.

"He said he had been sent by his master, the King Nyatsimba Mutota, to bring us the message that his Kingdom cannot provide the grain and the cattle needed for tribute this year. Instead, as we had agreed and decreed last year, they are offering to bring at least two hundred able-bodied men to serve in our army."

Hungwe turned and looked away from Shamai with a thoughtful look. Finally he said, "Well, we decreed it because last year we were hoping to start another campaign to conquer nations in the east but that has changed. Now we have to pay for our lack of foresight. If we had thought it over properly, we would not be in this mess. We have to live with our mistake."

He turned to look at his chief advisor and folding his hands on his chest, he said, "And today we decided on something else. We will accept their soldiers," Shamai opened his mouth to say something but Hungwe raised his hand in the air to silence him, "but we will use them for other things as my sons and others in the court suggested." Shamai breathed a sigh of relief. "Slaves and workers can find food for themselves. We will at least lessen the burden upon us."

"It saddens me though, my Lord, that the Mbire Kingdom cannot give us our annual tribute of grain and cattle. It is our largest vassal state and we need its support," said Shamai thoughtfully, rubbing his beard.

"What is on your mind?" asked Hungwe, for the first time becoming truly serious.

"Well, my Emperor, if they totally fail to give us the grain and cattle and provide us with men for the army, we will still be in the position we were trying to avoid at the court. I know that harvests have not been good for all of us, but from such large states, I think that we need to request a certain amount of grain and cattle, even if they cannot give us the required yearly tribute. At least, my Lord let us investigate to ensure that they cannot offer the grain before accepting their young men and women workers. The grain and livestock are more important."

"I see," said the Emperor, seeing sense, "I had not thought of us holding a thorough investigation. You are right. The Mbire is our largest vassal state and any misbehaviour from them could mean that other lesser states may follow. I do agree that an investigation should be conducted. Maybe they are lying about the grain and the cattle. How long will it take us to send a messenger back to their Kingdom?"

"About four days, my Lord, what did you have in mind mighty Hungwe?" asked Shamai, looking at him warily.

"I am saying delay their messenger for a few more days. Tell him the Emperor is too busy and he shall see him in three days' time. Keep him and his companions well. And we shall send our investigators."

"Very well then, my Lord," said Shamai, slowly as usual. He lingered on, just standing there as though searching for the right words to say. Hungwe looked at him, waiting for him to say something, then finally Shamai said, "There is the second issue, my Lord."

"Yes, go on, Shamai. I am listening."

"Well there is a shortage of salt in the Kingdom. You, my Lord, may not have noticed because we make sure that our mighty Emperor has enough of everything and some of the important people in the Kingdom may not have yet been affected. But with the booming number of people, salt is becoming short. I was hoping that you would sleep on it, my Lord, because this is a very important issue, and advise us on the steps to take. I shall be on my way, it is getting late. I shall, as you have advised, delay the Mbire messengers and in the meantime send our chiefs to investigate the truthfulness of the Mbire statements."

Hungwe blinked. Salt was indeed important in the Kingdom. It was a very important part of their diet. For how long could the nation go without eating food with salt? Indeed, here was an issue that he needed to sleep on. He rubbed his eyes. He felt tired. Each day had its own problems and some were quite difficult to solve. He felt burdened and fatigued.

"How about the salt we get from goat dung and reeds? Can it not suffice?"

"That, my Lord, is also not sufficient anymore. We have tried to make as much as we can, but at the current rate it is being used up and with the sudden population growth, I doubt that our salt reserves can last us very long." His voice sounded very dejected and made clear that the salt situation in the nation was close to hopeless.

"Well then, is there any place where salt can be found in huge amounts? We need to find that place, and if it is not one of our vassal states, we will if need be, trade with as much ivory and gold as we can to get as much salt as possible."

Shamai remained silent for a while as though thinking deeply. He always did that, especially when he knew the answer to a question the Emperor had asked. In the early days, this habit had irritated the Emperor but he had grown used to it. Then slowly he raised his head and looking directly into the Emperor's eyes, he said, "My Lord, I am sure you may have still been too young then. But I remembered something with the question you posed me. Many years back the Mbire also suffered a salt deficit." The Emperor was now listening carefully and noticing that he had his attention, Shamai went on to say, "The then Mbire King, Mutota's father Chibatamatosi, sent his servant, a man called Nyakatondo, who came back with large amounts of salt from the Mavuradonha Mountains. This salt came from the traders who trade along the Zambezi River. They say it was salt from the great seas. Rivers that are so huge you cannot tell where they end."

Hungwe just stared at him and finally, sighing, he said thoughtfully, "I see. The Zambezi area. That is far north. Very far from here. And who knows, maybe the salt traders are no longer there?"

"Perhaps, but maybe the salt is still there," said Shamai in a sombre tone that revealed he knew more about the Zambezi river trade than the Emperor did.

Hungwe looked up. Maybe the old man had a solution after all. "What are you saying, old man? Is there something you know about the trade at the Zambezi? We have a vast Empire that stretches all the way there, but we know little of that area. It was conquered so long ago by our forefathers. Now tell me, you are older than I, is there still salt trade in the Zambezi area?"

"Yes, there is my Lord," said Shamai, as a matter fact. "I have spoken to some traders who have visited the Kingdom. They say there still is salt trade taking place in the area and these are men who have traded with us for a long time. I hold their word in high esteem. This could be where our solution lies, my Lord, in the Zambezi area. The problem is the area is quite far and so many dangers lie along the way. We may be their lords, yes, but who knows how much respect they can give us if they are so far from the claws of the great Hungwe?"

Hungwe kept silent. He was thinking. Shamai was saying that the salt was there and that the area was under the Great Zimbabwe Empire, but it was still a dangerous place to go. In such cases, Princes would be sent in order to command the required respect, however could he justify risking his sons' lives for some salt? That was doubtful. Who would be willing to lose his life over salt for a nation that had remained behind sleeping, hoping the person would return home soon with the desired goods. No one.

Instead he said, "I hear you, old man, and thank you for your advice. Such problems are grave and it was kind and clever of you to note them early. Now leave me, the day has been long and trying. I will think about it. In the meantime, get ready three chiefs and an army of a hundred soldiers. They shall go to the Mbire Kingdom and see for themselves if what Mutota has said about his grain and cattle is true. They are to leave in two days' time." Giving Shamai a stern look, he added, "And let it be done privately, very privately, lest our aim is blown up right before our faces."

Getting the message Shamai nodded his head sombrely, as usual.

"Now go," said Hungwe, waving him away impatiently. Damn the salt issue, it had dampened his high spirits. Shamai clapped his cupped hands and, bidding the Emperor farewell, he left. Dusk was already present and once more the Emperor went to look out the small window. His spirits lifted up a bit as he looked at his promised new home. Soon he would retire to bed and tomorrow would be another day. He hoped to make it more successful than this one.

Later that night, just before he fell asleep, he suddenly shouted with joy. He had found his solution. All along it had been right under their noses. He called out to one of his guards who came running. He told him to go and call Shamai immediately. He was to stop the Great Zimbabwe chiefs from going to the Mbire Kingdom and he was to send the Mbire messengers back home tomorrow with an important message from him. Very soon, the two great men would meet face to face. Hungwe looked forward to that day.

His day had not ended so badly after all. And to make his night more endurable, the sentry he had appointed as spy over Chinake, his first wife, came with word that Chireshe had requested to see the Empress again and he had been allowed audience. The Emperor smiled to himself. He was amazed at how successful his plans were turning out to be. Sweet, cruel Chinake, his three sons, Chireshe, and very soon the Mbire King, Nyatsimba Mutota, would all be dancing to his mighty tune. He wished he had a drum to beat and dance to at the same time.

# Chapter fifteen

Chireshe went to see the Empress a few days after his request, feeling like an evil goblin about to reveal a wicked plan. As he walked to her place, he imagined the strain she was under, anxiously waiting to hear how far their dirty little plot had developed. She would look composed when he arrived because she was Chinake, the Empress whom no one could ever ruffle but right now, he could see her wringing her hands, hoping for the best.

His last thoughts were right. Back in her room, Chinake looked agitated. From the time he had requested to see her she had been waiting for the wretch, Chireshe, and only her desperate need and pride had stopped her from calling on him constantly. Now, after a painful wait, Empress Chinake hoped her dream for her husband was finally going to become a reality.

Chireshe arrived late at night and, in the bright light of the fire, he was surprised to find the Empress looking so fresh and composed, as though she had just left her bath. He had guessed well, she looked neither desperate nor excited. She was an accomplished actress and he admired and even desired her more for that. Once again, he had to strain himself to remain focused. This woman always managed to throw him off balance.

He greeted the Empress and after she greeted him in return, she offered him a stool. She sat directly in front of him on the floor and, giving him a serious stare which made Chireshe lose all his confidence, she said, "It has been long, Chireshe, since we met and spoke. I have been waiting eagerly for your return. Do tell me, please, if the maidens I sent to you were to your expectations."

He had not expected that question. She was supposed to have begged for the solution he had, but instead she had deliberately veered off track. What a cunning beauty she was, he thought to himself. Quickly he answered, "Yes, yes, my lady, they were and even more than that, they were so young, so innocent. Ah yes, you knew your servant's heart, my Empress. I must say your choice is true and rich," he said, nodding to show his gratefulness.

The Empress smiled a knowing smile and tilting her head ever so gently, she asked in her silky voice, "Then is my servant ready to give his Empress what she desires or does he need more time? My heart grows restless with worry. I dare not see my husband again and give him uninteresting news."

Already the Empress was trying to make Chireshe feel guilty. He had requested the meeting, but somehow the Empress had taken over the conversation. She would not let Chireshe command the situation, especially on her own turf, in her house. He, however, decided to let it be and answered, "My Empress should know that here stands a man of his word. Yes, I have a bright answer for you. I now know how to carry out the task you have given me. Do not worry. I will need your total cooperation though."

With a sigh of relief, she said to him, "It is good that you have been busy, Chireshe, my heart was growing anxious. I am sure that this is a tall order and it will take a lot of ingenuity and commitment to carry out, but I do trust you and am certain you will be able to overcome any difficulties. Had it been a war of the spear and shield I would not be worried, but this is something different and none of us have any experience with it. I do hope you will make me confident and happy"

Once more, she had cleverly taken over the conversation. But he let it be because he, too, had an ace under his cuff. "You are right," said Chireshe, "It is indeed a tall order and like I said, its success depends on your total cooperation as well. But there is a greater chance than we previously thought that your request may become a reality."

"Your words excite me, Chireshe. Tell me, please, just what it is you need and it shall be granted, as long as it gives my dear husband his peace of mind," said the Empress excitedly.

He stared at her for some time after she had finished talking. Either she was a great performer or she was a woman who loved her husband to a dangerous extent. He, however decided that she was both. Momentarily, he felt crushed but he brushed the feeling aside. He said casually, briefly dampening her joy, "Before I tell you what you want to hear, I need to inform you of the difficulties we may face."

Chinake's face fell. Just a moment ago, she had thought that they were on an unimpeded, gentle slide down to success, now this. She screwed up her face, looked dejected for a while, then gathering her composure she asked in a stately tone, "What could lie in the way of his majesty that should impede his desire for divine recognition? He has all the necessary qualities, all the wealth and all the glamour. Tell me, could there be anything in this whole world that could prevent my husband from becoming the being he deems to be?"

Was she pleading? Chireshe could have smiled because he sensed that she somehow had slipped up and he had gently taken over the reins. He looked at her and thought of how the pleading sound of her voice excited him. It reminded him of the two girls he had taken home that night. Their entreaties had done nothing to soften his heart, but had taken his ecstasy beyond control. Now, the Empress was pleading with him like a child and it thrilled him. Once again, he checked himself just on time. This was the Empress he was talking to, the Emperor Hungwe's first wife. He was on dangerous ground and he knew he had to tread carefully if he was to see tomorrow.

"My Empress," he said, clearing his voice, "your request, I must say, is quite a difficult one. The mind is a tricky place and is known only by its owner. One fact can hinder our progress as I discovered."

She glared at him because she was in no mood for boring briefings. He irritated her and she wondered just how she had become mixed up with him in the first place. But she needed him and he was her best bet, so she swallowed her pride. Quickly switching her mood to a more tolerant one, she asked, "Tell me then, my worthy mhondoro, just what could impede your actions and how much progress have you made?"

"Well, for one," began Chireshe, "I needed to know if the Emperor has a worthy support base. I went around talking to people and I determined that the masses like him." The Empress smiled. "But," went on Chireshe, and the smile quickly faded from the Empress's face giving way to a quizzical look, "that cannot be entirely true because, you see, the people know that I am a mhondoro and I am sworn to serve the Emperor and Mwari at the same time. Sadly for us, it is clear from what many said that they are rigid observers of their religion."

Empress Chinake saw their dream falling away and breaking into many pieces, like a dry clay mould on the floor. Chireshe noticed her crestfallen face and knew he now had her at his mercy. Now he would become the valiant soldier come to her rescue. His next words were the liberating hand she had been waiting for.

"However, do not despair. What is victory without a challenge? The more bitter the challenge the sweeter the victory. This country, my lady, is not ruled by the 'yes' of the masses but by the very few that matter and those are the mhondoros and chiefs." Her face relaxed and she became more attentive. "At the council of chiefs and mhondoros I saw that my Lord, your husband and our Emperor, has the support of these worthy men and as long as they give us the nod, which I know they will, he is home and dry. Now I need to ask you for a few favours which I am most certain will ensure the smooth sailing of our plans for you see, my Empress, it is the mind and the heart that have to be won over in this case. Let no blood be spilt and indeed, your husband will get his wish."

Slowly she nodded, as she recalled that her husband had said exactly the same thing. She realised that it was getting rather dark and it would not be safe to have this dislikeable mhondoro around at night, but she was eager to know all so she gave him permission to go on, lest time and chance would not allow them another meeting.

Chireshe said, "You will need to come to the next Emperor's court. It will be held not long from now. You are allowed, I'm sure you know, to attend any that you want because you are the first wife." She nodded gracefully. "Then I ask you to bring, or rather should I say, to invite the other wives of the Emperor. We know that they are not allowed to attend at will, but this time we need them. Let it be a gesture of good will from you. Your husband will not refuse because, as we all know, he respects and loves you a great deal." Once more, she smiled and waited for him to go on. "Please, do make sure that your sons will be present, all three of them. I have noticed how much authority and power they wield both in and out of court."

She breathed in and out with pride. Chireshe had her twirling right around his finger. He was enjoying this. As much as he was telling her his true feelings and plans he was also commanding the turf. This was now his game and he was playing it the way he wanted.

"Then, my Empress, I shall ask for another favour. I know that one of your sons, Perayi, is in charge of the army. I will ask you to speak to him and ask him to allow the army to give a passive show of power in the Kingdom. No, they will not hurt or frighten the people, instead they shall just parade throughout the Kingdom in full regalia. By the time we attend the Emperor's court, we need to have already reminded our people that the Hungwe is Lord and ruler of them all and that he has absolute power. The previous presence of the army shall serve to remind them of the truth of that fact. Trust me on this, my lady, I am a strategist of a different nature, I manipulate the mind."

The Empress was impressed. While she was not fond of him, Chireshe was indeed a brilliant strategist. As he spoke, she had summed up the importance of each of his requests. She had thought that the briefing would be boring but no, it had been interesting and fulfilling. She was actually eager to hear more. She had begun to think that it was not possible to become divine, invincible and immortal. If Chireshe believed it was possible, then it was, for there was no other mhondoro in the Kingdom as intelligent as he was.

"All things that relate to your husband's needs shall be said on that day. Do you desire anything else, my Empress, to be added to what we shall say at the court?" asked Chireshe.

She eyed him, telling herself that this man whom she was not so fond of was somehow now in control of the whole scheme, but at the same time promising herself that she would regain her charge of the whole affair. If the plan succeeded, she did not want to be in the shadows of some strange looking mhondoro, but needed to be at the forefront.

She got up and gracefully started pacing before Chireshe. He could not help thinking just how dramatic she was. Then hugging herself, she threw her head in Chireshe's direction and said, "He would want for me an enclosure of such strength and grandeur that it will last for hundreds of years. A home that will edify my beauty and worth. Its walls will be strong to show his might and high to prove his passion for me. Yes, I will have all the privacy I desire and no other wall shall be as mighty as mine."

She spoke so passionately that Chireshe was impressed. He was a man who did not understand love. He wanted women, needed them but knew he did not have that feeling called love. And here stood a woman who, despite her cold heart, had warmth for her husband. And for him to build such a home for her, he must truly love her. He gulped as a wave of jealousy swept through him and breathing in, he said, "So let it be, my Empress. If you desire to have such a complex built then allow me to say that you shall find the best builder, who should be unquestionably on your side."

"My son tells me that the new enclosure for my husband's other wives is very beautiful. He said an elderly master builder is constructing it. I am sure he can be of great use to my newly planned home. Do check him out and see that he is totally behind us," said the Empress.

"That should not prove to be too difficult," said Chireshe, in response to the request. "I am a good judge of character and I am sure he can be of great use to your desired enclosure. Your family wields too much power for him to decline. It is his younger brother, however, who may prove to be a problem. His name is Kwatara, a mhondoro, and a tough one for that matter."

The Empress seemed to recall the name then said, "This is too important to allow one scrawny, useless, so-called mhondoro to derail our plans. Deal with him accordingly, if need be. And he is but one man; what can he do against the undisputable might of the Emperor?"

Chireshe simply kept quiet. If only she knew whom she was talking about. One man was about to change the history of the Empire and that was her husband, one man was about to help him in his plans and so one man could certainly derail the Emperor's entire scheme, but he would let her remain happy in her ignorance of this. Rather let her sleep well. He did not reply, instead he politely said, "Right now we tread carefully, my Empress. Remember this is a new deity we are trying to introduce, which we shall introduce. We rule thousands of people and many of them, as well as those from our vassal states, are devotees of the present religious structure. We need to show both patience and force but," he said tapping his head, "we also need to use intellectual force. We shall reduce Kwatara at the Emperor's court, be sure of that and any who may desire to support him. That is where we shall rip him apart." He ended with a satisfactory tone.

The Empress nodded. She was happy at last, because now she saw the entire picture of prosperity in front of her. Very soon, her husband would be declared divine and gain immortality.

# Chapter sixteen

The following day saw further building of the enclosure that was to house Hungwe's other wives. It was near completion. Hombasha had woken up early and he was already busy giving orders to his supervisors and shouting at his builders. It was still chilly, but the old man was under great pressure to finish the enclosure. He did not want another ugly visit from the Prince, especially one that would catch him nowhere close to completing his task.

Kwatara had woken up early as well. He had failed to sleep well and so he had thought it better to visit his brother instead and see how he was doing. For the past few days he had been very worried. He could not help believing that the events at the last council of chiefs and mhondoros at the Emperor's court had a great bearing on his dream and refused to take the events for granted. As he walked to the building site to see his brother, his mind gradually went over recent events. He still did not think the boisterous behaviour of the Emperor's sons was in line. He believed that they were being given too much latitude and were steadily taking all state matters into their own hands. It was as though the Emperor no longer needed the voices of his mhondoros and chiefs, let alone his own voice. Besides the boys were still too young to carry the burdens of such a large state on their backs. They had called or rather commanded the shots and their father, the Emperor, had just silently looked on, secretly admiring their rude behaviour.

Then there had been the way the entire council had behaved, supporting everything said concerning the Emperor and everything said by his sons. Back in days gone by, he remembered that there would, at least, have been an argument, but it was as though, this time, they had come to cheer on anything that was said in support of the Emperor. He could not imagine grown men having minds that had been so dulled by their fear of the Princes and maybe also of the Emperor himself. He had seen Hungwe sitting there silently, like a gentleman, saying nothing. Or maybe was it like a snake, with small beady eyes which appeared not to see but could conceive everything. It was like he was watching a game being played, each side beating the other to death but he, the spectator, emerging the winner at the end. He shook his head to clear it and decided to concentrate on his journey. State matters would resolve themselves.

Very soon he came to the building site in the valley. Hombasha was busy giving fresh orders for granite rock and he hardly noticed his young brother standing behind him.

"I do not know why you strain yourself so much, brother, especially on such a cold morning. Men your age should be sleeping and waiting for their wives to bring them hot food to warm them up and heal their sore shoulders," said a voice behind Hombasha.

He turned sharply, cutting short his loud order to one of his builders and smiled when he saw his young brother, Kwatara, standing coolly behind him.

"You surprised me Kwatara, I wasn't expecting you," said Hombasha, still smiling.

"I couldn't wait till afternoon. I had to see how my sick, older brother was doing."

"It is good of you to think of me." Hombasha looked at his young brother closely and said in a concerned voice, "You don't look too good. Your face looks weary. Did you get enough sleep or were you on a dreaming spree?" He smiled a naughty smile with his last words.

Kwatara looked at him and he answered, "We had a hectic meeting at the Emperor's court. Too much was said which burdened me. But I will not bore you with my thoughts. I'm sure the matters discussed will be clarified in the coming days. How is your shoulder by the way?"

Hombasha understood his brother, state matters meant a lot to him. He lived to protect the nation.

"Oh I am fine now, of course there is a little pang now and then but I am fine," he said, flexing his shoulders.

"I see you are proving this by rising up so early in the morning and with your shouting, regardless of the chill. But I do hope your shoulder feels as good as your throat. It did not please me last time I saw it," said Kwatara, looking directly into his brother's eyes.

"Typical of all mhondoros, they think they know best, even how another man's body feels," said Hombasha. "But I must say it feels very good to have your young brother look out for you and to leave the warmth of his house so early in the morning to do so. Tell me, how did your wife take it?" asked Hombasha, with another naughty grin on his face.

"You know she never minds if it is you, and she, too, is concerned," replied Kwatara, as he advanced towards his brother. "Now, enough of the silly talk. I know how you are whenever you are trying to hide something from me," he said, placing his hand on his brother's shoulder, "Now let me see how the shoulder is today; it was badly swollen last time."

Hombasha tried to jerk his shoulder away but Kwatara was too fast for him. He quickly and expertly got hold of his older brother's arm before Hombasha could stop him, removed the cloth that covered his shoulders and was instantly taken aback. The swelling had doubled and the marks left by the Prince's nails, as they had dug into his shoulder, were an ugly green. It was clear that the older man was in still in pain. Hombasha stood like a criminal caught in the act, too powerless to fight off Kwatara, who had seen what he was not supposed to have seen.

"Why—why are you here this morning?" asked Kwatara, shocked and dismayed. "You should be at home, nursing your shoulder!"

"Maybe I am not one to concern myself with pain, Kwatara. Maybe I thought it better to be here working, rather than being at home paying attention to every pang that comes and goes. I did rest yesterday and that was enough," said Hombasha, as bravely as he could.

But Kwatara noticed something. This was not his brave brother speaking. He was clearly avoiding the mhondoro by looking sideways. Something was not right.

"Tell me why you really came to work. Is your wife giving you such a headache that you have to brave the cold wind with such a painful shoulder, or is it for the love of work?" asked Kwatara angrily.

Hombasha now turned to look at him and said in a stubborn voice, "Maybe I do love my work so much that I cannot keep away from it. Kwatara, why can't you just let me work a little while this morning and get this over with, please. I promise I will get some rest as soon as I am through," he ended, in a pleading voice.

"And by then you will be worse, my brother," said Kwatara, in a stern voice. "Look at you, you are not as strong as you used to be and not as young. You need some time off." He rubbed his temples wearily while Hombasha just stared blankly at him, as though he could not grasp a single thing his young brother was saying. "Goodness me, brother, you do not have to do this. What morbid fear of the Emperor's sons do you have that could lead you to work your aging heart away like this?"

Hombasha stared back at his brother and sighed resignedly. Shaking his head, he took Kwatara by the arm and led him to a small tree nearby. There, under the shade, despite the cold, they stood and stared at each other for a while longer. Kwatara made no effort to talk, he simply stared at his elder brother with a look of concern on his face. It was Hombasha who broke the silence by saying,

"When I woke up I thought I wouldn't come to work today, but the nasty incident with the Prince got me out of my covers fast and I decided to ignore my pain." Kwatara opened his mouth to speak but Hombasha raised his hand to hush him and looking into his eyes, he said, "Kwatara, being concerned about my health could mean the death of an entire clan. Do you think that if I stop working they will understand that I am sick? No, we are dealing with stubborn rulers who believe the greater the walls the greater their fame, and no sick old man is going to stop them from getting their glory. You heard them at the Emperor's court yesterday." Once more Kwatara tried to say something but Hombasha cut him short, "And please don't tell me that they should find another master builder, because they will not. They know I am good at what I do, and they know I can produce the best and they will use me until I drop down dead." He looked back at the wall they were building and said, "Tell me, little brother, for years the rulers of the Great Zimbabwe have been building these stone walls, but which ones look as neat and as strong as the ones I have built?"

Kwatara turned to look around and suddenly saw the truth of what his brother was saying. Certainly he was aware of his brother's skill, but he had taken it for granted. He now realised for the first time the great ingenuity that was being applied here. His brother's walls were straighter, more symmetrical and actually more majestic. Hombasha did have a gift and a gift for which the rulers of this Empire would certainly destroy his whole clan.

"You know that for years their glory has lain in building these enclosures. But now I sense that a ruler who is determined to build mightier walls is ruling us. I could have slept, but I knew what would happen if I did not finish at the appointed time. They use threats and they deliver the threats," said Hombasha, ending with a meek, dejected voice.

Kwatara's face turned serious. He grabbed his brother by the arm, making him wince in pain. "Tell me, my brother, have they threatened you, after all you and our family have done for them? Tell me, have they threatened you?" he ended by stressing his last words in his brother's face.

Hombasha just looked at him, too weak to answer, his silence telling it all. Kwatara looked shocked. He saw the answer written in bold letters on his brother's face, too clear to ignore. All along, he had thought his brother was addicted to his work; now he realised it was something more than that. It had been a push, a push too strong to ignore, a push from which he was protecting his entire family. He searched his aching mind for a solution to all this madness. Yes, he could tell his brother to face up to the Emperor and tell him that he needed a little peace, some rest, for a man his age could not continue to take such stress. The Emperor had his weaknesses, and although his sons and first wife were clearly evil, perhaps he would help. Kwatara hoped the great man was in no way involved in any of this.

Quickly he said, in a desperate voice, "You should have told the Emperor, my brother, he would have done something. He is a gentleman, you know, and yes, his wife and his sons are evil, but he could have protected you. I am sure he is one man who appreciates the services our family has rendered, for years, to the Kingdom."

But Hombasha remained passive, hands clasped below his belly. Kwatara stared back, confused at first as to his brother's silence then reading the look on his face, he covered his mouth with his hand. "Oh no, oh no my brother, tell me it is not real, no."

Hombasha looked back, crestfallen and with a weak smile nodded his head. Suddenly, the image of the Emperor at the court came back to Kwatara. Was what he saw on his face, as he looked at him, the expression of a conniving schemer? Did that face, which confused

Kwatara so much, hold behind it deep evils? He felt nauseous at the thoughts that were racing through his mind.

Hombasha, seeing the pathetic look on his brother's face, said in a low voice, "Do you think these mighty walls are built by soft hearted Emperors and pig-headed youths who stink of pride? No," he said, looking at the builders working on the enclosure. Kwatara turned to look as well with a sour look on his face. The builders started to hum a tune, which then turned into a song. He had always pitied the workers, but today the sight of them made him sick to the stomach. He now understood why they sang as they toiled, it was the only time they could open their mouths wide and express themselves. It was the only consolation they ever got, the only time their voices could be heard, through the songs of the Karanga tribe. Tears welled up in his eyes.

"Such majesty," said Hombasha, gesturing towards the walls, "has been created and built by kings with hearts of stone, not even as workable as the granite from which the bricks are made but harder than that. The desire of greatness is in their blood and they simply inherit their fathers' tyranny and iron will."

Looking back at Kwatara who was by now speechless, he said, "I am sorry I never told you this, but your blind servitude to the Kingdom and the Emperor was important. If you had known way back then your heart would have turned cold, it would have sold you out and you would have been wasted."

Kwatara looked at his brother, still speechless and Hombasha said, "Yes, the Emperor was the one who gave the threat. Of course, it came through his son's mouth that if the wall was not finished at the appointed time the whole clan would be wasted, but my junior master builder's brother is a sentry at the Emperor's royal chambers, he told me the decree was given by the Emperor himself. These are cold months and it so difficult to work the granite in this weather, but we have to do it. I never told anyone because I knew it was my war, my duty to protect my clan. They said if I never finished on time, or if I faltered, they would destroy us all. I am sorry, Kwatara, I am sorry. I should have been stronger but I—I . . ."

He broke down and tears ran down his cheeks. Kwatara suddenly realised the pressure his brother had been under all this time and wished he had known. A lump formed in his throat and hot tears welled up in his black eyes once more. The bond between the two was unmistakable.

They were the only two boys their father had had. Their mother had given birth to three children only, two boys and a girl, the boys being Hombasha and Kwatara. Because their mother had had problems conceiving a second child, their sister, Hombasha was some years older than Kwatara, but despite the age difference, the brothers had grown up very close. Kwatara had always helped Hombasha each time he was in difficulty, but now he felt useless. His brother had borne so much, alone without him, knowing simply that he had to save their small clan.

"You don't need to cry, brother, do not be ashamed. You did well. You worked to save us all. And all along I thought that the Emperor was a gentleman. I can't believe this. If one has a gift, why manipulate it? Why not talk like men and work out a plan and why the threats?" mourned Kwatara.

Hombasha said lovingly, "You are still young, little brother. Empires are not built by gentlemen, but by conquerors, pillagers and vanquishers with little regard for anything or anyone else. They will stop at nothing to achieve greatness. And mark my words, even those closest to them are cunningly manipulated because that is what they are, men who can only use others to their advantage, never able to love or show respect, but great believers in the unabated advancement of their own powers."

He stopped there and stared hard at Kwatara, pitying him for his shock. Hombasha could not bear the pain he saw on his young brother's face. He looked away and it was then that he noticed someone; and in an effort to avert attention from the present conversation, he said, "Ah there is a dear old friend, a pillager in his own right, the man of many words with a strange weakness for beautiful women, Chireshe."

Kwatara was momentarily diverted from his brother's horrors and he turned to look. He saw the man from afar, shaking hands with people and breaking into merry laughter. The sight of this mhondoro sickened him. He greatly disliked him. He knew Chireshe to be a man who feared no man, a man who had no scruples and who did not revere Mwari. He had a bad way with women married or not and that did not please Kwatara. His features changed from shock to disgust. It was then that he suddenly remembered seeing him on that strange night.

"Oh I saw him," he said dreamily, "I saw him and it was quite strange."

Hombasha looked at his young brother quizzically and folding his hands, he said, "You saw him and it was quite strange. Tell me, why was it strange? Your strange encounters are always so intriguing, little brother."

Forgetting their current problem Kwatara looked at his brother and, concentrating hard, he began to relate the dream.

"Just after recalling the entire dream," said Kwatara, ending his story, "was when I bumped into the girl and guess who came along, mumbling excitedly like a crazy mad man and rushing after the guards and the girls, none other than Chireshe himself. And like I said, they were coming from the direction of the Empress's quarters."

Hombasha nodded his head slowly and rubbed his chin thoughtfully.

"Mmm," he said at last, "that really was a strange dream and an uncanny coincidence. Have you been able to make out at least something about the dream or is it one of those that can only be understood as events slowly unravel?"

"I will tell you the truth, for years I have had dreams and I developed a way of knowing their meaning or what they relate to, but this one has baffled me, it has disturbed me entirely. It was like a story being told, more vivid than anything I have ever dreamt of in my life. It scared me, brother," said Kwatara, with a face that registered genuine fear. "It feels as though the dream walks with me, clings to me and will not leave me."

Moving closer to him Hombasha said in a calming voice, "I have never seen you look this frightened. The dream is strange and I see nothing of hope in it. But do not fear. At least you do not die in the dream; that's a consolation." He ended with a fake, encouraging smile.

Kwatara, with a half-hearted smile, said, "No, I do not see myself dying but, as you said, maybe it is one of those dreams that can only be understood as certain events unravel themselves. So we should wait."

Someone shouted a greeting. Both men turned to look in the direction the voice was coming from and saw Chireshe heading their way. He too looked in their direction and as happily as he could, he waved. He had a mission here, for he had made a promise to the Empress and he intended to keep it. They both smiled weakly and half-heartedly waved back.

"It is too late to move away. He will notice us avoiding him. Let us just stand and entertain him for a while. Later on, I will give an excuse to leave and you will follow," said Hombasha, turning to look at Kwatara.

"As though it matters, waiting and talking to him. He displeases me to the bone, notwithstanding the things that people say about the way he talks to ghosts at his house." said Kwatara, with a passion.

"I know it is not necessary to wait for him and I, too, have heard a thing or two about his conversations with ghosts, but do me a favour. I do find the way he handles his funny mouth quite amusing and his endless speeches can be such fun to listen to. It is amazing how he can sway the opinions of respectable and unguarded men and make them believe his lies," said Hombasha, turning to look at Chireshe who had stopped to greet someone else.

Kwatara looked at his brother and was amazed to hear him speak like that. He had never known Hombasha to have such an analytical mind. Yes, he knew Hombasha was intelligent, but not to this extent. Sighing in resignation, he said, "As you wish, brother; if it will put a smile on your face and make you forget your misery then let us entertain the mad man."

Hombasha smiled and for the first time that morning a twinkle came to his eyes as he saw Chireshe advancing towards them with a bright smile on his face. The mhondoro had decided to test Hombasha today, but he had not anticipated that he would see Kwatara. So far, he had succeeded with many chiefs and mhondoros, now it was time for the real test. Kwatara was never an easy man.

# Chapter seventeen

On the same day in the Mbire Kingdom, King Mutota sat in the very same position he had been sitting in the first time he came to make changes to the army with Tekeshe and his son Matope. He looked at the soldiers who sat in neat rows, spears at their sides. A lot of work had been done by Tekeshe, the army general, and himself, in order to choose two hundred men to be especially trained to lead the way to the new land the Mbire people were going to escape to.

None of the soldiers knew the reason why they had been chosen and separated from the rest; the fact of the matter was that they were going to be trained to protect the crown with their lives. Tekeshe had made sure that at least someone from each clan was chosen and from the bigger clans a higher number was chosen. This would prevent rivalry among the clans and he and the King hoped that it would build a stronger army, bent on protecting its nation.

On the other hand, he had cleverly involved his wife in the plot to break away as Tekeshe had suggested. He desperately needed the support of her people. Her tribe was the largest and her brothers and uncles the most popular among all the chiefs.

He had also remembered his elder sister Rungano, who was very influential and would definitely gain the support of other women for the King. She was the most talkative woman Mutota knew. Her height and their father's looks gave her an imposing appearance and not many dared to confront her or stand up to her in a confrontation. She had a way with words and information. Her wagging tongue was as sharp as her two ears. She could hear things and she could keep the King informed. Women heard of things from their husbands; they talked and surprisingly enough their tongues always loosened in the presence of the King's sister. Therefore, it would be up to Rungano his sister to wag her tongue expertly and motivate the women at the wells and at gatherings when the right time came.

The three men had decided that if questions pertaining to the training of a new, tough army were asked, the simple answer would be the restructuring of the army was for the payment of tribute and as soon as the training was done, the newly trained Mbire army would be sent as reinforcements to the Great Zimbabwe ruler, Hungwe.

Looking at his men from where he sat, Mutota saw new faces alive with curiosity and determination. They sat on the cold grass, in neat rows, with cloth covering their backs. A cold wind blew but tension was so high that none felt it. There was a new charge in the air. These men were eager to know what was to take place and they knew that they had been chosen, separate from the rest, for an important reason. They would get the best training, but for a long time the true reason for their selection would remain obscure.

Tekeshe now stood in the centre, a tall formidable figure, the wind flapping about the cloth he wore around himself. He stood erect and fearless and there in front of the men, there before the King of the Mbire and his son Matope, stood a true definition of a strong, Mbire warrior. He may have been in his forties now, but age seemed to have intensified the air of authority that surrounded him. His mere presence forced all the soldiers to pay attention and his renewed passion seemed to have radiated out to his juniors. Here, indeed, stood a man out to make warriors of the Mbire soldiers.

He lifted his spear high in the air and in a booming voice he said, "Men of the Mbire Kingdom, worthy soldiers, I stand here before our King, proud and boastful of an army that has always been courageous, powerful, resilient and respectful to the throne of the Mbire. Our King and all the royal families hold us in great esteem and we honour our King by our unfailing, unflinching service to his throne and to the Mbire Kingdom. Hail Mbire!"

"Hail!"

"Hail the person!"

"Hail!"

"Hail the first!"

"Hail!"

"Hail the son of the soil!"

"HAIL!" came a loud, united shout. King Mutota smiled. This was a new voice in his army; there was a new strength and indeed this was a new beginning. The King watched and felt the true Mbire fighter spirit flare up. He looked at his son and his son Matope looked back at him and smiled. Even he felt the vibration of a newborn army, a sleeping giant awoken and a defiant Mbire militia come to life. Both men saw the vision of a dream, dreamt just days ago, slowly become a historical reality.

Nyatsimba Mutota stood up from his seat and the soldiers with their heads bowed low began to clap with cupped hands. Casually, with newfound pride and dignity, he stepped down with his spear in his hand and walked to stand beside Tekeshe, his army general. The clapping stopped, and holding his spear more tightly, he swiftly and expertly lifted it up into the air and shouted,

"Hail the Mbire army!"

"Hail!"

"Hail to the army of the first born, the son of the soil, the son of the people! Hail to the protectors of the Mbire Kingdom!"

"Hail! Hail!" shouted the troops in unison, their spears also lifted up.

Slowly he walked past Tekeshe, who remained standing to attention before the King. Then, standing a distance away from the army general, he surveyed his army. In their simple attire they looked nothing like the Great Zimbabwe army and also lacked their ferocious demeanour. But the resolve on their faces gave the King a new boost of faith and confidence in himself and in his plans.

In a clear, bold voice he said, "I stand here today, tall and proud. In the space of a few days I have forgotten my age and I have forgotten my past. I stand a new man, a new King with new blood roaring in my veins." Indeed, he had spoken the truth, even his voice sounded bolder and younger. It roared above the rising, cold wind; the screeching of birds could not drown it out. None of the soldiers moved and such was their tension that they hardly felt the cold wind blowing.

Looking around slowly, he noticed that he now had the attention of the men and in a firmer voice he said, "We have met here, on these plains, many times over the past years. These have been our training grounds and I am sure the spirits of many late soldiers still roam around here. But what they are witnessing today is something different. It is something that never happened in their lifetime and I am sure that just like your King, they feel a great sense of pride swelling up their hearts." He stopped, took a deep breath, made sure that they were listening more attentively than before and beginning to walk down the rows of men, he said, "What I see here is new life, a new beginning. It is the birth of an army that will leave an unforgettable history behind. Look at you, your pride has returned, your blood now moves again in your bodies. You breathe air of the living once more. Your eyes are now wide awake and your faces show understanding."

He walked to the very back of the rows of men, expecting them to turn around with curiosity as they surely would have done in the past, but a newfound discipline ensured that none of them moved their heads. Shouting at the top of his voice, he said, "You wonder why you were chosen, I am sure. That is no secret. In you, we saw the deep desire to fight for a nation; we saw the faces of men who can take a beating and still serve the Kingdom with all their hearts. We saw men who are willing never to let go of their spears, but fight around the clock for their King's throne. We saw men willing to give up their freedom in pursuit of justice and willing to protect the people with their own lives."

He started to walk again and this time he went and stood in the centre of the rows of soldiers. He noticed that the worry that had previously been written all over their faces was now gone. It was a good sign. They were no longer foreigners to whatever was going on. His words had awakened their spirits and their faces now showed solidarity with their King.

A happier man, he now said, "We do not see a bunch of fools who will be led by the leash, but rather free men from respectable families who will fight for the honour of their Kingdom and for the survival of their families. We are here to create an army that will serve like none other, in honour and in respect and with the pride of true warriors. Hail the Mbire army!" said Mutota, lifting his spear high in the air.

"Hail!" responded the soldiers, their spears also lifted high in the air from where they sat.

Matope, still standing next to his father's seat, was surprised at the older man's new resolve and at the way the army had suddenly been transformed by a few words from their King's mouth. He was shocked to see how fast his father's dream was coming to life and how greatly the army had been transformed. These men had been chosen just a few days ago, but they now looked different and this made him feel proud of his father. He hoped that one day he, too, would lead a big army to amazing heights and his pride soared higher when he heard the following words his father addressed to the army:

"We will cease to be mere soldiers and become warriors. In the past we lacked obligation, but now we shall possess a new sense of duty, our commotion shall be converted to discipline, our infidelity shall become loyalty and no longer shall we be ruled by the passions of our bodies and hearts, but we are to be defined by the precincts set by the throne."

Now Tekeshe turned around from his position to look at the King. He had a slight smile of admiration on his face and he nodded his head slowly as the King said, in a bold challenging voice, "Once our sentiments were unguarded, but now we shall become immune to our emotions and nothing but servitude shall govern our actions and selves. You shall serve the throne to the last bit of will and strength in you. Do you have a past? That ceases to exist right now. You are going to be moulded into a new person and if you lived by the beer pot, it is time to break it into many pieces, because henceforth your thirst shall be quenched by an insatiable need for heroism. You shall live and breathe the throne's commands and never in your life, till the day you die, shall your spear leave your side. Today I marry you all to your spears! Hail the Mbire army!

"Hail!"

"Hail the birth of a new era!"

"Hail, hail, hail!"

After the King was done with boosting the soldiers' moral, Tekeshe Chingowo came and took over. The physical training began.

# Chapter eighteen

Chireshe had seen the two brothers from afar. He had woken up early hoping to find Hombasha, the master builder, alone so he could make his first attempt to sway him to his side. But now Kwatara was around. Though he had plans to speak to the mhondoro later on, this was quite unexpected. Chireshe may have been one who had a way with words and who many in the Kingdom knew and feared, but Kwatara was not included in the category of his many admirers and this unnerved him. Besides, the creepers had warned him that Kwatara had had a dream and though they had not been very clear, he trusted them. If only he knew what the other mhondoro knew.

He had the choice to turn around and go back home, but it would raise eyebrows. And looking on the brighter side, talking to both brothers would, if he was successful, give him a chance to catch Kwatara unguarded and maybe see where he stood. At the same time, the Empress was expecting results. Therefore he made a bold move, despite the presence of Kwatara, to go and talk to Hombasha and as he walked towards the two brothers, he decided on the method he would use to get the answers he needed.

As Chireshe approached, Kwatara folded his arms. Hombasha turned to look at him and noticed that already his little brother was on the defensive. His forehead was creased and his thick eyebrows were knitted together.

"Look at him, wouldn't you think he is a snake hissing to people and lying with a forked tongue," said Kwatara, venomously.

"Give it up, Kwatara. You shouldn't show your dislike for the man so openly. You know some people actually think you are jealous of him."

Kwatara turned his head sharply to look at his brother and said, "I do not like the man one bit. You know how he behaves at the Emperor's court. He has no respect for Mwari. And I do not care at all what the world thinks about the cause of my feelings; one day you shall all see that I was right."

"How can you say that, he is a mhondoro and all mhondoros are sworn to serve Mwari," said Hombasha, deliberately provoking Kwatara.

"Yes, all are sworn but not all are devoted," responded Kwatara, hotly. "And he is not the only one at that. Not that I am a saint, but I can see that our desires as mhondoros go beyond protecting our faith, calling, country and religion. We are after people's love, people's awe and we are taking advantage of the less privileged. Chireshe is the worst of us all and his love for women has an unnatural dark side to it. Beware of him, for the love of the female body he will do anything, even kill."

Hombasha blinked. He knew Kwatara was not fond of Chireshe, but though his summation was blunt and cruel, he had not lied at all. Still the other mhondoro fascinated him, he wanted to get rid of his rotten mood and Chireshe's funny ways would do the trick. Right now he knew he wouldn't win this particular battle with his young brother, so instead he sighed and turned to look at Chireshe who was smiling and standing just in front of them. He sincerely hoped that Kwatara was not going to spoil the comedy he was looking forward to receive from Chireshe.

The other mhondoro extended his hand to Hombasha first. "My dear master builder, always an honour to meet you, always. My, my, it is a blessing to meet with such an ingenious mind."

He took Hombasha's hand in both his and shook it so vigorously it could have taken away the chill of the whole month of June. Hombasha smiled back genuinely and warmly. He could not help it, Chireshe's mannerisms made fascinated him.

"And it is a pleasure to see my intelligent mhondoro. I am always honoured by your presence, my dear friend. It has been a long time since we met," said Hombasha.

"Yes, yes, indeed it has been. You see, I have been so busy with state business and things have been so hectic," said Chireshe with an air of importance that made Hombasha smile. He was already beginning to enjoy the show. It was so easy to make Chireshe move in one's direction. Almost at once he was performing as expected by the master builder. "And," he said, turning to Kwatara who simply stared at him with a blank look, "It is a pleasure to see you, my dear friend, you never know how lovely it is to meet a brother-in-arms. I did not get a chance to see you after the council meeting at the Emperor's court. Such serious business it was there, I must say, indeed I must. The Emperor's sons did make some very important statements about the great man who rules us."

He took Kwatara's hand in his and shook it firmly. Kwatara returned the handshake without much enthusiasm and slightly nodded his head in response. Chireshe, noticing the lack of friendliness in the handshake, quickly retrieved his hand.

In a new wave of gusto, he turned his attention to the wall that was being built by Hombasha. In his funny way of moving, he walked towards it and ran his hand along the granite bricks that balanced so well and tightly, one on top of the other. Kwatara stared at him distastefully and thought to himself that the mhondoro rather slithered than walked. Was it simply his imagination, his loathing of him or the bare truth that Chireshe had something snake-like about him? He shook his head as he tried to clear it from his thoughts and noticing his open distaste, Hombasha gave him a warning glance and said under his breath, "You had better not spoil this for me, little brother, or else I will hate you for the rest of the day. It's rare to get such learned comedians to entertain you and make your blood rush with laughter on such cold mornings. Bear with me, will you, for the sake of my foul mood?"

Kwatara found these words so amusing that he nearly laughed, but got a hold of himself just in time as Chireshe, with an excited look, turned and said loudly, "My, my. This is beautiful workmanship my dear master builder. Look at the craftsmanship of these walls and they are so even. All my life I have seen the enclosures being built, one after the other and I have seen others that existed before these, but none so even, so smooth."

Hombasha smiled. Already the mhondoro was beginning to spill out his crafty words to please the master builder. Kwatara looked on curiously. Why today of all days had Chireshe bothered to come to the building site and talk to Hombasha? Hombasha moved closer to Chireshe as though to encourage him to talk further. Kwatara moved a little closer too but still kept his distance.

"Tell me, master builder, just how are you able to keep the walls continuously even and beautiful?" asked Chireshe, with a genuine questioning look on his face that made him look even more comical.

Hombasha, moving right up beside the mhondoro, said, "Well, we have managed to rectify the problem of unevenness. You see, each layer is made so that it is slightly more recessed than the last and this produces a more stabilized inward slope. This has managed to produce the order and evenness you are now witnessing."

Chireshe did not understand a single word but deciding not to show his ignorance he asked, "This enclosure is for the Emperor's wives, right?"

"Indeed, my esteemed mhondoro," said Hombasha. "He ordered this enclosure to be made especially for his other wives."

"And you are a man who follows orders to the last dot, Hombasha. The Emperor Hungwe is a man of great taste. I heard he specifically asked for the enclosure to be beautiful. It is already held in high esteem throughout the Kingdom. I had to come and see for myself," said Chireshe, turning to look at Hombasha, as he broke into a grin meant to be a pleasant smile.

Hombasha looked at him curiously, a slight smile on his lips. Sensing something brewing, Kwatara advanced and stood in between the two men. He looked sternly at Chireshe and the older mhondoro went on instant guard. He had already told himself never to underestimate this young mhondoro.

Kwatara folded his hands on his chest and said, "You have taken a sudden interest in the walls of the enclosures, Chireshe. I am glad you find my brother's work a great delight but since you hardly know anything about building walls, I am sure that no matter how much Hombasha explains to you the intricacies involved, you will never understand. You need to be sharper in the world of art than in the nature of herbs my brother-in-arms." As he said his last words, he smiled a cynical smile meant to offend Chireshe.

Chireshe noticed this but he snubbed it off with a wide grin and a comment. "It is never too late to learn my dear fellow. I would not want to die without the knowledge of how such mighty walls are built. It would be a shame, would it not, my dear friend?"

Kwatara just stared at him and an uncomfortable silence ensued. It was Hombasha who broke the silence by saying, "It is good to find those who wish to know about these walls and how they are made. They are an undying legacy for our children and countless generations after them. It is a shame I do not have enough time to parley, otherwise I would have taught you a lot. If you would like to come one day when you are not too busy, I will certainly tell you more. It can get rather boring here with only these workers and their lack of wit as company."

Kwatara looked at his brother incredulously. Chireshe saw the shock on Kwatara's face and the earnest look on Hombasha's face and he was pleased. Now was his chance to finish his research.

"Oh yes, I would love to come, my dear man. What a pleasure it will be to spend time with a brilliant mind like yours. And the walls are truly astounding. They are a beauty to reckon, my man," said Chireshe earnestly and he went on blabbering, "I am sure that nowhere else can you find such mighty walls. Perfectly fit for kings such as ours and for greater beings as well." Smiling, with his large eyes widening, he said in a low, inviting and excited voice, "Imagine being asked to build such structures for those who are divine. Your hands will, Hombasha, my dearest master builder, forever be stamped with the mark of royalty. Ah yes, indeed, indeed, an honour it would be, my friend."

Hombasha looked at him slightly confused, not able to understand the divine beings Chireshe was talking about, then turned to look at Kwatara who shrugged his shoulders. Hombasha replied, "Of course, I am sure the spirits of our ancestors find it a pleasure to roam in these enclosures that we humbly build, and what a great honour it is for us that they do so."

"Yes, yes, I'm sure," said Chireshe, breaking into one of his unusual smiles meant to impress. Kwatara looked on and said nothing, but once more folded his arms on his chest. Hombasha became certain that the original show he was looking forward to had not gone as expected. Chireshe looked from one brother to the other and said with an air of finality, "I guess I had better go, brothers. I have enjoyed the conversation and indeed, indeed I have learnt a lot today. I must say again I have learnt a lot today." They both remained staring at him and he said, moving away, "Until next time, brothers, until next time, yes indeed, yes indeed, until next time." Suddenly he looked up at the wall and uttered, surprised, "By the way, I have noticed you have placed this lovely design on your wall, who designed it?"

Looking up, Hombasha replied, "Oh, that was ordered by the Emperor. It was described to us by his chief advisor and we followed instructions. The chief agreed that we had done the correct thing. As you know, the Emperor never comes down here so we rely on word from his chiefs and sons."

Chireshe nodded, admiring the pattern and Kwatara looked on. He broke into another smile and waving his hand, he walked away. Looking at him quizzically, they both waved back, uncertainly.

"Now what was that all about?" asked Hombasha, staring at Chireshe's disappearing form. "I thought he had come for one of his big, brainy showdowns but it was all so confusing. And what did he mean by his crazy talk on building enclosures for those who are divine?"

"Not confusing at all," said Kwatara, turning to look at his brother, "but rather mysterious. I do not think he wanted to see me, at all. His mission was with you. My presence threw his plans completely off track."

"It was funny the way he just tossed disconnected comments about," said Hombasha. "Very unlike him. He is usually so organised with catchy statements that intrigue me. So much for the usual brainy Chireshe show. I am really disappointed," he said, looking at Kwatara with a disappointed expression.

Kwatara found his brother's lack of amusement quite interesting. Shaking his head, he said, "What is truly funny is how you entertained him and even asked him over. And what makes you think he was throwing disconnected statements about? He knew exactly what he was doing. He is not one to waste time on uninformative talk. Believe me brother, I know him, he is as he says, my brother-in-arms. Chireshe is too intelligent to waste time on lame talk. You can never trust his delight in things, rather trust his disgust." He sighed deeply and looked at the ground thoughtfully.

Hombasha looked at his brother, grimaced and shook his head as though to clear a cloud. These mhondoros always confused him. They spoke in riddles, lived an obscure life and understood each other's mystifying ways.

"He will not come, he is too busy to waste time on a lecture on how to build enclosures," said Hombasha, calmly. "I simply meant to entertain him."

"And what in the world for? I personally hate the manner in which he forces his senseless philosophies on people. I hope he doesn't impress you with his fancy words," came Kwatara's hot response.

His years with the mhondoro had taught him never to trust Chireshe. Chireshe was simply, to him, a very bad dream waiting to become reality.

"Let me get on with my work," said Hombasha, eager to break the tension that was building up between him and Kwatara. "I am glad, though, that he found our zigzag design to be beautiful. Many are commenting on it. Come and see," he said, moving away from Kwatara and beckoning to him, "You saw it before it was complete, I'm sure."

Kwatara moved closer to the wall and looked up. The workers had begun another song, their work tools hitting the rocks. Behind them, many other workers went about their chores and a drummer was beating on a drum to boost their moral and singing. Hombasha was saying something, describing how they were designing the zigzag pattern with smaller granite bricks, but as he droned on he soon realised something was wrong and his excited voice and face went limp when he looked back at his young brother standing just behind him.

Kwatara was not even listening. He could neither hear the tools of the workers nor their song. He did not even notice them as they moved close behind him. He was oblivious, even, to his brother's excited voice, because he had seen something that he recognized from his strange dream. The exact zigzag pattern on the clay pot that had fallen from the girl's head in his dreams and crashed was the one on the walls his brother was building. This morning he had witnessed the second piece of the puzzle in his dream and he was greatly disturbed. The workers sang on, the wind whistled past and Hombasha rushed to him. He fainted.

Chireshe bustled away, oblivious to all that was going on at the building site, telling himself that he already had the support of many without their knowledge. What the two brothers did not know was that they had been part of a survey, a survey of a battle to come and from their conversation, Chireshe had already determined whether he would win or not. He decided that he would talk to more chiefs and mhondoros and sell his idea. By the time the real show came crashing down on them, they would be prepared to support the Emperor. Yes, both the Emperor and Chireshe would achieve their dreams. It was a game of one man gaining and one man losing. Chireshe would now deliver a message to the Empress.

# Chapter nineteen

Upon arriving home, he sent a message to the Empress, which simply said, "It is possible but there is still a thorn that has to be pricked". On hearing these words, the Empress made a date to see the Emperor. At least something was in motion and she did not fear to see her husband. The young, innocent looking sentry who was the Emperor's spy delivered her request, and the Emperor knew that something in line with his desire and plans had come up. Not wanting to appear too eager, the Emperor granted her request and told her to come two days later. He was once more amazed as to how smoothly his plan was working.

Elated at his ingenuity, he thanked his lucky stars that his plan had indeed triggered something. He anxiously awaited the visit from his first wife in two days' time. He guessed she would tell him she had found a way to make him divine but he would make her think it wasn't that important anymore and he knew she would beg for him to admit to her plans. He would stage it perfectly, from the time she walked in up to the time she spoke her heart and left. It all had to be perfect. Wasn't it wonderful to have people do your bidding without even telling them? Truly, the Emperor had every right to marvel at his strange gift.

When the Empress was granted audience with the Emperor she breathed a sigh of relief. It had been some time now since she last saw her husband. She had dared not go to him lest his agony would torment her heart again.

When she went to see him and walked into his chamber she found him staring again at the hill, which would one day be his new home. This time her heart did not sink, rather it rejoiced, because she knew that she would give him what he wanted and no longer would he live on the same soil with the common sons and daughters of men. He was Hungwe, Emperor of the Great Zimbabwe. He deserved more than this raw deal he was currently getting. Already she had fallen into his hands and was dancing to his tune.

She greeted him with a smile and with all the dignity she had. He returned her greeting with a warm and welcoming smile that encouraged her further to break the good news to him. He then invited her to sit beside his throne and she obliged. Gracefully, she sat down and he looked at her and smiled once more.

"My Lord, it has been long since I last saw you and my heart has ached over your last words. How do you fare, my King?" she enquired, with her large eyes showing genuine concern.

Hungwe looked at her and wondered. Did this woman, who had such a conniving heart, really have a spirit that could ache for him in this manner? It was amazing to discover the kind of people who could love you when they could hardly feel anything for the rest of the world. He breathed in and smiling slightly, he said, "You amaze me, woman. Did you really take seriously the words of a bored King and husband who has nothing better to do than to dream of homes on hilltops and the gift of divinity? I am impressed that you still had my crazy thoughts in your pretty head. But do not worry, I am fine now. I suppose if the world you live in cannot give you what you want, you have to be content with the best there is and I already have you, my sons and all this, what more could there be beyond what I already see?"

He was so clever. She did not see it. She played right into his hands. "But my Lord," she said, getting up and wringing her hands, "What makes you think that a man of such wealth, such valour and such fame, a husband so worthy and a father so caring should deserve less than a place among the ancestors in the skies? I took your words seriously because I believe in you. You are a man who does not parley with words; you are too great to allow lame thoughts to roam your mind. You deserve the greatness you dream of."

She spoke passionately and he was touched by her sincerity. He looked at her and nearly lost his guard from the pity he felt for her. But he checked himself in time and said in a low tone, "I was beginning to think that the Arab was crazy. Maybe he was, maybe he wasn't," he said, shrugging his massive shoulders. "And in any case, if he wasn't crazy what can be done about it? I rule a people who believe in another deity. Leave the people be, they have enough to honour and a worthier being than me on top of it all."

"Do not speak like that," she said, kneeling before him. "Why do you underrate your might and your prestige? It is sacrilege to speak like that. Never before have the people of this nation been ruled by a King of such worth and yet you speak so humbly about yourself." She continued to plead with him, "My Lord, did you not stop to think that there is every good reason why the Arab told his story and on that very night? Is it coincidence that you invited him to dinner on that night and he was impressed by your greatness? No, I do not think so. You say that this nation has another deity and enough to worship but I disagree; they can be made to see reason, to see the truth that before them stands a man, a supreme being who deserves their gift of praise."

She was so good, he thought to himself. He wondered if Chireshe knew that he had a worthy competitor. Now he saw for himself that he had an ally who would even lose her life to see that he got what he desired. He stood up and said, "Tell me then, do you think that the people can be forced to leave their religious order? I wonder what they will think of me if I make them do it? And what would they benefit from it that they have not already. I am just a mortal. They are not fools, they know whom to worship as they have known for years."

She nearly sprawled down before him but gracefully got up and said near to tears, "You have always been a gentleman; a man who rules with a heart. Who will force them? No one. But they will be made to see reason. And who says they will leave their Mwari, no one. But they will see that you deserve a place among those who live in the heavens. They will see that you deserve as much praise. And Hungwe, what have you not given these people? You own all that they have, even their lives are in your hands; you allow them to live and your armies protect their very breath and health. Then why shouldn't you be awarded the worship and praise of these people so that you can gain the immortality you wish for? You are not Emperor because you chose to be but because the ancestors and Mwari saw it fit that you sit on this throne. You therefore deserve to reside among the ancestors and Mwari as well."

He stared at her, disbelieving and amazed. His wonder at this point was genuine. She really meant what she was saying. And she did have facts too, dangerous ones for that matter. Facts that could see the conversion of an entire nation's religious beliefs. Maybe the Arab had spoken the truth. If many people shared this woman's passion and faith in him then could he not become divine? He was excited. He checked himself again.

"My wife, my wife Chinake, I see the faith you have in my dream. I am glad. I am sorry I doubted you." he looked deep in her eyes and said so sincerely. "Tell me then, my wife, what I should do. If not for me, then let it be for the faith you have."

She was touched. She looked into his eyes as well. She breathed in a sigh of relief and said, "I have thought of a few ways to make the masses believe us. Do not waste your breath in speaking but let us sit and I will tell you everything I have thought over. I hope you will not think of anything I shall say as too ambitious."

Sitting down beside his throne, she told him, "We have people, important people in our Kingdom at your side, my King. I have set about trying to see if people who matter can be won over to your desire and it is possible. Do please, bear with me, I have asked the favour of one who may not entirely please you but you do know yourself that he has a brilliant mind." She looked at him eagerly.

"And who may this one be?" asked the Emperor without looking at her.

"None other than Chireshe," she now spoke quickly, "I know he is not to be trusted with women but you know your wife, my husband, never can she ever be unfaithful to you for any cause. My body is more of yours than it is mine. But I have noticed he is the one man who can be courageous enough to sway the people to understand and uplift you to your heavenly status, my Lord." She was now out of breath. She dared not say he had suggested the man to her himself.

He stared at her and for a long moment he said nothing, then from nowhere he let out a laugh so loud and ruthless which Chinake found disturbing.

"You are so daring, Chinake, to see that weasel under my roof without my permission." She was now feeling afraid, but she was Chinake, she had set out to do this for her husband, he had, in fact, suggested the man himself and she would not be moved. She looked at the ground and said nothing. He glared at her.

"But I know you; still he is a man, a clown yes but still a man. You seem to have more faith in all this than I do, to take that weasel into your trust."

"I do, my husband and you must too. What good can come out of anything if faith in it is absent? You are more than this, my husband, you are more than this."

With deep red eyes that did not reveal his thoughts he stared at her once more. Then, as though tired, he said to her, "I think you at least deserve the benefit of the doubt. What can I do once you have set your heart for your husband and King? And I trust you did not tell him anything about my desire to stay on the hill." His eyes were now blazing.

With wide open eyes, she said, "Oh no, my husband! I heard you when you said I should not tell a soul. But please listen to me, my husband, listen to me and I will tell you how things can work. Please, just this once."

He snorted and got up. Then slightly, without facing her, he raised his hand and he waved her on. Quickly, she scrambled after him and kneeling by his side, she told him how best they could win their cause. She was good at narrating facts, she was desperate to please him and she was his perfect pawn, too loving, so blind and very easy to fleece.

When Chinake was through, the Emperor remained quiet. She was glad, at least, that he had not been gruff and unkind. He neither said he would go along with it nor did he say he would not. Instead he said, "I am tired, Chinake. I am very tired but you have already gone this far. Your love for me is great." That was all; once more he would not completely commit himself, in a bid to make her resolve greater.

She did not flinch. He was amazed at her nerves of steel. She was willing to do anything to please this man before her. It was amazing what the power of love could do. Or was it something else other than love; perhaps a crazy desire to please a man whom she worshipped so that others would worship him as well? He shook his head. Still, he was acting it out well enough.

"Come, Chinake," he finally said, without even concluding the matter, "Why should I let you starve? You love me, my wife and your faith in me is amazing. You have a mind of your own and you are my Empress. I am hungry. Come, let us dine."

That was his way of saying yes, carry on with the plan. He was too proud to ever say it outright and Chinake knew him well. She was relieved. After talking, they ate lunch. Later, when it was dusk it was time for Empress Chinake to return to her quarters. She had spent a lovely day with her husband and she left a happy woman. He remained behind a happy man. And as soon as she was outside, he went back to his favourite spot by the opening in the wall and looked out. For the first time with no hesitation, he visualised himself sitting on that big rock and holding his court. He saw his enclosure there on the hill and he felt invincible. From where he stood, he soared up like the fish eagle, a royal bird untouchable in the sky. He saw himself looking down at his first wife's enclosure. And he already had a name for it, it was to be called, Imba Huru, The Great Enclosure.

Her enclosure would be easy to build, but his home would not be so easy. Nevertheless, time was on his side and he still had bright ideas up his sleeve. Tonight, however, he could afford to sleep a happy man knowing that soon he was going to be immortal and live like the spirits in the heavens. Dear Chinake; no wonder he had found her fascinating from the beginning.

*   *   *

As soon as she was outside Chinake stopped, looked around and allowed herself to calm down after her elation. Two sentries walked up to her to escort her home, but she shooed them out the entrance of the Emperor's enclosure. She needed to be alone in this place that had once housed many other Great Zimbabwe kings.

Once alone, Empress Chinake slowly turned her head around as though to take in with her eyes every single detail of these walls that surrounded her. This place usually had an effect on her; it made her feel weak in the knees. She was a worshipper of power and superiority. Just as men weakened in the presence of her beauty, she felt giddy in the presence of royalty. She loved the feel of this place where her husband had lived. Other Kings had resided here and their spirits lived on in this very place. She always felt as though she could feel their presence, as though the spirits of the dead Lords who once lived here had landed upon each reigning ruler, accumulating to make a force that would cause the next King in line to be greater and more powerful than the one before and so she lauded this place. But that was before today, because all of a sudden, with the coming to fruition of her husband's plan, she saw this place which she once worshipped as dreary and lifeless. Today, the grandeur and power of these walls were surprisingly gone.

Sighing, she gingerly walked to one part and, reaching out her delicate hand, she gently stroked and felt the grey rocks that made up this enclosure. Then she breathed in, closed her eyes and listened to the stones as though they lived and were sending out a secret message to her. A message which only she could hear and comprehend.

This had been her secret act each time she was on her way out and alone, but today the walls would have to listen to her as her voice travelled through the granite rocks to the hearts of all those who had lived in this complex before. Today she was the one to deliver the message.

Placing her mouth against the wall she whispered inaudibly into the grey bricks, "I pray to you, forefathers of the Great Zimbabwe, forgive me for what I am about to do. It is not that I despise your majestic dwellings. You have stayed within these walls through generations but there is one of you who has chosen to defy your norm and it is my husband, the reigning Hungwe. He shall leave your spirits behind in these walls and start his own existence high above the world, overlooking mere mortals. He has decided to leave the marshes behind. He shall soar and live like the Hungwe, his totem. Yes, my husband shall fly and be a great divine being, he is the true Hungwe, the true fish eagle." Then her face turning icy and her voice cold and challenging, she looked up and she added, "He shall be greater than all of you. Yes, my husband shall be the mightiest Hungwe to ever rule in this nation, ever! And the people of this whole country shall know what it means to be under the talons of the Hungwe."

As soon as she had finished speaking into the walls, she felt a sense of freedom. The Empress was already living her husband's dream. It was as though she had set him free. He deserved to start his own life unbound to his forefathers, to these walls and to the past. She halted, looked up at the sky and smiled a dreamy smile filled with visions of greatness.

Then she snapped out of her reverie and breathed in, satisfied that she had completed her other mission here. The first rock of the Emperor's new home on the hill had been laid.

# Chapter twenty

A day after Chinake saw her husband, the messenger and his companions who had been sent by Nyatsimba Mutota of the Mbire returned to the Mbire Kingdom and they were given audience by the King at his court. Nyatsimba Mutota, who had been anxiously awaiting the return of the chiefs, was sitting on his rock. His son Matope, Tekeshe and his other chiefs were present at the *dare*.

Once greeting formalities were complete, one of the King's chiefs asked the messenger to relate to Mutota the news he had brought back. The messenger told them that the mission had not been so difficult. They had been treated well by the Great Zimbabwe Emperor, but instead of getting a straight answer to their pledge of giving the Emperor an army of soldiers in place of the usual tribute, they had been told to tell their King that he was requested to come in person to the Great Zimbabwe and see Emperor Hungwe.

There was a hush. Nyatsimba Mutota blinked, cocked his head slightly as though attempting to hear better then licked his lips that were now suddenly dry. He sat there immobilised by what the messengers had said. Everyone in the court was stunned. Someone coughed but Mutota did not hear; his world had stopped and unintentionally he wiped off tiny droplets of sweat that had gathered on his forehead.

Gradually life returned to the gathering and murmurs arose from the chiefs and mhondoros present. The men present knew that Emperor Hungwe was a busy and no nonsense man. He did not have time to entertain trivialities and he hardly ever called upon his kings to come and see him. They all guessed that most probably Hungwe had not been impressed by their humble request and that spelt trouble.

Tekeshe looked at his King with a genuine look of worry written all over his face. Right now he could read his thoughts, clearly understanding the anguish that had enveloped the King from the Emperor's request. It also meant that their plans with the army could be disturbed if Mutota was to go to the Great Zimbabwe. What omen was this that could have swept their way to make a dream, near to completion, suddenly fall from their grasp?

The atmosphere in the court became tense as slowly, one by one, the chiefs and mhondoros turned their heads to look at their King whose mind was clogged with painful thoughts. It was a relief when one chief stood up and boldly asked,

"Has not our offer pleased the Hungwe?"

"He did not say, maybe because we never got a chance to see him face to face. We arrived on the day he was holding court with his council of chiefs and mhondoros. What we have come with we were told by his chief advisor."

"It is not comfortable for a mighty man like our Emperor to desire to see our King after our failure to give him the usual form of tribute," said another chief.

"It was not of our own doing, there was a drought which also affected the Great Zimbabwe and all other states. Further to that, the Emperor decreed that this year, upon failure to pay tribute, the vassal states should present soldiers to the crown, therefore surely there is nothing wrong with what we did." said another chief.

The others agreed and a mhondoro stood up and said, "Would it then be wise for our King to go? The Hungwe rules with an iron fist and we all know that. Maybe the Great Zimbabwe inhabitants see him differently, but we are his vassals and we know the other side of his nature and besides, his sons are ruthless. I fear that this may be a trap to harm our King."

Murmurs of agreement arose as the chief, who had spoken first, said, "If the court may excuse me I would like to agree with what has just been said. It is no lie that second to the Hungwe is our King, Nyatsimba Mutota. It is again no lie that our population numbers are increasing. The Hungwe may be afraid of all this and hence he may be trying to lure our King on a journey that will see him harmed. We need to tread carefully."

Once again, the men agreed. All the while Mutota remained silent, digesting the strange request from the Emperor and what the other men were saying. He, too, had found it rather uncomfortable to be called upon after sending an excuse for their annual tribute. Matope looked at his father and saw the concern on his face. He turned to look at Tekeshe as though for some moral support. Tekeshe gave him a knowing look and nodded his head ever so slightly. He seemed to be saying it was going to be alright. Matope hoped he could believe that.

"Then shall we all agree that our King should not go until we have enough tribute to give to the Hungwe and until we have fully consulted with our mhondoros; we need the guidance of our ancestral spirits and Mwari on this," said the chief and the whole court burst out in agreement.

It was at this stage that, silently, King Mutota stood up and raised his hand in the air. Of course he had been badly shaken by the news, but he was still their King who was supposed to be brave and composed. The final decision lay in his hands. The whole court became silent. He stood in front of them and remained silent for a while, then in a calm voice he spoke, "I am impressed that I have a court full of men who fear for me and care for me so much. I understand your concern because I have been called upon under unusual circumstances. Believe me, I am also of a heavy heart."

The men murmured in support and he went on to say, "However I will say this, let us never speak evil of the Emperor, he is our Lord and to him should all respect be awarded. It is not good for us to think of the negative before we have heard what the Emperor wants from me. We may promote evil from our dark thoughts. At the same time there is no reason to consult with our mhondoros; it would be good, yes, but I have been requested to travel to go and see the Emperor in person and that shall not change. I may find it rather uncomfortable but remember the Emperor is our master, he rules over us and so I have to obey my Lord, otherwise my folly and pride could harm an entire nation and our future. Just as I am sworn to protect and serve my people, so I am a servant of the Great Zimbabwe throne and so let the Emperor's voice be obeyed."

A disgruntled murmur came from the men present and a chief stood up to say, "It is true that the word of the Emperor is the law and that it shall not be refuted, but really it is not wrong for us to be informed of the reason he intends to see our King?"

126

"Then that would undermine his authority and if I do request knowledge of his intentions would I still be his humble servant? No," said Mutota, in a low firm voice. "I am his servant, I say again, and so are we all. Why should I place my nation and position in jeopardy? You know the way they deal with insolent subjects. Let us be loyal to the throne of the Hungwe."

There was silence. No one moved. All eyes were on him. Matope looked lovingly at his father and felt sorry for him; Tekeshe admired this great King who would do anything to protect his people. Finally, one of the chiefs said in a sombre tone, "Our King is right. We must obey the voice of the Emperor and also the wish of our King, Nyatsimba Mutota. Then shall our Lord go with an army of at least forty men because the way there is dangerous." The chiefs and mhondoros once more consented.

"Thank you," he said, sounding relieved. I shall be accompanied and I shall leave at my earliest convenience. Two days from now will be the most. We just pray for the best. Let us then look into other state affairs, I am sure this matter is resolved."

The men agreed grudgingly and went on to other state affairs. Mutota did his best to contribute but his mind was not settled. Something was wrong and something was strange about it all. He wondered how his first wife was going to take it. She had just begun to see a new life for them, now this strange request. He would tell her the following day and hopefully she would not fall apart.

After the court meeting when the others had left, Tekeshe Chingowo remained behind and said to the King in a hushed and pained tone, "My Lord, my heart is also troubled by this strange request, I shall get ready forty of our best men to accompany you on your journey. I pray it will not take too long and that it will not hamper our progress."

With a heavy face, Mutota looked at him and managed to say, "I do not think that it will as long as you remain behind and see to the training and discipline of the army. I shall be alright. It's just that the demand has been badly timed, especially after our failure to provide enough tribute and just when we are beginning to make something out of our army."

"Do not worry," said Tekeshe, "That will be well taken care of, as you said you shall be leaving in two days' time. Let me hasten then and start to prepare the men you require. I wish you all the best my Lord."

They clasped hands and as Tekeshe was about to make his leave Mutota gripped his arm, making the giant stop and stare at his master in shock. He saw his master's eyes turn red and fill with tears. Never before had he seen his Lord look so broken. Now Tekeshe knew that, truly, his Lord had taken the news rather badly.

Mutota's lips quivered as he said, "Tekeshe Chingowo, my friend, my nation suffers because of an Emperor whose word is indisputable. He is infallible and his decisions are like a heavy wind tearing at us, drawing us back." A tear flowed freely from his eye, rolled down his cheek and dropped to the ground. As it fell, Tekeshe's heart sank.

"Master," he managed to say, "do not—please do not cry like that."

"I cry, not because I am afraid to go, but because I am leaving the only family I know and worse, I am leaving a dream behind. Who shall follow it through for I know not what will happen to me? You have heard of the way the crown Princes are and you know our Emperor, he has called me and maybe it is for my demise. If we had paid tribute it would have been better." Tekeshe opened his mouth to refute but Mutota raised a quivering hand to hush him and went on, "I want you to do something for me, Tekeshe, my friend, only you can I trust and not any of my own blood. Take them away from this place and begin a dream for my people, please. Make an oath right here and now that the dream of an Mbire Empire shall not fail."

Tekeshe mouthed something, unable to speak and Mutota looked him deep in the eyes. He had no choice, his master's mind was made up.

"Y-y-yes master," he nearly choked, "Yes, I shall honour your dream and I shall honour the crown Prince, but I shall honour the hope, too, that you will be back for the love and sake of your vision."

With cheeks covered in tears, Mutota sniffed loudly and managed a thin smile. Once more, he squeezed Tekeshe's hand and after giving the King a reassuring smile, the soldier, like a drunken man, made his leave. Weakly, Mutota went and sat on a stool, sighed loudly and covered his face. He wanted to think but he could not. It was as though his mind had stopped functioning.

Moments later, Matope came in from the other entrance and seeing his father seated and looking despondent, he said with concern, "Should I accompany you, father? I dare not remain behind and think of what can befall you in my absence."

128

Mutota looked at his son lovingly and said, "It is not as though I am going to my death. I will be fine. It is only that the Emperor is unpredictable. It is rare to be called upon by Hungwe. But you need to remain behind. You need to sit on my throne. I will make arrangements that your mother and my chief advisor assist you in my absence. The throne cannot be left vacant. Tekeshe will also be there despite the fact that he is busy with the army right now. But I know he will assist you in times of need. And besides, you still have a lot of military training to catch up with."

They spoke for a while longer and ended up joking and recalling many events. They even planned for the future and that helped lift their spirits. Matope finally left his father. Alone, this time he was able to think and he started to very seriously. What did the Emperor want with him? It was true that the Mbire Kingdom was steadily growing strong and more populated. Could the Emperor deem it now to be a threat? Or maybe he wanted to tell Mutota personally that they would not accept soldiers from such a large nation as his for tribute payment? Or maybe, worse still, had his worst nightmare come to life?

Had the Emperor heard about what they were doing with their army and guessed why? But who could have told him and even if the person had said anything, training an army did not necessarily mean he was planning a revolt. Mutota knew that, in his silent ways, Hungwe was also a very intelligent man. He hoped that Hungwe was not planning to send his investigating army during his absence. He wished he was right and that whatever it was the Emperor wanted him for would turn out in his favour.

It was not wrong for his chiefs to have negative feelings about the whole affair, no one in his Kingdom ever trusted the Emperor. Still, not going could have its own repercussions. So he would go and he would show his people that he was no coward. He would show them openly that he was a disciplined subject and hoped that in return they would behave in a similar manner.

He sighed and got up from where he was sitting. Now he felt hungry. He would call for lunch and after eating there was a lot to do. He had to make his journey to the Great Zimbabwe brief so that he could return home in time to complete his plans. Of course he trusted Tekeshe, but he needed to be around. He needed to continually supervise the progress of his dream. His son was still too young to carry out his father's orders in their entirety. Since he was the one going, he had to organise an appropriate gift for the Emperor with his advisors and make proper arrangements with his wife and his sister as well as with Tekeshe. Time was not on his side. Soon it would be night and he had only three days to prepare. He had not seen the Emperor for a very long time, too long in fact. He wondered what the big man looked like now.

All other things aside, deep in his heart Mutota felt that what the Great Zimbabwe Emperor had just given was an outright challenge. And he could not have been more right.

# Chapter twenty-one

Back in the Great Zimbabwe Kingdom, nighttime had crept in. The former cold air of July was slowly being replaced by the gusty winds of August, which carried a slightly warmer current. Life was now more bearable. Here and there leaves were lifted up and twirled in the air by the blowing winds. Heavy tree branches creaked and groaned as they were swayed by the force of the blustery weather. Sleeping on his back and blinking into the darkness, Kwatara found the whistling sound of the night wind comforting. It was not like the dark silence of July, which had nothing better to offer than bitter cold.

He had woken up beside his wife who was fast asleep and for the last hour or so had been silently listening to the wind blowing and rustling the leaves outside. Having lost sleep for a while, his mind gradually trailed back to the strange events that had occurred the last few days and he started re-evaluating their impact. He recalled the impact the zigzag pattern on the walls had had on him. Then his brother's anguish clouded his mind and he felt a lump at his throat. He had noticed the pattern before but that had been before his first dream about the girl and the clay pot. How could something so simple have such an effect on him. He felt helpless.

He sighed and just then the crazy face of Chireshe came to his mind. Desperately, with a little anger and disgust in him, he hoped that he would not have to encounter Chireshe again for a very long time. There was something about his brisk behaviour that was a bit out of line these days. He was behaving like a dog sniffing around for a thief or for a bone. Every now and then he would see him talking to chiefs and mhondoros, making his strange gestures. Kwatara could not help feeling angry at the man and in his anger he clicked his tongue.

So much was happening and it was all too jumbled up for him to make any sense of it. Maybe he would think better tomorrow with a clearer mind. Feeling tired and sleepy, he turned onto his side and came face to face with his wife who was fast asleep and had begun snoring lightly. Once she started, Kwatara knew that it would be long before he found any sleep. Nevertheless, he closed his eyes gently and waited for sleep to overcome him.

Suddenly his eyes fluttered open. Something had surely awoken him but he could not place it. Though he was now wide awake he also had this odd sensation that the he had not really slept that long. He blinked and tried to focus in the darkness. Strangely, he discovered that this time he could see much better. The darkness that had shrouded him now was no longer so intense. Had daylight come so fast, he wondered.

Something whimpered and impulsively he turned towards the sound but got the shock of his life. His neck was stiff and the slight attempt to turn sent a bright white light bursting in his eyes. A sharp pain raced through his head making him feel dizzy. Numbed by the pain he wondered how and why he had suddenly developed a very stiff neck when moments ago he had been just fine.

He shut his eyes as a terrible throbbing started inside his skull. He could hardy think let alone breathe and when he tried to lift his hand to rub his temple a gruesome discovery awaited him. Both hands were painfully stiff and aching so intensely. He could barely lift or move them. It was as though, here and there, he had been bruised and the tender areas were now hurting him. What had happened to him? Terror ripped through his mind and triggered a new wave of pain that shot throughout his entire body.

Kwatara moaned from the aching and his throat joined in the pain parade. It was dry, sore and in dire need of water. He felt like a man who had not been nourished by a refreshing drink for ages and a desperate need for water formed in his hurting mind. He could not call out, but at least he could do something, he could reach out for his wife. He did but lo, his painful hand ended mid-way, she was not there. Were his hands fooling him?

"T—Tari," he whispered, inaudibly. He wanted her to answer, hoped for at least some movement to show she was there, somewhere near, but the terrible truth that this was not going to happen was bare in front of him. His heart raced and fear engulfed his entire mind. She had been sleeping and snoring beside him minutes ago and he had fallen asleep. Then what? Why was his wife not there? Maybe she still was sleeping where he had left her and it was he who was somewhere else.

Where on earth was he and how had he ended up here? Moments passed as he raked his mind for an answer but found none. The sudden realisation that he was in an unknown place, all alone, overtook him and with that, fear started trickling in. He started to sweat. Something was very wrong and he needed to get out away from this place, hurting or not.

Fright and the urge to escape from wherever this was pumped adrenalin into his veins. He was a man with a sixth sense and he realised that this place was not safe nor was it sane to remain immobile, pain or not. Slowly, ever so slowly, he balanced on one hand, pain exploded through his body and his head nearly burst with throbbing. Trying his best to ignore it, he carefully balanced on the other hand and tried to sit upright. Dizziness caught him and fighting to remain awake, he slumped against something. It was not a wall and had a coarse feeling to it. He tried to figure out what it was because his head hurt too much for him to turn back and look. Then it struck him and nearly blew him away. He was leaning against the bark of a tree. The comprehension made the aching in his entire body worse than before. He was stunned. Where indeed was he?

With his heart pounding madly in his chest he looked about, suddenly unaware of the pain in his neck and with his hands he felt the ground where he sat. He was not sitting on the floor in his hut but on a pile of leaves and twigs that rustled and crumbled under him. From above, he saw streaks of light gradually forming and falling to the ground. He could make out the canopy of numerous trees and looking feverishly about him, sweating profusely from the pain and fear, he saw huge trees surrounding him, unkempt and growing wild. He realised he was in the heart of a thick forest and that realisation once again sent fresh pangs of terror through his mind. And as though to enhance his newfound fear, from nowhere wild dogs began barking in the distance, barks so loud and which sounded so near Kwatara nearly swooned from the mere thought of being eaten alive. He groped around as though searching for somewhere to hide and finding himself once more immobilised by his pain and his foreign surroundings, he clung to the bark of the tree against which he had slumped, petrified.

Then the trumpet of elephants joined in, mingled with the crazy giggles of numerous hyenas and accompanied by the roar of a lion. Together the sounds of all these wild animals formed unearthly noises that threatened to drive him wild with fright. He closed his ears with his hands. This was crazy, was he losing his mind? One moment he had been sleeping beside his wife, now he was here in the wild with all these crying animals which were nowhere to be seen. He shut his eyes as the sharp shriek of a bird rang across the forest. He could not bear it anymore. Despite his pain, he screamed and the scream ended with the agonizing sobs of a very scared and broken man.

Then suddenly there was silence. A deep uncomfortable silence. Slowly he opened his eyes and warily looked around. He did not know which was better or worse, the screaming animals or the deep silence, both were just as terrifying to him. He looked about furtively and wiped away beads of sweat that were freely running down his face.

Brighter streaks of light that stole in through the gaps in the canopy that formed above, gradually took over the darkness in the forest. Now he was going to be exposed to the crying wild animals as soon as it became brighter. Everything that was happening around him offered no solace at all.

"The master said that we should leave you here," said a voice from beside him.

His breathing stopped and his eyes dilated. Quickly he turned to look at his right side. Before there had been no one standing there, but now there stood a soldier in full regalia beside him, face taut and eyes looking straight ahead as though he could not turn his head to look at Kwatara as he spoke. Kwatara's heart stopped and he let out a small whimper like a cornered puppy. Was this a ghost that had so suddenly appeared?

"He ordered us not to even touch you but to leave you here for the wild animals to do as they please with you," came another voice from his left side. Once more he sharply turned his head and saw, to his surprise, another soldier dressed in the same manner and also looking straight ahead, intentionally ignoring Kwatara. Where had they appeared from and what cursed forest was this? He moaned and nearly fainted.

They remained standing like statues and together they said, "Let it never be known that you were left here and may your name be erased from the lips of the inhabitants of the people of this nation."

He couldn't stand this, why was he being condemned? What had he done?

"W—Why?" he managed to croak. His throat was so dry it hurt when he spoke. "Where did you come from and who are you? Who sent you?" They did not even seem to have heard him because they remained posed as they were, as though they spoke to someone of utterly no significance at all.

"Because," they both spoke at once, "They that oppose the divine supremacy of our Lord should suffer a death worthy of those that cannot recognise the existence of such a high being. You dared open your mouth, now here you are in the heart of savages like you and thus you shall perish."

They turned to look at him with eyes blazing like flames. He wanted to scream but nothing came out. They looked like evil creatures with faces of men who had come to guard and to torment him. Looking angry and hateful, they opened their mouths and revealed toothless black holes from which ghostly moans escaped. Scared, Kwatara clung to the tree and as though it was the only shoulder to lean on, he cried against its rough bark. Then in unison they turned their heads, looked straight ahead and started to walk away, marching like soldiers at a parade.

The sound of feet breaking twigs and crunching leaves reached his ears. He looked up. He was indeed being abandoned to the horrors of this forest. Crying like a child he held out his hand, he wanted to tell them to stop and wait for him but nothing came out of his mouth. As evil as they looked, they were his only hope. He tried to get up and follow, but the pain from his throbbing head shot like a sword piercing his entire body and he crumbled to the ground. He began to sob. How had this happened? What had he done? How could he have ended up like this, a worthy mhondoro like him who had only wanted to work for Mwari and to help his people, his nation that he loved so much? Was this the reward of faithful servants? He sobbed uncontrollably, suddenly letting out a wailing sound like a woman crying for a lost child. His heart ached and he felt so lost, so unwanted and so desolate.

Then in between his sobs he heard another voice. This was much warmer and it said, "If you allow me to show you the way then promise me that you shall teach my son the ways of being a spiritual warrior, for being a warrior of the sword is not enough to hold a mighty nation together."

Shocked he was jolted out of his mourning and he looked up. Right there in front of him stood an elderly man whom he was sure he had seen before. He wore a black cloth tied around his waist which came to his knees and tied on his back was the hide of a Leopard. Kwatara blinked as he tried to place the face and to fully focus on the figure standing before him, but before he could comprehend what was being said, the older man turned and started walking quickly away, "Come and I will show you the way out. Be brave, there is only one way and you shall know it by the creepers that grow alongside it. See, they have big white flowers."

He looked and saw that, indeed, there were creepers growing up the trees and there was a small, nearly indiscernible path that was winding away from where he sat. The older man kept on walking. Seeing that once more he was being left alone, Kwatara tried to get up. This time, despite the pain, his fear and desperation propped him up and like a drunk he followed the older man through the forest.

"Take note, take note, do not forget. For with this path you will meet the King and he shall know that I have sent you because you shall show him this." The older man abruptly stopped, slightly undid the cloth around his waist and just where he tied the knot was a scar, the maul of animal claws. Kwatara gasped. The scar was ugly and though it had healed a long time ago, it showed that the man had been cut deeply by whatever animal had attacked him.

"No one else knows, apart from him, that the animal that did this to me is the very one that is on my back," went on the older man, "I always told them it was a lion. And when you tell him of this scar he shall surely know it was I who sent you. Now hurry, you have a lot to teach my son and time is not on our side."

Once more Kwatara was not able to ask anything for, in a twinkle of an eye, the other man was some distance ahead of him and Kwatara had to hurry after him, taking note of the road. Finally, the older man stopped before a tall, baobab tree with fruits ready to pick and said to Kwatara, "Now lie here and wait for my son, as he heads north he shall pass by. He shall find you and he shall take you with him. He is the King." And before Kwatara could ask anything the man turned, quickly walked away and suddenly stopped some way off to look back as though he had remembered something very important.

"Do not, I tell you," he seemed to shout, "take my son through the plains because they are awaiting a Prince. Take the woods and avoid the trap. I cannot afford to lose a son." And then he disappeared among the trees. Now more perplexed than before from what he had heard, Kwatara was left alone, wondering what was to become of him. He sat down, too tired to think and slumped onto the heap of twigs that was under him. He was swimming in confusion and try as he did to make sense of everything, his mind felt too tired to join the facts together. He could not help but to succumb to the fatigue that was so overwhelming. He closed his eyes. In no time at all, he blacked out into a deep sleep.

From somewhere far away a cock crowed. It crowed again and this time Kwatara heard it like a small child's distant cry in his sleep. The third time the crowing was louder. It woke Kwatara up with a violent start. His eyes opened wide and he blinked against the morning light that flowed into the hut in which he slept through the tiny opening on the wall. Gasping for breath he felt his bedding and looked around, eyes wide with fright.

Gradually getting more accustomed to his surroundings, he turned to look beside him and saw his wife sleeping peacefully. He felt his skin on his hands and his legs. Everything told him he was not injured, but fine. He was back home and the realisation that once more he had had a bad dream concerning his nation and himself struck him with full force. Frustration filled him upon the sad comprehension that again he was unable to interpret the meaning of the dream, but was certain that very soon the events in the Kingdom would reveal for themselves the meaning of what he had just visualised in his sleep. Painfully he sighed and he wondered when it all would end. Little did he know that his dream signalled the beginning of the real story.

# Chapter twenty-two

The Mbire King Nyatsimba Mutota could not have chosen a worse day than this to begin his journey to the Great Zimbabwe Kingdom. It was now mid-way into the month of August and cold gusty winds blew against the faces of numerous people who had come to see their King off. Among these were his first wife, his other wives and his entire court of chiefs and mhondoros. They had come all the way from their homes to wish him a safe journey to the fear-inspiring Kingdom of the Great Zimbabwe.

Many were not as jubilant. They, like their King, despised the Hungwe and they feared for the life of their King, but the Emperor's word was the law and all his subjects had to abide by it. The King's first wife, Tashonga, made no brave show. She actually shed some tears as she stood close to her husband. In between tears, she said, "You go to see the Hungwe, he is a lion that roars and he is a mighty man. I fear for you my husband."

"It is not as though I am going to die, Tashonga, please," said Mutota. "Your tears do me no good. Do you wish for me to travel with a heavy heart? It will bring me ill luck I tell you. Now stop crying and wish me well on my journey." She wiped away the tears and looking at him, tried hard to smile. "I am not going to see a lion but a man just like me. He may be my King but I have not done him any harm. I am a man and I will stand my ground for my nation, my life and family. Believe me, I will come back." She merely stared at him, shook her head then turned to look away. The King sighed deeply and speaking in a low, soothing voice he said, "Then you should remember that I, your husband, am a

King in his own right and one to be feared too. I will be back home safe with good news." He smiled and hoped he had not lied.

Soon after, he was speaking to Tekeshe Chingowo and he said, "Remember our deal, you made an oath."

"And I am a man of my word, my Lord. Remember, I said you would also come back, for only the dreamer of a dream can bring it to completion," replied Tekeshe. Mutota nodded and Tekeshe smiled.

"Farewell, my brother", said his eldest sister, Rungano, as she came to stand next to him. "Do not worry about her," she said as she turned to look at her sister-in-law who was looking lost and torn. "She shall be in my safe hands. I will do my best to console her. I, too, am very worried but I will hold onto the faith that you shall return. Now go and be brave. We have bigger and more real battles ahead of us. Nothing will stop the future conqueror of nations."

She smiled warmly and reassuringly and he smiled back. At least she had lifted up his spirits a bit. He looked at his wife and this time she gave him a tiny smile, he smiled back. Then raising his hand in the air he signalled to Tekeshe that he was ready to leave. His son Matope came to him and gripped his hand. "It is well, my father. You will be safe. Dreams like the one you have cannot be cut short, lest history will never be made. Travel well and I will look after your throne and mother. I will for the few days you shall be gone guard your Kingdom."

Mutota felt very proud of his son. It was amazing just how fast he had grown in just a few months. He was certain things would be fine. He turned away and waved to his people. They clapped and the women ululated. His first wife tilted her head slightly and gave him a proud smile.

"Hail our King!" shouted Tekeshe.

"Hail!" the people shouted.

"Hail to the first, the man of the soil!"

"Hail!" the people shouted once more, clapping and ululating. Mutota smiled proudly and thanking them for the last time, he straightened the leopard hide that he wore over his head, turned and walked away with his soldiers. The wind did not abate and it was long after he had gone that the people turned to leave. The only ones to remain were his first wife and his older sister. Only long after he had gone did they morosely turn and walk back to their homes, each one lost in thought.

Mutota did not look back lest he felt his legs weaken and his heart sink. Instead he walked proudly on until he was out of sight. The fact that the invitation from the Emperor came at the wrong time still weighed upon his mind. He wondered if he would be back and if he would, if he would be back on time and in shape to lead his people away. Silently, he wondered why the price of independence was so steep and if ever there was anyone who could pay for it in full and find his freedom from the Great Zimbabwe Lords.

*   *   *

Three days later the Mbire King and his soldiers arrived at the outskirts of the Great Zimbabwe. They would have arrived the previous night, but a persistent gale that was blowing across the country delayed their progress. Added to that, the hot August sun forced the men to rest every now and then from fatigue and thirst.

Standing on a hill that overlooked the Kingdom, Mutota saw the massive grey walls of the city's enclosures standing out. While on any other occasion the granite enclosures would have appeared awesome, it was not so today. They looked like bleak and dreary imprisoning forts set against the howling wind that sent a melancholy sound into the plateau, doubling the already miserable mood of the King and his soldiers.

He breathed out and looked around. He knew that the numerous scouts dotted all over and hiding from view had already spotted them, but since they were expected, he was not alarmed. However, he decided that it would not be prudent to go on with his men and he sent out three soldiers who would herald their arrival before they advanced to the gates.

He looked at his men and saw anxiety written all over their faces. It would not do to march with them into the great walls with such burdened hearts and dejected looks, so he decided to speak to them in words that would not be misconstrued by the scouts nearby.

"Fellow soldiers and servants of the Great Zimbabwe throne, we are here today upon the request of our mighty Emperor, the Great Hungwe. We shall therefore walk into his Kingdom with faces of warriors true to the throne to show the great awe and respect we have for our Emperor. Do not hold dejected faces for they do not honour the crown, but hold your heads high as true Mbire warriors loyal to the throne of the Hungwe."

They got the message and immediately the spirit in the camp changed. Slowly the anticipation and fear left and they sat down in neat rows. But he could not blame his men. There was something about this place. It held a daunting stamp of authority that was unavoidable. Had it not been for the zeal he had to flee he would have buckled, but in his desire to run away he had found a new self and the much needed strength to enter into the Kingdom like the King he was and meet with Emperor Hungwe.

Sitting down, he patiently waited for the return of his soldiers and word from his Emperor.

# Chapter twenty-three

It was a long wait, three hours later they returned with four Great Zimbabwe soldiers who were to accompany them to the entrance. They were huge men and spoke very little. The air of self-importance surrounding them immediately made Nyatsimba Mutota aware that though he was King in his own land, in this Kingdom he was nothing but a servant. Mbire was just a good dream, this was where the reality was and today he was wide-awake in the land of truth. His heart ached as he yearned for the day when even those mighty Lords who dwelt in this Kingdom would see him as an equal.

On their way to the city, the Great Zimbabwe soldiers led the way. Mutota and his men had travelled far and were weary, but their King had told them to hold their heads high and so they did. They went down the hills strewn all over with granite rocks, into the bushes then into the valley. They went past cattle herders and boys herding goats. They passed women on their way to and from the river. All these people stopped and stared. To Mutota it was ordinary. People stopped and stared at new faces. But what he didn't know was that they had noticed that here was a King with his men and soldiers who appeared as though they had nothing to fear, yet they walked on the very same soil which the Great Zimbabwe Emperor treaded. For years, kings and traders had stepped into the Great Zimbabwe territory but not one group had the same dignity exuded by Mutota and his men. An aura of greatness surrounded these men and it was as vivid as a flash of light to the eyes. By the time the Mbire King and his men reached the valley of the Great

Zimbabwe, it was close to midday and news of their arrival had already spread throughout the Kingdom.

As they neared the city gates, they saw here and there groups of Great Zimbabwe soldiers sitting on rocks or casually strolling in full army attire. Mutota wondered what the battle gear was for. Was his crime this bad, he wondered, that already soldiers were in position to prevent his way of escape? His heart felt heavy. Little did he know that the charade by the soldiers was not even meant for him.

A few days ago, Perayi had managed to convince his father that the civilians needed a reminder of who the Hungwe was. If their vassals could ignore the rules set by the throne, then the same worm could find its way into the hearts of the Great Zimbabwe inhabitants. The presence of the army would serve to remind them of their allegiance to the State. Hungwe had agreed, not because he agreed with Perayi, but because he knew just how far this would promote his goal. The final battle needed minds dulled by any psychological weapon present.

Just outside the valley, Mutota and his men were told to wait for the Emperor's permission for them to enter. A reed mat was laid for him to sit on and two hides were placed on top to make it more comfortable. Only the soldiers guarding the King remained standing. Mutota realised that the wait would be a long one.

Looking at the large granite walls, he realised the power of the rulers and people within. Stories of new and more beautiful walls being built had not failed to reach his ears and he wondered what they looked like. Very soon, the Mbire King would know.

They waited and the day advanced to late afternoon. Still they waited and still they did not complain. Hungwe was their Lord, they were merely his servants. In the silence and throughout the long wait, the King planned and re-strategized his moves. The servant was scheming right at the gates of his Lord.

Meanwhile, Shamai was standing before the Emperor who sat like a man bored with life, yet his mind was as alert as ever. Today, in fact, it was more alert because he had been informed hours ago of the arrival of the Mbire King, Nyatsimba Mutota.

"Tell me, Shamai, is that why you have disturbed my line of thought, to tell me that my servant Nyatsimba Mutota has arrived? Is it so unusual for a King to visit the Emperor that it warrants that I should be disturbed?"

He gave old Shamai a hard stare who returned it with a humble look. He was used to this kind of treatment. It was not that the Emperor was uninterested in Mutota, his visitor, for he had personally called him here himself and Shamai clearly remembered the excitement in the Emperor's voice and on his face the night he had asked Shamai to send for Nyatsimba Mutota. Hungwe was just trying to sound important, and like always, Shamai would play along for the sake of progress. More pressing matters awaited his attention.

"It is true, my Lord, that I have intruded on you at such an inconvenient time," he said in his deep, humble voice, "You are correct, kings of minor importance like the Mbire King should not disrupt the day-to-day running of our Kingdom. More important matters await my Lord's attention. Would it not be prudent, for the sake of my Lord's peace, for him to see the Mbire King and get it over with?"

Hungwe looked at Shamai and pretending to consider the proposal, he said, "Very well. Let him be told that he will see his Emperor soon. Like you say, we have more pressing matters. Right now his issue is not as important as is this Kingdom and the people within these walls." Shamai kept silent and remained looking at the King with no emotion whatsoever showing on his face. "Now tell me, Shamai old man, is there anything else you need to discuss with me?"

And as though the Emperor had not offended him at all, Shamai automatically opened his mouth to give a list of other pressing matters within the Kingdom. The Emperor looked at him as he spoke and wondered just how the old man was able to do his job with absolutely no show of emotion. Sometimes the old man's character plainly irritated him, but grudgingly he always admitted to himself that there was no better choice for the job. Hard to understand or not, Shamai was certainly the best. He turned his mind from these thoughts and listened to Shamai as he spoke.

It was just a few hours before early evening when Shamai, already tired from the business with the Emperor, went to meet King Mutota at the city outskirts. As he forced his old legs to move, he silently cursed the Emperor because he would have to walk all the way back into the city with the visitors to show them their lodgings. His business with the Emperor had left him feeling too tired to entertain anyone and he hoped his mission would be brief and painless.

Two sentries accompanied him and as he approached the Mbire King and his companions, a surprise awaited him. These men had arrived hours ago and were supposed to be very tired from the long journey they had taken, but there sat in four neat rows of six soldiers each, soldiers who showed discipline by their postures. The bored and expectant faces he had anticipated were absent. Instead, men who showed no pain and men who were taking the treatment from the Great Zimbabwe Kingdom with all the dignity they possessed greeted him. For the first time he felt a wave of guilt hit him. These were not like other men who had visited the Kingdom. These men deserved more than the treatment of mere servants of the Emperor.

He stood in front of Mutota who stood up with a clear face and Nyatsimba Mutota remembered this old man from a long time back as the Emperor's chief advisor. He bent low on one leg and cupping his hands, greeted him in a voice filled with genuine respect.

"Greetings my Lord. We are honoured at your presence and for sparing your time to attend to us humble servants of the Hungwe, Emperor and Lord of the Great Zimbabwe." His men cupped their hands as well and assisted their King in greeting Shamai.

In all his years he had never been given such royal respect by those from outside the walls. He was touched. He had heard of the Mbire King and of his popularity with his people and now he knew why. He also admired the leopard hide that Nyatsimba wore over his head. This rejuvenated his spirit and despite his tired self, he said, "I am indeed sorry for being late, but I had important business with the Emperor. Now if you and your men could please rise and follow me. It is getting late and very soon it will be dark. Let me show you to your lodgings."

The King got up and stood erect in front of Shamai. In the early light of dusk, Shamai saw a man of muscular build, tall, dark and with a face that showed all the markings and makings of a King. It was as though royalty just freely flowed from him affecting all those nearby. He breathed in heavily and told himself, "Here is a worthy opponent of the Emperor."

Mutota ordered his men to get up and they did, maintaining their formation. The weeks of hard training and discipline that had been drilled into them were finally paying off.

With his keen eye Shamai took note of all this and marvelled at the solidarity these men had with their King. He remembered a time when the young King's father had visited the Great Zimbabwe. He too had come with his men and accompanying soldiers to protect him on the journey. Yes, the old King had looked exactly like his son in stature and features, but his army and his men had looked nothing like these that stood before him. Upon his son, the royalty of all the late kings of the Mbire had been poured. He also remembered twice as many years ago when Nyatsimba Mutota had visited the Kingdom to pay his respects to Hungwe with other lords from other kingdoms. On both occasions, he had not impressed Shamai like this. Time could really change people and nations, thought Shamai to himself, and the Kingdom had every right to be wary of this man.

Shamai led the way and Mutota followed, with his men walking after him and his guards flanking him. Once more, people stopped and stared. He was a great King, the mightiest of the Great Zimbabwe vassals and his stately composure, as well as that of his men, proved it. They did not stare back at the people, nor did they look sideways, but simply marched on following their King. From the corner of his eye, Shamai noticed all this and he was suitably impressed. He decided to be more friendly and dropping his step to walk beside King Mutota, he said, as they went past the new enclosure being built, "Look at these walls, this is the new enclosure being built by our master builder, Hombasha. He is good."

Mutota noticed this too and he agreed. The walls were straighter, more organised and had a beautiful zigzag pattern on top. He promised himself that he would one day build walls of such grandeur and if not, walls of at least some grandeur. Shamai noticed the King's admiration and with great pride, he went onto explain more about the walls, detailing the way the new ones were being built. Mutota responded with true enthusiasm, all the while studying the architecture and the beauty of the granite walls. Impressed by this enthusiasm, Shamai took a liking to their new visitor and he took him the long way to the lodgings, showing off more structures and explaining in detail, despite his exhaustion, the workmanship and craftsmanship involved in the making of all the walls.

Workers moved back and forth, busy finishing off their day's work. They looked worn out and tired. Mutota was glad that he had not already sent some of their young men and women as tribute to work on the walls of the Great Zimbabwe. The Emperor was a man who seemed more than happy to drain every slave and worker of his or her strength for the sake of his massive granite walls.

Tired and hungry they finally arrived at their lodgings and Shamai left them with four Great Zimbabwe soldiers to guard their enclosure. At the rate at which they were assigning soldiers to guard him, Mutota wondered whether it was an act of kindness or the fact that he was a force to reckon with. Chuckling to himself, he chose the latter.

It was way into the night that he finally managed to rest, but best as he tried anxiety kept gnawing at him. Why had Hungwe called him here? He wished he had been given the chance and the right to ask. This was one time that he felt what it was like to be a true servant, there was no peace and no trust. His desire to break away to the north grew and he silently prayed his visit here would not blow away his chances to do so.

# Chapter twenty-four

News of Mutota's arrival spread throughout the city at lightning speed, even the dead granite walls were aware that the Mbire King had arrived. There was so much speculation over his visit that already people were placing wagers on his head for everyone knew that he had failed to pay tribute and that the Emperor had not been all too happy about it.

The only person who seemed unaware of the arrival of the Mbire entourage was Kwatara. His last dream had left him a very disturbed man, so much so that he had locked himself in his own little world, allowing nothing but worry to be his companion.

Today, once again broken in spirit, he found himself at his favourite spot among the rocks. With an expressionless face, he looked around but his mind registered nothing and his ears remained deaf to the voices that filled this place. Alone, surrounded by the granite boulders, he felt at home, far from people, with only the morose sound of the howling wind winding its way through the rocks to keep him company.

As if in prayer, he absentmindedly looked up at the sky, it was not a pleasant sight and did little to soothe his confused mind. Clouds were rolling by, dark grey clouds folding and unfolding into each other. On occasion, they would block the sun and give way to cold winds, and then when they parted they would expose a blistering sun that would scorch the earth mercilessly for those few seconds. Sullenly, he looked away and began to study his hands as though he was a fortune-teller searching for an answer in his palms, an answer to the meaning of his dreams, for he badly needed one otherwise he would soon lose his mind.

Who could blame him, on both occasions he had been physically thrown into the dream and the terror, pain and confusion had been so real they had transcended into the actual world after he had woken up. Never before had he been so badly shaken by dreams and both had left a deep scar of fear and confusion in his pleasant character. His wife had tried to shake him out of this state and to make him open up. She had failed and had finally given up. Now alone, he wondered if he was being unfair to her.

From the morning he had woken up from his dream he knew he would go mad if he told no one, but he had been too burdened to find the strength to go and tell Hombasha. Hombasha was his best friend and from years of mutual understanding, he would never think otherwise of Kwatara. True, he would not be able to explain the dreams, but opening up to him would certainly offer a degree of sanity. Feeling that he urgently needed to confide in someone, Kwatara made a decision to go and see his brother before doubt crept in and kept him rooted in his dilemma.

He got up and headed towards the building site. Children, running to the river, went past him laughing and oddly, their laughter was a strange reminder of the laughter of hyenas in his dreams. Momentarily, he stopped and like a crazy man he looked around frightened. Only the small amount of rationality left in him rang a bell and from somewhere far away, he realised the abnormality of his present action. He looked about and saw people staring at him, most probably wondering why such an important man was behaving like a demented fool.

Hugging his cloth close to his chest he quickly he made his way to the enclosure, as though afraid he would change his mind or lose it before he arrived.

Finally, he arrived at the walls and saw workers moving here and there. A song was in the air and at certain points the voices of the singers were carried away by the blowing wind, leaving in its place the whistling of the gale. The song was slow and sad, and added weight upon his burdened soul.

Resting his hand against the granite wall, he gathered himself together. Those close to where he stood looked at him strangely. He knew it was because of the way he was behaving. He could not possibly present himself to his brother before the workers in such a state. It would kill Hombasha. He went and leaned against a tree and breathed in and out. Slowly calm returned and he looked about seeking Hombasha out. Where was his brother? He decided to ask one worker who pointed to a section of the enclosure and said he was behind that wall with a few men.

Kwatara thanked him and as steadily as he could, he walked towards that direction wondering who the men were, hopefully not the Prince and his entourage again. As he came close, he heard his brother talking in a loud voice. It was as though he was giving a lecture. Funny, thought Kwatara, how so many people these days were interested in the construction of the enclosures. Surely, Hombasha must have built the greatest one ever.

Going round with a feeling of urgency to talk to his brother he stopped dead in his tracks, for there in front of him, with their backs to him, were five men, two chiefs and three mhondoros and among them, of course, was his arch rival Chireshe.

Kwatara disliked the man so much that he even knew him from his back. Momentarily forgetting his demise, a feeling of dejection filled him and he thought of turning back and heading home to bury himself in his dark thoughts. Here he had come to seek solace and there was his brother busy giving a lecture of some sort from the sound of it to men on how the walls were being built. And worse still, among the men was Chireshe, the one who simply never failed to irk him. He wondered why he was everywhere with mhondoros and chiefs these days and what his interest in the walls was all about?

He creased his forehead, thought for a while and deciding not to intrude lest an argument with Chireshe ensued, he turned and gloomily started to walk back home.

"Kwatara!" called Hombasha. He had suddenly noticed his kid brother.

Kwatara stopped, shut his eyes and breathed out. A sharp pain crossed through his head making him feel dizzy. He had to make a choice and a choice that was not only for his benefit but for his brother's as well. Not wanting to humiliate him, he turned back and stood facing Hombasha without making a move to get any closer.

"Come closer, brother and meet your fellow men. I was just giving them a lecture on these beautiful walls. It is good to have gentlemen of such great esteem pass by and pay homage to our heritage." Hombasha was beaming brightly and Kwatara wondered how he was managing to feel so good about everything despite his aching arm and pressure. His brother's mood was in stark contrast to his own.

There was a murmur of agreement and Kwatara, not wanting to humiliate Hombasha, moved towards the group with the brightest look he could force upon himself.

"I am sorry, gentlemen, I did not wish to intrude," he said apologetically.

"No, you are not intruding at all," said Hombasha, "The gentlemen were just passing by on their way to pay condolences at Kwashi's house. You heard, I am sure, that his mother is now late."

Kwatara tried to remember, Kwashi was a mhondoro and a family friend who had lost credibility after his addiction to beer. He had been as outspoken as Kwatara before he fell prey to the beer pot. Kwatara must have heard about it, then it hit him like a bolt and he felt ashamed. Yes, he had from his wife.

"I did," he said quickly, "and I was going to come and ask you to accompany me," he lied. Hombasha knew him well, he noticed the lie and the broken face. Something was not right. Instead, he said, "Good of you, as soon as I am done we shall go." Kwatara forced a smile noticing that he had been caught out.

"We, too should be on our way; thank you Hombasha, you have opened our poor, blind eyes," said one of the chiefs. "And how we took your valuable skills for granted all this time. Indeed, this is a heritage to last a lifetime and there we were ignoring the very best of our art right under our noses." Hombasha smiled.

"Quite true," added another chief, "Quite true. It is good we passed through this place. Your hands are doing the Empire good."

"Oh, do not give me such credit, gentlemen," said Hombasha, earnestly, "Many hands have passed through these walls and mine have copied from those before me."

"Well said," said Chireshe, "But yours have given the best touch to the walls. For where else can you find such grandeur and ingenuity as this? Am I wrong, gentlemen, to say that this symbolizes an age of greatness, an age of total change and an age of total supremacy?" he said with an exaggerated gesture of his arms.

The others agreed and Hombasha sensing something coming up, looked desperately at Kwatara with eyes that screamed, help. Kwatara's head was aching badly but he knew Hombasha needed him and somehow he, too, sensed that the conversation, as it had the last time, was taking the wrong direction. He was tired but he did not like Chireshe and he was suspicious of his sudden interest in his brother, Hombasha.

"Each age has its own degree of intelligence, Chireshe, let us not forget that," said Kwatara, folding his arms and coming to his brother's aid. He knew Chireshe never spoke positively about anything or anyone without an ulterior motive. Immediately Chireshe knew that a battle of words was about to begin. Here was his chance to spread his gospel and to garner support for the Emperor's dream.

"Very true, my brother-in-arms, I do not dispute that," "he replied in a most humble voice, to counter Kwatara's hot tone, "but each age also supersedes the other if minds and hearts are there to make a great change. I still say that this is the age of undeniable greatness. I mean, brothers, can you not feel it in the air, an energy, the birth of a new era of physical greatness and if I am not wrong, of spiritual change as well? For what else could these powerful walls symbolise other than the dawn of a new everything?"

His companions agreed but Kwatara did not give up.

"And I still say let us respect all that our ancestors did for us. They gave us the original idea and we perfected it, but we are not greater than them. They are great in their own respect," he said, life coming back to his eyes. "And I don't think it is proper of you to put thoughts of superiority in my brother's head. He is a humble man, he works for the Empire and its pride, not his."

Chireshe was not discouraged. His dream was coming true. Already he saw the final scene at the Emperor's court, he against Kwatara, his words convincing the entire nation. He said, "Oh, but I put nothing into his head, I simply say what is plain to see. If greatness is plain to the eyes let it be given the praise it deserves. If one is more superior let him be given the acknowledgement worthy of him. Is it wrong to praise he who deserves it?" he asked, looking about with an expression of genuine surprise on his face.

"Certainly not," echoed the others.

"It would be unfair and an act of jealousy," said a chief. "Anyway, let us be on our way, we will meet you there. And Kwatara, what ails you young man, you do not look so well."

Chireshe screwed up his eyes. He had noticed that something was out of place when he first saw Kwatara. Feeling trapped at being caught unawares, the young mhondoro lost his composure and, unlike himself, stammered, "N—nothing. The wind has been giving me a headache, a terrible headache. I feel nauseous too but I am sure I will be fine."

"Ask for a cure from the best," said an old spirit medium with a bright smile, patting Chireshe on the back, "He knows everything."

"It will be my pleasure as long as it is just a headache and nothing spiritual," said Chireshe, looking at Kwatara squarely in the face.

"I am not that sick and neither is it spiritual," he replied coldly. "You are running late, noblemen." They all stared at him and then at Chireshe, no one understanding what was going on, then one by one, they said their goodbyes leaving Kwatara and Hombasha alone.

As they moved away, Chireshe began to think. The creepers had not lied, Kwatara's face showed it all. His usual coolness and composure were absent and his face looked haunted. It could be he was aware something very disturbing was about to happen in the Kingdom, but so what, that only made the battle tastier. Oh, how this turned Chireshe on, to imagining how he was going to launch his surprise attack at the Emperor's court with Kwatara behaving and looking like a mad man; all the odds were certainly against the young mhondoro. He relished the thought and went along with the others to Kwashi's house, a happy man.

Back at the building site moments passed before Hombasha said, "If I am not wrong, this is the second time I have heard that funny mhondoro talk about the walls symbolising divine beings. And what about you, you look as though death paid you a visit and showed you your grave. What is wrong with you?"

"I thought you would thank me first for saving you from that obnoxious weasel," said Kwatara hotly. "What is it with him and other mhondoros and chiefs? All of a sudden he is interested in your work and the nation's supremacy. I know him he always says something for an evil benefit."

"And I think you should answer my question and now," Hombasha said, meaning business. "Chireshe is who he is and you can never conquer his ways. Or do you only need the presence of Chireshe to fire you up? What is wrong with you brother?"

Hombasha was not relenting at all and right now, this was not the pressure Kwatara needed. Suddenly feeling very tired, he slumped against the wall. He rubbed his forehead and looking ahead, he said in a dreamy, husky voice, "I had a dream, I had another dream." With that he gave Hombasha a scared look that told him his little brother was about to lose his mind.

Hombasha quickly went to stand next to him and said in a concerned voice, "I'm sorry, brother, I was harsh with you. What is wrong, what kind of dream can get you so worked up again? This must be worse than the first because you look too shaken for words."

Kwatara looked at him but seemed to be looking past him. "I was there, Hombasha, I was there in the forest with the wild animals and with the soldiers. I felt the pain as much as I can feel the ground right now and I felt the fear and confusion, I could even taste the sweat."

Hombasha did not want to believe his brother. If he had been anyone else, naturally, he would have dismissed Kwatara as paranoid but he was his older brother and something about his haunted eyes and tone told him there was more to his story than just attention seeking. Still he had to try to shake it out of him in case Kwatara lost his mind.

"It was just a dream, Kwatara, like all the rest. Look at you, you are a mess. And everyone can see it. Do not lose it over a vision that will come, explain itself in the long run and leave. Like you said, this may be something that we cannot change and if you worry yourself to death, how then can you help the nation. Get a grip of yourself and see this through, I will see it through with you."

Shaking slightly, Kwatara looked at his older brother who sat next to him and with a shaking hand, he wiped away the sweat that had formed on his forehead and was trickling down, disturbing his already blurred vision. For a moment, his emotions were stirred. Just weeks ago he had been the one who was strong, the one offering a shoulder to lean on to Hombasha. Now he, the mhondoro, protector of the nation was weak and felt like a mad man. Was this the price of trying to save a people and a country you loved so much? Was this the reward of a gift you could not ever deny? He looked once again and saw tears well up in his brother's eyes. Kwatara nearly choked and he closed his mouth with his hand trying to stifle a moan. Hombasha placed his hand on his shoulder to reassure him and said, "Tell me, little brother, what did you see?"

Slowly Kwatara ceased to cry. He sniffed and wiped his nose. Then in a shaky voice he did his best to relate the dream. "It was like-like I was abandoned, alone and no one was in sight and what scared me, what really scares me," he ended, "Is that I was led away, away from home and from my family, to a land I do not know. It is better for me to die, Hombasha, than to lose this land, my home, my family and you." Tears started to fall freely down his cheeks.

Hombasha was at a real loss. He wanted to tell Kwatara that the dream would not come true but he knew it would be a white lie. His mind was numb; to lose Kwatara was to lose himself. And to make matters worse, the dream was just like the first, it gave them no clues as to what event was going to happen. If it had they would know how to evade the impending horror. Then something hit him.

"You said he had a leopard's hide with the head on his head?" he asked, shaking his brother.

Kwatara blinked a bit, wondering what on earth had excited his brother.

"Is that correct?" he asked again. Kwatara nodded his head, confusion clouding his already perplexed features.

"Your dream, it has foretold of a man who truly exists. He is here in this Kingdom," he said excitedly, hoping that maybe there was a chance to interpret the dream.

"I-I do not understand," said Kwatara, squinting his eyes. "And how come I don't know him. He looked like a King?"

"And you are right, he is. He does not stay here but he came just yesterday, Kwatara. Word is all around. I do not know how it slipped my mind when you were talking."

"Stop playing with my mind Hombasha, who is he?" asked Kwatara, suddenly very awake.

"It is a King, the Mbire King, Nyatsimba Mutota and he is here."

Kwatara was too dazed to speak, his head started to ache again. How was all this connected and how on earth were the two dreams related? On the face of it, they had absolutely nothing in common, but yet looking deeper there were connections between the two. Could it be that an intricate web was slowly being woven? And who was this spider that was weaving two events with totally different scenarios but connected nonetheless? Kwatara's vision became fuzzy again and he felt nausea rise. He knew the Mbire King, he had heard of him and had even seen him once from afar. But what on earth was he doing in his dreams? Kwatara was a dreamer for the nation of the Great Zimbabwe and he had never had a dream concerning another nation. It was Hombasha's final statement that did him the most damage.

"Oh no, Kwatara. I am not a mind reader nor can I translate dreams but tell me, little brother, could this King have come for you? No, I will not believe it, are they going to sell you to him as a slave?" Hombasha nearly wailed in despair.

It may have sounded absurd but Kwatara did not have the energy to dispute it. He realised one thing for certain, he and the King had a lot more in common than either of them knew and both had an end that was connected. A sharp pain nearly cracked his skull and his strength gave way. A foreign King, what was going on? He collapsed in a sorry heap at his brother's feet.

# Chapter twenty-five

The next morning was cold and windy. Dark clouds had gathered in the sky threatening to paint the atmosphere with a bleak grey hue. He had started his journey in bad weather and now his audience with the Emperor was on a day cursed with bad weather again. Nyatsimba Mutota wondered, as he journeyed to the Emperor's court with Shamai beside him, if this was a foretelling of impending doom.

Like any normal servant summoned by his master under unusual circumstances, he was pensive and apprehensive but he managed to hold his head high. As they went past the smaller enclosures, Shamai explained what Mutota was supposed to do as soon as he came into the presence of the Emperor. He was to kneel just a few steps from the throne, cup his hands and with his head bowed, he was to greet the Emperor Hungwe. And no, he was not allowed to get up or to look up before the Hungwe gave him the order to do so. Shamai did not have to tell Mutota the consequences of doing so.

As they walked to the Emperor's court, people stopped and stared, children pointed at them but Mutota was oblivious to all this; so much was going on in his head, nothing else mattered. He was about to meet his Lord for reasons unknown and like a clay doll, his entire life and planning could be remoulded by that one man, and lose its whole purpose. He was one dejected King.

After some time they arrived at the Emperor's court. It was a small granite brick enclosure guarded at the entrance by four huge soldiers. They eyed Nyatsimba Mutota and his men with disdain, but greeted Shamai with total respect.

"I am here upon the Emperor's request. I have come with Nyatsimba Mutota, King of the Mbire," said Shamai in his cool, deep voice. He was addressing a dark, heavily muscled soldier who appeared to be the commander.

The commander nodded and slowly turned to look at Nyatsimba Mutota who eyed him back. Mutota's firm look must have irritated him for he sneered and flexed his massive shoulders. All the while, Shamai remained silent and from the old man's coolness, Mutota realised that the chief advisor was by now used to such treatment from the Great Zimbabwe royal guards.

Finally, the commander grunted and walked down the entire line of the Mbire soldiers who had accompanied Mutota. He looked at them with his small beady eyes like a trader scrutinising a common piece of earthenware. Finished, he flared his nose proudly and grunted once more.

"Master Shamai, you can go in," he said walking back. "And yes, you can announce King Nyatsimba Mutota but none of his soldiers shall enter the court with him, only those who bear gifts for the Emperor shall and that is if they are called upon at all."

Mutota realised the snub, his gifts meant nothing to the Emperor and he was to enter alone to ensure that he was at his most vulnerable. Whatever happened in there, no one from his Kingdom would ever know. Shamai nodded, cursing the proud soldier beneath his breath and casually he entered the court leaving Mutota behind. The soldier took up his position and eyed Mutota with displeasure. This time Mutota ignored him totally. Seeing this, the soldier spat on the ground and clicked his tongue. Moments later Shamai returned and nodded to Mutota. It was time to enter.

"I shall announce you and then you shall enter, remember where you are to stand. You will bring in with you five of your most senior men," Shamai said, as coolly as always.

At this, the soldier grimaced and said vehemently, "But he cannot, who knows what lurks in the minds of his barbarians. I will not allow it, he will go in alone."

"And I, as chief advisor to the Emperor, have said he shall take five of his men inside with him for the sake of the Emperor's greeting. Or is it not that important?" asked Shamai, heat radiating from his last words.

The soldier blinked thrice then wiped a bead of sweat that had suddenly formed on his forehead. He had understood the message. Grudgingly he stepped aside and allowed Mutota to choose five of his most senior soldiers who would help him greet the Hungwe. Mutota dared not look into his eyes lest he was spat at.

Shamai entered the court and once inside he called with a loud voice, "Let Nyatsimba Mutota, King of the Mbire enter!"

Mutota breathed in and straightened his leopard hide. He closed his eyes, concentrated and as boldly as he could, he entered with his five men close at his heels. Inside he stopped, just where Shamai stood.

"The King of the Mbire has come at your request, my Lord Hungwe. Now kneel, Nyatsimba Mutota and greet your master Emperor Hungwe as a loyal servant should."

In one sentence, he had been placed in his rightful position and had been ordered like a child before his father. He knelt on one knee and so did his men. Cupping their hands, they clapped and greeted the Hungwe.

Hungwe looked at the man kneeling. So this was the man Nyatsimba Mutota, this was what the man now looked like, the only King who was a fear to reckon in his vast Empire. Now he knelt before him like a beggar, begging for leniency before he knew why he had even been called here and what his judgment was.

When they were through, Nyatsimba Mutota remained kneeling. Shamai turned his head to face the Emperor for more orders and surprisingly he received nothing but a very slight nod of the head and a wave of the Emperor's stick. That meant that he had been dismissed for the time being. As always he showed no reaction at all, he simply stepped aside.

With his head still bowed low Mutota noticed Shamai moving away from the corner of his eye. He realised the time to face his master the Emperor had arrived. He waited for the Emperor's command for him to rise up.

"Rise Nyatsimba Mutota and face your master," the Emperor said in a clear, deep voice.

Mutota rose. He was in an open circular court, made of grey granite blocks. Here and there, trees had been left growing and they cast a shade with their huge branches and leaves. The place was clean and showed signs of recent sweeping.

Before him, on a high stool made of strong dark wood, sat Emperor Hungwe. The legs of his throne were carved like the claws of the fish eagle and in his hand, he held a staff with the face and beak of an eagle. He was a dark, huge man nearly Mutota's age, with a beard and deep red eyes. Wound around him was a black cloth which looked quite new and of good taste. His hands were adorned with numerous shiny copper bangles and colourful beads dangled from his neck. Flanking him on high stools, were three young men, two on the right and one on the left.

All three young men had a resemblance to the Emperor, and Mutota concluded that these were the Emperor's sons. His eyes fell on the shorter one who sat on the Emperor's immediate right. It was Chikomo. Chikomo returned Mutota's gaze with a sneer. He sniffed and flared his nose as usual. His arrogance was so apparent and he made no effort to hide his immediate dislike of Mutota.

The one who sat next to Chikomo gave Mutota an uncomfortable long, deep stare that unnerved him. He looked quite young and had in his hand a knife of foreign origin. It was long, curled up at the tip and its shiny cruel blade, glinted in the light of the sun. The young man was Tapera. He played about with the knife like a toy as he sat and his stony face refused to be lit even by the bright light of day. It was as though he was there and yet was not. This one, Mutota believed, was dangerous. He reminded him of some soldiers he had seen in battle, not real fighters but just cruel and irrational.

On the Emperor's left side sat the third young man, Perayi. He appeared to be the oldest and had a striking resemblance to the Emperor. He was dressed like a soldier and had a superficial air of self-importance. Nyatsimba Mutota saw the young Prince casually rub his chin and saw his red eyes study him closely.

A few other people were present. From their dressing, Mutota concluded that they were either chiefs, mhondoros or army officials. They all sat behind the royal family on much smaller stools.

His mind was called back to the present when the Emperor said, "So what does my servant have for the Emperor, his master, or is his Kingdom so drought-stricken that he has dared to come with nothing but another excuse?"

Mutota blinked at these words. The Princes looked at their father and then at him, so did all those present. He looked like a little boy who had come to his teacher for a tough reprimand.

"No, my Lord," he finally said, "I have come with gifts fit for my Emperor but humble gifts nonetheless because my land, your land, was struck by a severe drought. The gifts lie outside with my men, ready for the Emperor to see."

He had a firm voice with a royal yet humble ring to it. Perayi looked at him talking and immediately felt jealous. Nyatsimba Mutota's natural confidence and the genuine respect he showed the Emperor infuriated him.

"Should the gifts for the Emperor be brought forth?" asked Shamai.

"No, chief advisor, they can remain outside and at a time convenient for the Emperor he shall view them," said Hungwe. Mutota felt crushed. Once again, he had been shown that his gifts and status meant nothing in this Kingdom. Shamai nodded and stepped back.

"How then should you stand before your master, feigning humility and yet you defied him," said Hungwe, once again bringing about the issue of tribute in a subtle way. Mutota opened his mouth to speak but the Emperor raised his hand to silence him and looked away, as though disturbed by the mere presence of this defiant subject.

Hungwe was a man who hardly spoke but today he was speaking. This was a sign that he was not happy. Perayi gave his father a concerned look and those present began murmuring and shifting uncomfortably in their stools. Mutota was confused and fear started trickling in. His men looked at him, feeling uneasy. The atmosphere had become rather awkward for Mutota and his men.

"See how you have offended my father," said Perayi, getting up and looking at Mutota with accusing eyes. "Once again I am forced to see his crushed countenance because of kings like you who dare think that they can do what they desire to the throne of the Hungwe. You are mere ants and the price of being subjects who are allowed to rule is payment of annual tribute."

He was compelled to say something to defend himself because it had not been his fault, but he knew better. Instead, Mutota kept his silence and like the disciplined servant he was, he bent his head and waited for the next accusation.

"They say they have no tribute and yet look at them, they remain strong and their soldiers look even better than during the years of abundance," said Chikomo, in his raspy voice as he also stood up.

He, too, had been offended by Mutota's boldness, albeit natural to him. Mutota's heart skipped a beat. Had he been found out? He had to remain calm lest he sold himself out. Fearlessly, like a man with nothing to hide, he raised his head and looked at Chikomo as he spoke, all the while wondering why the young Princes had so much freedom, even with kings.

"So you dare feed your men, you dare feed your worthless citizens," said Perayi, "while the great army of your Emperor suffers, while the workers at the stone buildings go without proper meals and while the royal families and precious citizens of this nation struggle to save every crumb of food? Is it right that the walls of this great Empire should stop being built because of infidels like you? Look at what you have done, now all the states have declined with their tribute. You have started a rebellion and the price for that is death!"

"Correct, true indeed!" shouted the men in the court, as some stood up to support their Prince.

The atmosphere abruptly changed from awkward to life threatening. All of a sudden, accusations came hurtling at him from all corners. Everyone present seemed to have something to say and a judgement to pass. He looked about at the charged excited faces of those present and felt their words hit him like daggers. His heartbeat quickened and his breathing became laboured. He thought he had been careful and he was certain that only four trustworthy people knew about his intention to break away. But it appeared as though the people in this court were aware of his plot. So, he had been right, he had come to receive his judgement, his death penalty, because he had dared to dream. He had to wriggle out of this and he had to know if his plan had been exposed.

"No—no my Lord," he said at last. "Even the Mbire are starving. We have never failed to pay tribute and the crown knows this. But all your nations have been struck by the drought and because we respect the throne of Hungwe, we did as you decreed."

"And you wish to give us more mouths to feed while you are left to gobble up your food, our tribute!" shouted Perayi, his face riddled with anger.

Words of agreement arose from the whole court. They had not even listened to Mutota's words. He felt their pride and their anger as a wave of heat against his flesh and he began to sweat. The Mbire King was openly standing alone among a pack of merciless wild dogs, gnashing their teeth at him and howling for his blood.

"Let their soldiers be brought and let them come with their own food!" cried out a chief as he rose up. "Better to have them than nothing and next year a double portion of tribute."

Mutota's men looked about frantically and searched for some hope on their King's face. He was too engrossed in his attempt to escape the accusations and provided them no recourse.

"Indeed, indeed," cried the whole court. Mutota swallowed; the Emperor noticed this. He had him cornered. With simple words and actions, the Emperor had wormed his way into the people's brains and hearts. He was softly preparing his chiefs and sons for the final slaughter, this was just a forerun.

To all this only Shamai said nothing while Tapera, the knife in his hands, coolly studied Mutota, most probably wondering what his blood would look on the blade of his weapon.

"Enough!" said the Emperor as he rose. "I see that all of you are angered by this man and truly you have an unmoving love and support for your Emperor, but," he said, turning to give Mutota a stony stare, "he is my subject and mine alone."

The shouting turned to silent murmuring and slowly, save for the two Princes, all those standing took their seats. Emperor Hungwe stood up and went to stand before Mutota who immediately knelt.

"You have such respect for my throne when I stand before you and yet under the covers of your Kingdom you do what you please." His voice was now serpentine cool. "They say that you should bring your subjects here to work for us, fine, but why? Why punish an innocent people for the sins of their master?" He became silent and so did the whole court. Mutota could hear the man's breathing and could feel his suffocating presence. The Emperor moved away from him and stood before his throne. Tension was high in the court.

"I will not punish *my* people because of a man who will not acknowledge his master. And neither will I let off a Kingdom that incites indiscipline among other states. You are our biggest vassal and your actions determine the actions of others. So let me say this," Mutota's heart stopped; the court was silent and Shamai slowly turned to look at his Emperor, "you shall pay for this sin and it is just, for a worthy King goes ahead in battle and dies for his Kingdom. If I have heard well, you are one such very responsible King."

His last words were a chilled knife that sliced through Mutota's heart. The judgement had finally come and his men looked at him unbelieving and dazed. So, he had been right, he had come to lose his life right in front of his soldiers. His lips trembled. He wanted to cry but he was a man and a King; whatever was going to befall him would not make him bow out in shame.

"Hear what the Hungwe has said!" cried an old chief, "Let his words be the law henceforth." And the men agreed loudly.

"What punishment should then be given a man like you Nyatsimba Mutota, answer your master?" asked the Hungwe, his voice mocking.

Sounds of shock and dismay escaped the mouths of the men in the court. The Princes turned to look at their father with questioning glances, but Hungwe deliberately ignored them all. He was the Emperor with a mind of his own and the life of his subject, Nyatsimba Mutota, was his to do with as he pleased. Silently he hoped that all those present should keep this in mind and use their knowledge on the fateful day Chireshe would declare him divine. For a long while, Mutota remained silent. He had thought the Emperor was about to take his life but he had been wrong.

"Answer or we shall answer for you," said the Emperor.

Finally, Mutota said, in the steadiest voice he could, "One that befits the Emperor, for in his hands is my life and the future of my subjects. I have nothing of my own."

A hush filled the court; he had not begged for his life. Eyes quickly went to the Emperor, the choice was his, to give or to take his subject's life. Hungwe was impressed, even with the threat of death before him, the man Nyatsimba Mutota would remain arrogant and die like a royal fool.

"A brave man you are Nyatsimba Mutota, a very brave man indeed," he said, as he gently rubbed his beard. "And your honour of the Hungwe throne astounds me. Then this is what I shall say," he stopped for just enough time to get people worked up, "let your bravery assist you on an errand I shall send you on and let your honour of the throne make you return with that which I shall require you to bring."

The people in the court gasped. They had not expected him to get off so lightly. Stunned, Mutota stopped breathing. His head started to spin. Just minutes ago he thought he was about to lose his life, now this.

Perayi tried to say something but Hungwe raised his hand up to silence him. Chikomo coughed and Tapera stopped playing with his knife. Shamai looked on, now highly interested in the goings on.

"Look at me, Nyatsimba Mutota," said Hungwe, with a serious tone. Mutota looked up, still uncertain if he had been given a second chance or if the spear would have been better than what was to come. "My salt reserves have depleted and I hear that among the Tavara in the north, salt still exists in abundance. Your father once went there and I know he must have told you something on how to reach the place and there must still be someone in your country who remembers. So I say, go and get your Emperor salt and only when you return shall I forgive your offence."

He had said it so coolly but his verdict was quite heavy. Realising the weight and obvious consequences of his sentence, the men in the court once more became excited and started talking among themselves. Certainly, the spear was better than the long journey to this unknown land this man had been sent to. Shamai frowned, now he understood why the Emperor had excitedly called upon Mutota that night. The Emperor was indeed a deadly schemer. Only this time he had fallen right into the hands of Nyatsimba Mutota.

Stunned once more, Mutota slowly shook his head. He could not believe his ears. Had he heard right or had his mind been so clogged with worry that the Emperor's words had come to him as the opposite of the truth. One minute ago he thought he was about to die, now here his dream had been spelt out for him. He had been ordered to go north.

After months of planning, a door of opportunity had been opened by a crime that had nearly killed him. He was shocked, he looked dazed. Truly this was not happening. His eyes filled up with tears and slowly they fell down his cheeks and his lips trembled as though to say something that just couldn't escape.

Hungwe felt pleased with himself. He had rid himself of a promising pest with clean hands. As soon as Nyatsimba Mutota was out of the way, he would take his people and make them work on his enclosures and there would be no one to oppose his religious coup. He folded his hands on his chest and gave Nyatsimba Mutota a satisfied look.

"M—my Lord, my Lord," said Mutota, finally able to speak, "My Lord, the north, the Tavara, so far away, away from home, my Lord, so far away from what I have always known. No, it cannot be true." He looked shocked and Hungwe, together with his court, mistook his words for pain and his look for desperation.

"Now leave this court Mutota. There is no time to waste, by tomorrow you and your men should be out of this Kingdom and I will give you only two days to prepare once you get home. I shall send my chiefs to see if you have left and if you do not return with the salt in a month's time, I shall kill your family, even the unborn baby, and burn your houses, then I shall take all your soldiers and put them to the spear. You would have run away for nothing."

Mutota nodded slowly like a man unable to comprehend what the Emperor was saying. He felt too stunned to even rejoice in his heart.

The Emperor nodded to Shamai who said to Mutota, "Nyatsimba Mutota of the Mbire Kingdom, the Emperor has ordered you to go on an errand and, since the issue is critical, you shall leave now. Go and you shall be seen out of this Kingdom by the same soldiers who accompanied you here. Your gifts shall remain with the soldiers outside."

Gradually reality came upon Mutota who knelt once more and clapping with cupped hands he thanked Hungwe and his court. He stood to go and turned, accompanied by Shamai, to the entrance. He could not believe it. The north, his dream, it had been handed over to him and he would not leave alone with a few soldiers but with all his people, as soon as they arrived he would leave. Tekeshe Chingowo would not believe this lucky break. He almost stumbled and they thought that he was crushed. His soldiers felt sorry for him and secretly hoped they would not be chosen to leave with him.

"Father," said Perayi, "you dare not let that untrustworthy King leave and go on his own. He is willing to give his people to us for tribute, do you think he cares about what happens to them if he does not return? And in any case who says he will?" The whole court agreed to this. They had wanted to see his blood flowing freely, but the Hungwe had disappointed them.

Hungwe smiled and went to sit on his throne. Everyone looked at him, wondering what would happen next. Suddenly he boomed, "Nyatsimba Mutota of the Mbire, stop." Mutota stopped and looked back. Now what, why did everything have to be so difficult and full of suspense?

"Your King is not like you, Mutota, he is not foolish and he cares for his subjects. I care for your safety. Why should I risk your life?" Mutota looked at him, confused, his heart beating. Had he rejoiced for nothing? "So I will give you fifty soldiers to accompany you, chosen from our special force. You shall go with them and yours shall remain behind. In the event that you do not return, I shall make an example of them before your very people. Let one of the soldiers who shall accompany you be Torasha, the one you met at the entrance."

Mutota's mouth opened, his features crumbled. The court rejoiced and the soldier at the door heard and sneered. Perayi was satisfied and Chikomo sniffed. Tapera licked his mouth while Shamai stood taken aback. Was there going to be an end to these surprises?

"Now go!" ordered Hungwe. That was an order but Mutota could not move, the Emperor's last words had nailed him to the spot. His mouth opened to protest, but strength failed him. In disbelief he looked from one man in the court to the other as though begging for mercy, but cold stares glared back at him until finally his eyes rested on Hungwe. There was no clemency on the Emperor's face but a satisfied look. Had he actually planned the Mbire King's demise and all along Mutota had been made to believe it was something to do with tribute? He could not believe this, the Emperor had never wanted him to go and simply look for salt but to leave everything behind; to go to his end and not to his dream. He was no fool, the Emperor's soldiers would never bring him back alive.

Anger rose up his chest as the truth hit him. The Emperor wanted him totally out of the way. From the pitiful stare came a look blazing with anger and hate and for a moment the two men's gazes locked. Mutota's lips trembled and his fists clenched. Hungwe looked at him, slightly coked his head and sneered. Nose flaring, Perayi became alert, ready to defend his father.

The truth now stood bare before Mutota. Like the bird of prey he was, Hungwe had lain in wait for his vassal and at the very right time, he had swooped down, gripping Nyatsimba Mutota by the throat. He had then dashed him to the ground with just enough force to cripple him and cause an internal injury that would lead to his slow painful death and that of his Kingdom.

Feeling tension rising, Shamai took Mutota by the arm and said, "It is time to go, Nyatsimba Mutota. The Emperor has given you a quest and you need to follow it through. Come, let us leave." Mutota turned to look at the older man with an incredulous look. Shamai tugged at his hand and finally, like a very ill man, he walked, his feet heavy with gloom. The soldiers who had accompanied him into the Emperor's court filed out after him, feeling sorry for their King but more afraid for themselves.

Standing at the entrance, Torasha greeted Mutota with a wide grin and he laughed a guttural laugh which made the thick muscles on his chest dance about. Mutota looked at him with a hurt face; Torasha winked and sniggered. Now Mutota knew for certain that he never should have underrated the Hungwe. He was his Emperor and he, himself, merely a servant, servants never dream of empires, those are dreams for mighty men, he thought to himself.

Shamai looked at Nyatsimba Mutota and saw a man broken in spirit. It was difficult for a father to leave his family, so it was worse than death for a King to be ripped away from his Kingdom. An observer of politics like he was, Shamai knew that Mutota had been both legally and politically annihilated.

Printed in Great Britain
by Amazon